HEX-PERIMENTS

A DARK BIOTECH ANTHOLOGY

KEITH ANTHONY BAIRD ROSS JEFFERY
KEV HARRISON TRACY FAHEY VILLIMEY MIST
DAVID SODERGREN PAUL KANE DAVE JEFFERY
DEMI-LOUISE BLACKBURN SARAH J HUNTINGTON
ANTHONY SELF DENIS BUSHLATOV
EYGLÓ KARLSDÓTTIR WILLIAM MEIKLE

Introduction by
C. J. TUDOR

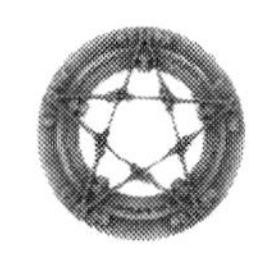

To request permissions, contact the publishers at kabauthor@gmail.com & rossjeffery@storgy.com

ISBN: 9798767393411

First eBook and paperback editions December 2021

English Translation courtesy of Natalja Saint-Germain (@bjorn_stjerne)

Cover art by Hubert Spala 2021

CONTENT WARNING

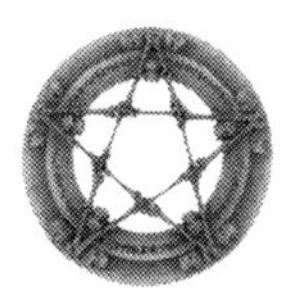

If you would like to see the content warnings for this anthology, please go to the end of the book where you will find a page that details these for you.

The proceeds from this anthology will be going to The Bristol Methodist Centre which serves the homeless and vulnerable in Bristol. It is a place where people feel welcome and safe, whilst being sustained in their daily lives and nurtured in growing and making positive changes in their lives.

The centre has been offering shelter, sanctuary and support to the homeless, vulnerable and excluded in Bristol for almost 100 years and the dedicated staff team will continue to serve this community for as long as it takes to address the issue of homelessness.

The Bristol Methodist Centre provide on a daily basis food, showers, access to computers, laundry services, a clothing store, healthcare clinics, 1:1 support, access to drugs and alcohol support services, housing support and benefit advice, as well as friendship and the options for additional support when needed.

You can find out more about the project at
www.methodist-centre.org.uk

FOREWORD

BY C. J. TUDOR

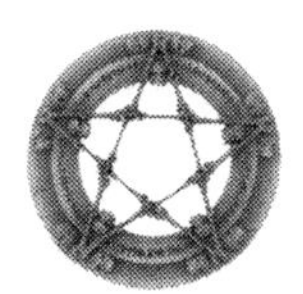

I often think that the scariest stories are the shortest.

There's something about horror that lends itself to the medium. A burst of adrenalin, a spike of terror. That moment before we clutch at our chest and laugh a little, because it was just the wind or a floorboard or the house settling.

Except when it isn't.

My first introduction to horror was through reading short stories. But I also grew up on monsters and sci-fi: *Doctor Who, The Twilight Zone, Star Trek*. Okay, so some of those monsters may have been comprised of washing-up gloves and tinfoil, but the terror was still real. I guess in a way we all grow up on monsters. From mythical beasts to childhood fairy tales - full of witches, dragons and angry giants - to classics such as Dracula and the creature in Mary Shelley's Frankenstein.

The abominable have long crept around in the dark corners of our imagination – once, as a way to explain things we couldn't understand and, in more modern times, to serve as a warning to man: that to push the boundaries of our knowledge, to test our morality too far, can come at a price.

In this anthology the monsters are a result of experiments, exploration and human tampering gone awry. And like the best of tales, they tap into our darkest fears and 'what ifs'.

From a sentient forest to children used in a hellish experiment with nature. Explorers discovering an ancient evil to a more contemporary evil in a Nazi concentration camp where scientists confront the results of their own unthinkable experiments. A lockdown ends up with a woman unleashing spirits from another portal. We encounter a mysterious vessel and a terrifying gaoler, our worst nightmares made real and an invasion of mankind from the inside out . . .

It would be trite to say that the real monsters in these stories are of the human variety. But in a way, our monsters *are* a part of us – a reflection of our fears, our follies. Monsters are not born. They are created.

Of course, the great thing about fiction is that we can contain those monstrous creations within the printed pages, facing up to our fears from the safety of a comfy armchair. That is, as long as we don't let them linger for too long inside our heads. Because monsters tend to take root . . . and feed.

So, proceed with caution. The alarm is sounding, the locks have been released. You are about to enter the Biohazard zone.

See you on the other side.

Well . . . maybe not all of you.

Love and scares,

C. J. Tudor

THOSE DAMN TREES

BY DAVID SODERGREN

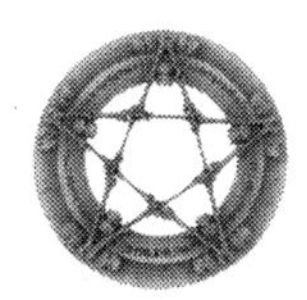

'They're getting closer,' said Margaret. Tom Campbell looked up from his morning paper. His wife hovered by the kitchen window, her hands fidgeting across the worktop.

'Eh?' he said, in no mood for conversation.

She turned to him, a worried look creasing her face. 'The trees.' She broke into an unconvincing smile. 'If I didn't know better, I'd swear they were...'

'I don't want to hear it,' Tom interrupted. 'First the cows were looking at you funny, then it was too quiet at night. Now it's bloody *sentient trees*.' He raised his paper and shook his head. 'Get a grip, Margaret.'

He watched her over the top of the broadsheet. She turned back to the window, the sunlight streaming over her face, making it glow a serene yellow. From upstairs came the sound of small feet thudding across the floor.

'Nicky!' shouted Tom. 'Keep it down! It's half eight in the bloody morning.'

'He's just a child,' said Margaret, though when he looked at her she was still staring out the window. 'Tom,' she said.

'What now?'

Couldn't a man get any peace in his own house? Was he doomed to be forever interrupted from his morning ritual?

'Someone's coming,' she said.

'Oh, aye. The fucking trees, I suppose, on their way to sell us some encyclopaedias.'

She tore her eyes from the window and stared at him. 'No. It's *them*.'

Tom nodded, folded his paper, and pushed his chair back from the table with a screech.

'Stay here,' he sighed. 'I'll get the shotgun.'

HE OPENED the door before they had the chance to knock. There were three of them this time, three men impeccably attired in identical, neatly pressed suits. One of them shuffled forwards holding a briefcase, an insincere smile etched on his face. When he spotted the shotgun cradled in Tom's hands, he hesitated.

'Mr Campbell,' he said. 'Pleased to meet you. I'm—'

'Dinnae give a shite what your name is,' said Tom. 'You're not welcome here.'

The man started to open the briefcase, his nervous fingers clumsily fumbling with the latches. Beads of sweat trickled down his forehead.

'Mr Campbell, please, I'm sure we can come to an arrangement. I have a new offer from Mr Robbins, and I think you'll find it quite agreeable.'

Tom took a deep breath. 'How many times have I told you wee arseholes that I'm not selling my fucking land?'

'A number of times, I believe.'

'Do I need to get it tattooed on my face?'

'That won't be necessary, Mr—'

'Then why are you still here? Why are you bothering my family?'

'But Mr Campbell, this new offer is significantly higher than—'

Tom raised the shotgun and pointed both barrels into the man's chest.

'Get the fuck off my property and don't come back. This land has been in my family for centuries, and I'll be damned if I'll sell it to some cunts to build a bunch of student flats.'

'Not flats,' said one of the other men, bravely stepping forward. 'This is prime space for an outdoor retail experience and—'

'Fuck off!' roared Tom, thumbing the safety on the shotgun. They backed off, and when he fired into the air they turned tail and scurried back to their car, tripping over each other in their haste.

'You'll regret this,' one of them shouted as he scrambled into the vehicle and slammed the door. Black fumes belched from the exhaust pipe as the wheels skidded in the dirt, and then they were off, careening through the thick forest. Tom watched them leave with a wry grin.

Funny.

From where he was standing, the trees *did* look closer.

For Tom, that was the last day when things still felt normal. The men never returned, and life lumbered inexorably on, but something was up with Margaret. Nicky, of course, never noticed. What can you expect from a four-year-old? His life was all tantrums and Paw Patrol. To him, the acres of forest that surrounded the property were a giant playground, nothing more, nothing less. But to Tom, they had taken on a sinister aspect. He blamed Margaret. Her behaviour was becoming irrational.

One morning, he came down the stairs in his slippers and dressing gown to find her standing in the doorway, her hands gripping the frame with white knuckles. When he touched her shoulder, she jumped.

'Good grief, woman,' he said. 'You're on edge.'

She looked away from him, but not quickly enough. He could see the red around her eyes from where she had been crying.

'It's so quiet,' she said.

'Aye,' smiled Tom. 'That's why we moved here, remember? To get some bloody peace.'

She stared out across the land, land that had become theirs when Tom's father had passed away two years ago. 'But it's *too* quiet.'

'Oh, come on! You—'

She looked at him, eyes wide and frightened. 'Listen!' she hissed. 'Just *listen.*'

He did. 'What am I listening for?'

'For anything. Don't you understand? There's nothing. No sound at all. You hear any birds, or animals?'

'Never been one for nature,' he said with a shrug. He placed a hand on her arm, and she wriggled free.

'Those damn trees,' she muttered, brushing past him and creeping back inside. Something about the way she moved bothered him.

It was as if she were afraid the trees were watching.

NICKY WENT MISSING the following day. When the call from Margaret came through, Tom was busy flirting with the office secretary, leaning over the desk and trying to peek down her blouse.

'It's Nicky,' Margaret had sobbed over the phone, her voice frantic. 'He's gone! I can't find him!'

The words rang in Tom's ears as he raced his car down the single lane country road, the trees whipping by in a frenzy of greens and browns. The sky was grey, leaden with clouds that threatened to burst. He took the turn-off past the loch and followed the unmade road that led towards the mountain, at the base of which sat his ancestral home, so perfect in its sombre isolation. The heavens opened, the deluge turning the dirt track into a thick brown sludge.

Gnarled branches clattered against the windshield. The willows drooped low, heavy with rainfall, his windscreen wipers struggling to keep up. Tom flicked on his full beams to penetrate the darkness, the canopy of trees refusing to allow any light through.

He emerged into the clearing, into the daylight. A figure in red hurried towards him, slipping in the mud.

'Margaret,' he shouted as he threw the car door open and ran to her.

She gazed into his eyes, her red sweater soaked through. 'They took him,' she said.

'Who... those men?'

She shook her head, her wet hair flicking against her cheeks.

'No,' she said, her breath coming in tight gasps. She gripped his arms and wept. 'It was the trees.'

'Margaret, please, you—'

She regarded him with crazed, tormented eyes, and grabbed him by the lapels of the wet shirt that clung to his body.

'The trees took my baby!' she screamed.

Tom stood before the forest. He felt no fear in the presence of the great trees. Margaret was being absurd. It wasn't the first time Nicky had gotten lost in the woods. On the last occasion, Tom had found him playing by the fallen pine tree barely twenty feet into the woods. He was four, and couldn't get far on his stumpy wee legs.

'Nicky!' he shouted, casting his torchlight between the trunks. The light made the shadows move, but Tom was a pragmatic man. Margaret's belief in occult bollocks like astrology had initially drawn him to her, her carefree nature the opposite of the boardroom stiffs he worked alongside. But he had assumed motherhood would have knocked that nonsense out of her head, not made matters worse.

He brushed aside some branches, snapping a glistening gossamer spiderweb.

'Nicky!'

No response.

'I'm not angry, I promise,' he lied. 'Just come home. Your mother's worried sick.'

He crossed the perimeter and entered the forest. A deadening, curious silence greeted him. He headed towards the fallen tree, where he himself had whiled away countless hours as a child, climbing up the trunk, pretending it was a pirate ship, clinging on to the make-believe mast.

But now it wasn't there.

Impossible, he thought. *It's been there as long as this house has stood.*

He walked further, questioning his memory. Something caught his eye, a glimpse of royal blue through branches that entwined unnaturally and forced him to duck his head to pass. He squeezed uncomfortably between two trees. Had he put on weight? Perhaps. Working a desk job could do that to you.

He crouched, reaching for the blue object. It was one of Nicky's action figures, an anthropomorphised dog wearing a policeman's hat. So he *had* been here. That was good. He glanced up, and there was the downed pine tree, still sitting at its forty-five degree angle, the bark white and dead, the roots bursting angrily from the earth. Something was different, though.

Something was off.

The trunk bulged, a circular mound protruding grotesquely near the top like a rodent caught in a snake's belly. Tom took a step closer, placing his palm against the bulge.

It was warm.

'What the fuck,' said Tom, and then something inside the tree lashed out, the dull thud reverberating for miles across the silent forest. Startled, Tom fell backwards, watching as the trunk split, hot blood oozing from the cracks like sap, pooling on the ground and steaming in the misty, frozen air.

'Daddy!' came a shrill cry, but by then, Tom was hurtling through the forest, the branches lashing his face, reaching for him, trying to curl around his arms, his neck... and then he was in the clearing, breaking free of their grasp and collapsing on the sodden grass. He looked back to where he had come from, at the trees curling around each other, slithering into obscene knots, their bark splintering and raining to the ground.

Tom turned and ran for the house. He needed a drink.

'WHERE'S THE POLICE?' said Margaret. She paced back and forth, biting her nails. 'I called them hours ago.'

Tom had no answer.

Margaret stopped by the window.

'They're getting closer,' she murmured, her voice tremulous.

'Don't be ridiculous,' said Tom, already on his fourth brandy. He hadn't told her about the tree, because he no longer believed he had seen it.

Trees didn't *bleed*. They didn't cry out, and certainly not in the childish voice of his missing son.

That's right, he told himself. *Now drink up.*

'It's those men,' said Margaret. 'Call them, Tom. Call them and tell them you'll sell. Nicky might still be... they might have him somewhere.... they...'

She trailed off, gazing through the rain-streaked pane.

'The police will be here soon,' said Tom. His brandy glass was empty. He tottered to the cabinet and opened it. As he lifted the bottle, he spied a thin green weed curled in the corner. Eyeing it with distaste, he tore it out and stamped it underfoot, grinding the plant beneath his heel.

Outside, the wind whipped through the trees, making it sound like they were screaming. Tom closed his eyes and drank straight from the bottle.

'The police will be here soon,' he repeated, as Margaret put her forehead against the glass and quietly wept.

THE POLICE NEVER ARRIVED. Tom lifted the receiver of the phone in the hallway and started to dial.

The line was dead.

He staggered drunkenly up the stairs to the bedroom. It was almost ten. He entered to find Margaret hurriedly stuffing clothes into a small suitcase.

'Where the devil do you think you're going?' he slurred.

'I can't stay here,' she replied without looking at him. She closed the suitcase and pressed the lid down. 'I'm going to drive into town. I'll speak to the police myself.'

'And where are you planning on staying?'

She zipped the case up and stared at him. 'Anywhere but here.' She sounded small, frightened. 'If Nicky comes back, will you—'

'You're acting like a fool,' he snapped. 'There's nothing out there.'

She glared at him. 'Then why aren't you out there looking for him? Why are you hiding in here with me? Your son is missing, and you're—'

'If he comes back, I'll call you.'

He just wanted her out of his house. A headache gnawed at his temples, and he wondered idly — not for the first time — whether Nicky actually *was* his son, or the offspring of that college lecturer he always thought Margaret had fancied.

His wife brushed past him, lugging the suitcase to the door. She stopped, and turned to face him.

'Come with me, Tom,' she said. 'It's not safe here.'

He sat down heavily on the bed. 'If... *when* he comes back, I'll call you,' he repeated.

She didn't reply. He watched her leave, listening to her footsteps on the stairs. The front door slammed shut, then an engine grumbled into life.

Tom lay back and let sleep overcome him.

When he woke, it was morning. He shook his groggy head and coughed. Something scratched irritatingly in his throat, and the light hurt his eyes. He got out of bed, still wearing yesterday's clothes, and reached for the shutters.

'Fucking impossible,' he whispered, his hands dropping to his sides.

The trees weren't just closer. They were right outside his yard, the white wooden fence buckling against their mighty trunks. They must have moved fifty feet overnight.

'You're still drunk,' he said, but he knew he wasn't.

He backed away slowly, his heel nudging the empty brandy bottle. His throat tickled like he had smoked a twenty deck the night before. Something was caught in there. He marched to the en suite bathroom and leaned against the wall, looking at his haggard reflection in the mirror. Opening his mouth, he peered down his throat.

He gagged when he saw it.

There was a plant in there, thin and green. He reached two trembling fingers in, the weed recoiling from his grasp. It was wrapped around his tonsils.

Heart hammering, he yanked open a drawer and rummaged inside until he found the tweezers.

'Get out of my mouth, you wee cunt,' he said, opening wide and reaching in. The tiny pincers jabbed at the back of his throat. He placed them around the stem of the weed. It writhed angrily, winding its way over his hand, moving with alarming speed. Tom reflexively jerked the blades closed. He winced in agony as they caught his tonsils, cutting them. He spat into the sink, the weed splattering against the porcelain alongside his own blood.

There was a knock at the front door.

'Fuck off,' he gargled, dropping the tweezers into the sink and running from the bathroom. Grabbing his shotgun, he jogged down the stairs to the hallway. Blood trickled down his chin. He walked to the front door, grabbed the handle, and threw it open.

There was nothing there. The trees were in his yard now, their branches swaying languidly. Margaret's red sweater dangled from one of them, the fabric shredded.

Aside from the cool morning breeze, all was silent.

Tom stepped cautiously over the threshold, the shotgun heavy in his tired hands. He spat a mouthful of blood onto the grass.

'Come on then,' he said. 'What're you waiting for?'

Nothing happened.

He stepped forward and snatched Margaret's sweater from the branch. It was wet with blood, the trees regarding him with the cruel indifference of nature. He pointed his shotgun at the nearest one and fired, the trunk exploding in a shower of bark, and suddenly the branches were alive, whipping around like fire hoses, lashing across his exposed face and arms, wrenching the shotgun from his hands. Tom threw himself backwards, the branches following like obscene, groping tentacles. He slammed the front door, trapping one of the branches. Still it writhed, striking out towards him. More plants sprouted between the cracks of the door, edging their way in. The door started to warp, a thick branch bursting through the letterbox like a twisted jack-in-the-box.

Tom scrambled to his feet and ran for the basement, skidding on the expensive John Lewis rug Margaret had wasted his money on. The whole house seemed to shrink as the trees closed in. Wood splintered, glass shattering all around. Tom opened the basement door and tumbled helplessly down the stairs.

There were no windows here. No way in.

And no way out.

That didn't matter. He pulled a cord, a single bare light

bulb illuminating the interior, and hastened to his workbench. There, hanging above the selection of scattered tools, was what he needed.

His Stiga chainsaw.

'Come to papa,' he muttered, lifting it reverentially from its shelf, cradling the powerful tool like a baby. Loose debris rained down around him from the ceiling, the house shrieking.

He laid the chainsaw down and snapped off the leg from a chair he had been reupholstering, wrapping an oily rag around it.

'This is my fucking house,' he said, lighting the rag, half-closing his eyes as the chair leg erupted into a vicious blaze.

The basement door split down the centre. The trees were inside the house. Tom opened the throttle of the chainsaw and tugged on the chain. After a couple of pulls, it roared in fury.

The branches were slithering down the stairs.

In one hand, Tom held the torch. In the other, the chainsaw. It purred contentedly in his demented grip.

'Come on then, you bastards,' he growled. 'Fucking have at it.'

He started up the steps. The branches moved back, the heat from the torch keeping them at bay. Tom stomped into the hallway. Two pine trees blocked his escape, their roots churning against the floorboards like oversized maggots. He waved the torch before him, but they remained in place.

'Get the fuck out of my way!'

He lunged towards the nearest tree, holding the torch to it. It screamed.

The damn tree *screamed* as it went up in flames.

Two burning branches reached out to him. Tom batted

them away, then ploughed the whirring chainsaw into the reedy trunk. Amber sap gushed out in a torrent, hot and bubbling, spraying over Tom, the walls, the floor. He withdrew the blade, then plunged it in again. With a loud crack, the trunk broke, the tree toppling over into the second one, bringing it to the ground. Tom set them ablaze and hopped over the fiery remains, heading for the door. The wail of the trees pierced his ears, drowning out even the savage fury of the chainsaw motor.

He reached the front door and stopped, his passage blocked. Dozens of branches formed an impenetrable web across the exit. And there, tangled amongst them, was his wife.

Margaret.

Her clothes had been stripped from her body. Branches penetrated her flesh. Her breasts, her torso, her legs, even a couple of smaller ones through her face. One disappeared up her nostril, another through the torn skin of her cheek.

She gazed at him through soft, lifeless eyes, her body red with her own blood.

'Help me,' she mouthed at him.

Tom stared at her in disbelief. 'Fuck that,' he said.

He raised the chainsaw and brought it down on Margaret's shoulder. She threw her head back and cried as the spinning blade cut through her skin, making short work of the thin bones. Blood fountained across the room as Tom kept cutting. He angled the saw towards her crotch, the branches that held her powerless to withstand the awesome force of the power tool.

Margaret was dead by the time her belly opened and her steaming guts flooded the floor. As she split fully in two, Tom stepped over the heap of viscera that had once been his wife and left the house.

The trees formed a circle around him, but they didn't dare come closer. Still, he had to hurry. The torch wouldn't last forever, and he wasn't sure how much fuel remained in the saw. He jogged towards where he knew the road to be, following the peak of the distant mountain. As long as he headed in the direction of Cook's Point, he would find the road.

The trees circled him, trying to confuse him. Was that possible?

They're trying to kill you. Anything's possible, you daft shite.

The torch wasn't strong enough to dispel the darkness, but it kept it at bay. Tom broke into a jog, the roots of the trees scurrying alongside him like millions of spider legs. He saw lights ahead, red and blue flashing monotonously.

The police car. He passed by, the occupants of the vehicle torn apart and splattered across the interior. The window had been smashed, and the remains of one cop dribbled pathetically down the side of the panda car.

Tom moved on.

A pine cone struck him in the face. He winced. Another hit him, then another, launched with such velocity that he felt blood trickling from a gash in his forehead. He swung the torch, trying not to think of just how insane his current situation was.

'Fuck off,' he said as he strode onwards, hoping he was walking in the right direction. Sure enough, the trees parted for the first time since he left the house. He saw the sun glimmering off the gentle ripples of the loch, and ran to the water, wading into it, drenching his trouser legs. He splashed along the bank, heading for the old boathouse. The trees kept pace with him.

Tom raised the torch as a warning, and at that moment — with the perfect timing of a Scottish summer — it started to rain.

The trees closed in as the torch flickered and died.

Two birch trees seemed to lunge for him. Tom swung the saw in an arc, slicing them in half. The tool slipped from his grasp and disappeared into the water. He turned from the trees and dived into the loch, keeping below the surface, pulling himself along by the rocks below. When he bumped his shoulder off a support beam, he surfaced to find himself in the boathouse, the rain drumming off the corrugated tin roof.

'Can't catch me,' he sneered desperately, clambering into one of the two fishing boats, nearly capsizing it. The boathouse shook. Wood smashed, falling in around him as he untied the rope that moored the boat to the thin walkway.

He pushed off from the pier as an enormous Douglas fir wrenched the boathouse roof apart, towering over him in all its hellish majesty.

'Aye, come and get me, you fucking wanker,' grinned Tom. He gripped the oars and worked them hard, not stopping until the boat rocked gently in the centre of the loch. He looked at the trees leering impotently on the edge of the water. 'Fucking wee pricks,' he laughed, his whole body trembling with adrenaline. He dropped the anchor and waited for his breathing to slow.

Now there was nothing to do but wait.

TOM'S EYES FLICKERED OPEN. It took him a few seconds to remember why he was lying in a boat in the middle of the loch. Had it been a dream? Had it fuck! He wiped blood from his face and sat up stiffly. Row boats were not designed for comfortable sleeping, he decided.

The sun was setting, spreading its golden-red light across the sky.

Red sky at night, shepherds' delight, he heard his mum say. He looked over to the shore. The trees were gone. Had they given up? Was it over? He thought it best to row the other direction and head into town. No sense in taking any chances. First, though, he had business to attend to — his aching bladder. He stood carefully and unzipped his fly, then pissed over the side of the boat, the gentle splash of the water pleasing to his ears.

The stream cut off abruptly.

He looked down at his cock, then screamed wretchedly as pain wracked his genitals, coursing through his body. He collapsed into the boat, making it rock from side-to-side. His penis jerked with a life of its own, rearing up like a cobra. Something green emerged from the tip.

A plant.

'No!' he cried, reaching for it. His dick moved to the side, avoiding his fingers. The plant emerged further. It was getting thicker. He felt like his cock might burst. He tried to grasp it again, then noticed the thin green veins emerging from beneath his fingernails. His thumbnail cracked as a vine erupted out, but Tom didn't notice.

The pressure in his skull was too great.

Something slithered through his guts, heading up his throat and scratching his insides raw. He put his hands to his ears, feeling the ferns that sprouted there tickle his palms. His neck bulged as something pressed against it, trying to get out, and then his vision was gone, his eyeballs popping wetly, two glistening red flowers blossoming from his ruined sockets.

His last thought was of that bottle of brandy from the previous evening.

Margaret had always told him he should drink less.

He tried to laugh, but the movement forced the sapling through his stretched jugular in an eruption of gore, and then Tom Campbell was no more.

TRISTAN ROBBINS STOOD with his arms crossed, smiling as the diggers fired into life. He clutched the blueprints for the retail complex in one sweaty hand. It was more for show than anything — he was a businessman, not an architect — but several journalists were coming today and he needed to look important.

As the house that once belonged to Tom Campbell shuddered from the impact of the wrecking ball, Robbins' grin grew even wider. He couldn't believe the serum had worked as well as it had. He really ought to give Pierce, his chief scientist, a raise. Well, maybe not a raise, but at least a bonus. He motioned to the man, who walked over, the hard hat balancing precariously on his curly brown hair.

'You did good, Pierce,' said Robbins. 'I have a few friends overseas who could put your serum to good use.'

'Military application?' asked Pierce.

Robbins nodded. His smile faltered, and he looked intently at Pierce. 'You sure we're safe here?'

Pierce chuckled. 'Absolutely. The effects last a maximum of one week.'

'You ever tried it on a human subject?'

Pierce shuddered. 'Yeah. Best not to talk about that. It's almost lunchtime.'

Robbins smiled. He could see the TV news van coming up the road. He straightened his hard hat and adjusted his tie. Years of planning were finally nearing fruition. It had cost Robbins a lot to buy off the local council and the forestry commission, but soon it would all be worth it.

When the press arrived, Robbins offered them his usual facile soundbites about 'retail-led lifestyle districts', and then it was time for photos. Robbins ushered Pierce out of the way, replacing him with a pretty seventeen-year-old in a high-legged blue swimsuit and silver tiara. Helen Lamb was the winner of this year's Miss Badenoch & Strathspey contest, and she was there because Robbins knew that a glimpse of teenage cleavage was as good a way as any to get folk excited about his new retail development.

He helped Helen adjust her satin sash, letting his fingers linger against her skin as the photographer set up the shot, and then the pair posed in front of the forest, each holding one end of a vintage crosscut saw many years past its glory days. The wind whistled through the trees behind them.

'How about a shot of you cutting a tree down?' suggested the photographer, a bearded man who looked no older than Helen. 'And hurry, we're losing light.' He shook his head. 'Those damn trees,' he muttered.

Robbins and the girl got into position. They raised the saw, holding the blade to the tree. Helen struggled with the weight, in danger of toppling over, while Robbins mugged for the camera, giving the lens his widest smile.

'Those cameras rolling?' he asked. When he received a nod of confirmation, he launched into his prepared speech. 'I, Tristan Robbins, hereby christen this the very first tree to make way for The Robbins Nest, the Highlands' premier Relaxation and Retail Therapy Complex.' The photographer started snapping pictures as Robbins pulled the saw towards him, the teeth grinding against the trunk.

The tree screamed.

Robbins looked up at it. He glanced at Pierce, but the scientist was already backing away, his face ashen.

'Did you hear that?' he started to say, and then Helen Lamb screamed as a rogue branch punctured Robbins' chest, emerging with his still-beating heart impaled on the tip.

The other trees followed its lead.

They moved with an aching weariness, remembering the

way the people had treated them over the centuries; chopping them down, burning them, carving symbols into their hard skin.

The trees had lived long lives.

They had a lot of time to think.

And they were very, very angry.

DAVID SODERGREN

David Sodergren lives in Scotland with his wife Heather and his best friend, Boris the Pug.

Growing up, he was the kind of kid who collected rubber skeletons and lived for horror movies. Not much has changed since then.

Since the publication of his first novel, The Forgotten Island, he has written and published a further five novels, from slashers to Gialli to folk horror to a weird western co-authored with Steve Stred. He is currently working on several more novels, including a trilogy of violent revenge stories to be published in 2022.

You can follow David on Twitter and Instagram.

TURNING TO THE SEA

BY EYGLÓ KARLSDÓTTIR

When I place my hand on the mirror the glass feels cold to the touch. My handprint forms on the glass, mist shaping my hand.

Reflections are different though; I can't touch those.

I stare at my own impression in the still bay water. It makes me think of all the cracked mirrors in this forgotten village. I see my face, small ripples on the surface that is almost possible to pretend are the wrinkles of age, if I just squint a little the illusion is perfect. I can see the entire pier and all the houses on the nearest street reflecting in the water. The church tower, the seaport administrative office, the old kiosk and a few houses all wiggle in the water, fronting the town that lurks behind it. I stand on the foreshore with my feet in the water. The weather is warm enough and when I stand here, I can almost pretend that the town is whole, that nothing is wrong, that everything is as it used to be. That this remote Icelandic town hasn't faced the curse alone and been forgotten.

I can pretend, for a moment, that she's still working in the tourist shop and that all I have to do is walk in there to see her.

That I never found that message in a bottle, never meddled with powers I didn't understand. Never became immune to the plague that devoured everyone around me.

A shadow hovers up above, reminding me of his roughness and his abrasive nature. He is excessive, scaled, with fragile, glaring eyes, blue as the heavens with a tint of black holes in the middle. If you get caught in their event horizon you are done for, like I am done for, bound to spend an eternity orbiting the disaster that followed my own shortcoming. He looks so frail but so terrifying.

Mostly, I'm all alone. The cabin I live in is old, but it has everything I need. A stove, a refrigerator, a soft bed, a fireplace, a sofa to sit on, a dining table and it even has a porch, facing the ocean. I spend my days finding ways to survive. I collect wood, to keep warm. I find fish, and fungi, to eat. It's not hard to find fish around here, but it's hard to find one that isn't either dead or mutated to look like some aquatic demon, nature gone livid, fighting back the black curse of the ancient Seiður.

It's hard to find food that isn't poisonous.

Each day I traverse through the decaying town, trying to find items that will help keep me alive. I've walked these roads so many times, climbed stairs and gone into houses, each and every one. They are all in a different state of blight. The wood has gone soft, dissolving under my feet, or it turns to mud at the touch. Everything is damp and the fog never seems to lift, so I can hardly remember what it feels like to be out in the sun. It's just a soft halo in the sky, drifting over the firmament ever so slowly. I get water from one of the wells. It's not clean exactly, and what killed the people of this town is surely mixed with the water, mingled until it became like everything else, tainted, ill-willed and deadly.

It doesn't seem to affect me much, and so I drink it because my body cannot survive without water. That's one thing I know for sure. I still need sustenance. Of course I do, I'm human after all. I haven't changed, unlike everything around me. I am as I always was, perpetual, while others transformed, went through their own personal metamorphosis, or died.

I remain the same, for better or for worse I guess the ritual protects me still, even if it was meant for something else entirely.

Each morning I go down to the beach to walk in the sand while the light is still gentle. I don't use the boardwalk, it's too murky and full of gunk and sludge from fish crawling on land. Dead things. It's not just disgusting to step in, but awfully slippery as well, and so I avoid it. The stones on the beach aren't much better. I stick to the sand, glaring out into the foggy distance, wishing myself away from this dreadful place, this place that used to be my beautiful hometown, but has died a sad, pathetic death.

And I think about Andrea, and what we almost had.

The night snuggles over the town, like a mother hen brooding on her eggs, waiting for something to be born out of the magic that is her life. I usually can't stand the beach during the night. The fog lifts, showing the vastness of the sky above. The stars in all their glory make me feel a sense of vertigo. It's a lonely infinity up above and it frightens me, the empty space above. It frightens me that we live on this earth that is drifting slowly through empty space.

It never used to scare me, but now it does.

And so, I go home whenever I see dusk nearing, because it feels better to spend the dark hours in the confinement of my own home, whatever it is, than to stare into the face of darkness, knowing what's out there.

The memory of the bright, green town often plagues my mind. The houses used to be full of life, living people, children running in the streets with yellow rubber boots, waiting to play in the sand by the sea while their parents leisurely watched. This used to be a fisherman's town, turned into a tourist trap.

Now it's just a prison.

I sometimes go into the trinket shop, look at the souvenirs that brought money into this far-off place. The town was never blessed with riches, except for fish, fittingly. Ironically, the shop was called Enough Fish in the Sea. Now I wonder if what's here is fish at all.

Each time I climb over the shop's threshold, however, I hear my father's voice.

'What have you done?'

I can see his pale face in my mind's eye. It felt like he became bigger then, grew to extreme proportions until he couldn't fit, was just a shadow high above.

I browse the shop, always the same circle. It wasn't a big shop that my father owned, but there were a lot of small items in it. Necklaces in the shape of the anchor that used to decorate the town square. The anchor itself is just an incoherent mess now, one of the arms has come off, the shank has a strange, mutated dolphin stuck on top of it, slowly decaying as the scales, the beast developed late in life, slowly transform into nothing more than ordained life goo. There's a lot of growth on the pedestal as well, but it's not green and lush, like you'd expect growth to be, but fungal, a strange combination of The Devil's Tooth, that makes it look like the earth is bleeding, and a Brown Brain, that has lost its lustre. The fungus is everywhere, mostly it's White Beards that grow on the houses, on the pier and the boardwalk. It hangs white and sad on everything, an outpouring of white icicles giving this dark town a sense of innocence it doesn't deserve.

The shop has other trinkets. Scarfs and shawls, beanies and caps with the town logo imprinted on the front. It looks a bit strange now that everyone is gone, and I can't bring myself to wear any of it.

I often think about Andrea, who worked the register the last summer it was open. She had dark, straight hair, beautiful brown eyes and a smile that seemed to welcome anyone into her heart. I liked her. Maybe a little too much. It started as a wonderful crush but morphed into something else, something dark.

An obsession.

It was dark love and like a river, all my feelings flowed in one direction, and I got nothing back. It became harsh, and it was impossible to get away from its current.

'Sorry, I'm not into girls,' she said to me, ever so plainly, and not unkindly either.

I had to take matters into my own hands. The message came to me in the form of a drifting bottle, a note that taught me the enchantment, the Seiður, a spell that would make her like me back. The idea was firmly planted in my head.

Then things changed and he arrived. The town started to decay, rot from the inside out.

And I was all alone. Everyone else either gone, dead or too affected by it, morphed beyond recognition. Taken over by the evilness that beset everything.

I still encounter them at night, howling, slithering, dead stares in their hollow, distorted faces, and the worst part is that I can still identify them all by the way they move, or tilt their head, or by the way they look at me. It's in the subtleties.

I come to the shop to remember what used to be real, before this aquatic hell took place, to remind myself what is still true. I come here to remember what this place used to be like, because apart from my own home, this shop seems to be the only place that hasn't completely lost its battle to this dark plague, this festering boil the town has turned into, this soft malevolent curse determined to end us all, turn us all into monsters.

I'm inside the tourist shop when I see it walking leisurely between the houses. It looks like a cow, skulking near the old town hall, which has seen better days. The roof has caved in, the second floor collided with the first floor months ago, but there is something left of its grandeur. The walls still stand bravely refusing to let go of their former glory.

The cow looks my way, as if it senses my presence inside the house. I stare at it as it slides in between the houses and vanishes deeper into town. It is a strange being, this thing. So different from the scaled beasts that roam the town, the beasts that sometimes stare at me through the window as I lay in my bed, completely still as not to alert them. Some of them used to be my friends before they turned and walked into the sea.

The stench in town is horrendous, though you get used to it like everything else, but when they get closer the smell becomes unbearable. The entire town reeks of rotten fish, sulphur, and something else as well, something they all smell of - life and death in one hideous sense of rot.

They look odd, with their bodies covered in barnacle beds. Everything seems to be covered in barnacles, as if the sea has laid claim to everything, just not engulfed it all yet. Sometimes when I look at my reflection in the sea water, when the ocean is completely still, I get the impression that I'm looking at the real town and the thought that I am the one under the sea strikes me. The sea has devoured me, made a resting place for the living. I'm not sure what I did to deserve this hell though. Maybe he engulfed me, this monster that interrupted me and now lurks above, or beneath, and I am just a living reflection, a single memory of a life that used to be. Unable to touch what is up there, the real town, continuing the way it always did before. Maybe I am nothing more than a reflection of something that occurred, hunkering in the depths of the devilish sea where nature turned violent, evil.

Sometimes the loneliness is just too much, and my mind wanders in strange directions. That's all it is.

The cow is different though. It comes into my bubble and disturbs the equilibrium, disturbs the finely tuned life I lead in the middle of this mayhem, and though it hurts my soul to do everything the same way day after day, it does provide a continuum, and a way of life. Whatever it is.

I see it again just an hour later as I am sitting on my porch, waiting for the darkness to engulf me. The cow looks at me with its intelligent, tangerine-coloured eyes. It glares at me through the fog that is slowly lifting as the darkness takes over. It tilts its head, as if it's as surprised to see me as I am of seeing it and it lingers for a while before it vanishes, trotting slowly down the road.

It's here to stay. It's here to ruin everything. It's here to make sure I succumb to the curse too, like everyone else has. It is here to make sure the barnacles or the limpets can live on my flesh, like they do the others. It is here to kill me. The cow with the intelligent eyes comes from the outside to remind me of what I am, what I used to be, what I did, and I don't want to remember any of it.

I will never be allowed to leave, but because I am immune to the plague, the force that enthrals the town has made me a slave. I am supposed to be the last reminder of what was, the exception that proves the rule. The sole survivor.

When I see the giant monster slowly traversing above the houses, I feel a sense of panic.

What if I am wrong? What if there are people somewhere out there? What if the nightmares I have of the deep are the truth and the town is still unscathed up above?

What if everything I believe is actually upside down? What

if I am just a horrendous mermaid that did something to deserve this curse long ago?

It's so easy to succumb to the voice of anxiety.

He swoops down, lingering above my home, waiting for me. I go outside and stand completely still. I know he can smell fear on me. Fear that hasn't been in my bones for a long, long time. He will become suspicious and no matter how much I stare into his black-holed eyes, and no matter how long I orbit around their beautiful event horizon, he will notice, and he will not be affable.

My fear was logical in the beginning, but after all this time I have become used to him and this existence. I know him and his ways. I know how he moves and what he does, and he has tolerated me and my presence. He has tolerated the fact that I am not like the others. Tolerated the fact that I live, and even if it's a desperately lonely life, I do want to go on. I want to live. I don't want to die. I never wanted to die.

I think of the life I led. The mistakes I made. The things I never got to experience. All the bad decisions. And I think of what has been taken from me, and what I have been given in return.

I've seen the apocalypse come and go, nature turned beast. Not many can say that. I've seen the people around me collapse from the inside out, transform into monsters or die trying to fight it the best they could. I've walked the town every day, from the time it still looked as if people lived in it, till now that it is just a shadow of its former self. I've walked in the fog, and I've stared out to sea and sometimes I've even yearned to walk into it.

Maybe walking into the sea is the only answer. Maybe that's what he doesn't want me to do.

I've been holding onto my humanity while living on rotten fish and mutated fungus, but what is really left of me?

I was so certain that his eyes told me the truth of the universe. A truth larger than anything religion or stories could hold. Larger than the small life I lead, but for some reason the cow has me questioning everything.

Maybe the ritual backfired. Maybe I'm alone in the mayhem.

His eyes are full, like the moon, and as dark as the night. I'm under his spell. My head lulls forward in submission and I fall to my knees. My heart is thumping with the new ideas and no matter how much I try telling myself that it doesn't matter, that it's all the same and that whatever doubts I have should have been whisked away in the wind a long time ago I still find I can't battle it.

I summoned this thing.

My heart is thumping, beating hard.

Fear tastes salty.

I can feel his hesitation. Usually, he looks at me for a while, puts one of his feelers on my head, or strokes my chin. His abrasiveness tantalising, the touch reminds me of what it used to be like to be human. What it felt like to be hugged and what it was like to talk to other human beings. And each evening he gives me a reminder, in this single courtesy. It is a soft comfort that he is not like anything else in this universe. The delicate one. The cursed one.

His eyes are the gemstones of the world, the thing my entire existence revolves around, the thing the entire world revolves around.

But then there's the cow. I can see it in the periphery. A white imp, almost as if it's just a hallucination, luring me in, ruining everything.

I need to be able to live without being terrified. I was a prisoner to fear for such a long time, until I succumbed and bowed my head to him, looked into his big, dark eyes and got lost in him.

It is the purest form of love. Purest form of nature. Love transgressed into everything else that fills my senses. It is all I am. Being in his presence. It is all I can be.

The cow comes close to me, lifts its head up in the air and lets out a groan, a disgruntled moo that seems to transgress my very soul.

I run and I fall.

I come to think of her. Andrea and her soft skin, the girl who told me she didn't do girls and then did anyway. The girl who rejected me and then kissed me late at night in a dark alley. I told her I loved her and all she could do was hiss at me and run away, vanishing into the town that later rotted and died underneath my feet.

Her skull is still resting on the floor in the tourist shop. I don't know what happened to her. The dreams I have are just that, dreams, stressful scenarios that never really happened. In the dream, she is running away from me, and I catch her. The spell is supposed to be working, but she still runs. I try pulling her close, but she tears herself away and falls, hitting her head on the corner of one of the tables in the shop. She falls to the ground and the blood pools beneath my feet. The smell of spearmint in the air. A broken spell. A broken promise.

That's the worst part.

She must have died like all the others, succumbing to the plague, whatever it is. Then he crawled out of the sea and made a home in the town he poisoned, where people morphed into witless monsters. I fear his nefarious nature, but I love him too and perhaps he loves me back.

It's a feeble thought. I am too small for him to care one way or the other, though he enjoys toying with me.

The cow has to go. It is an abomination. It doesn't belong in the town.

It's still dark outside, but I can't wait till the morning. It needs to leave so that tomorrow will be just another day like any other. There is a spear near the administrative office. It's heavy, but I can wield it and though I am not going to kill the cow I might be able to poke it, drive it away.

I know he is lurking. He's always close, often shading the stars at night, though I sometimes see them reflecting in his eyes. I know he's there, watching me. Testing me. The cow doesn't belong.

I run down the street where I last saw it, glancing in between the ruins, careful where I place my feet. I find it standing in front of the wall that used to be the town hall. It's chewing on something. I rush towards it with my harpoon, but it doesn't care, just looks at me and continues to chew the cud. When I poke it, it takes a few steps and then a few more, looking at me with suspicion, but not fear.

I can make it go a few paces at a time by poking its behind, but I can't make it go the way I want it to. Instead of driving it out of town it goes down to the beach, traversing the sand.

The image of a cow on the sand is disturbing.

It steps into the water and for an instant I see a change flash by, though only for a moment.

This is no regular cow at all, but a sea cow. Friendly, sailing through the water.

I see the ripples on the surface, the town reflecting in the water. The houses look whole, they look fine, as if the barnacle beds never caught hold, as if people wake up every day and proceed to go to work.

As if Andrea hit her head on that table, and everything just continued as usual.

I look up and I see him. He's watching me. The darkness

complete, and all I want is for him to devour me, for him to end this miserable existence before it's too late. If only nature would do me the kindness of devouring me like it did everyone else.

I poke the cow with my harpoon again, but it just glares at me. Then it swims away, back into the town behind me.

But I can't let go of the reflection. It's even eerier in the dark. Strange ripples, the waves surging, except I realise that I am the reflection. Someone is standing on the pier above. They are looking into the water, sad tears in the corner of their eyes.

I look back, but the sea cow is gone. All I can see is the dark seaweed wiggling between the ruined houses and the shadow of the monster above. I want to look into his eyes, get caught in their event horizon again, be mesmerised and forget, but he is merely a shadow now. Nothing more.

I walk a step, then another and before I know it, I feel the air playing with my feet. Soft whisks. The feeling is tantalising so I continue to walk until it's as if I've dissolved. I am merely ripples on the water.

I caused this.

She died after a severe head injury as I chased her through the shop trying to make sure the spell would work on her. The ointment was supposed to touch her skin.

I can still smell the spearmint.

Then blood pooled beneath my feet.

All because I couldn't take no for an answer. I couldn't let her go. I just wanted a little more. And so, I performed a ritual sent to me by the sea, by him. I walked right into his trap.

And woke up the dormant dread of the deep.

The realisation is thick, so painful that I dive back into the sea. I see the town before me as my body succumbs to the water once more.

The town itself is as it ever was. There is no fungus, no barnacles. There are no dead fish on the pier, or on the boardwalk. The boats are quietly rocking in the harbour. The tourist shop stands tall, as does my house. There is no dead dolphin on the anchor.

And then I see him. He's standing on the pier, staring into the water. Staring down at me, because my face is underwater, forever underwater, watching the up above. Watching that town where I used to live, where I was born, and where I should have died.

His words echo through my mind.

'What have you done?'

I've been living in the reflection all along. Forever alone in the aftermath of what I did, when walking into the sea was the only course of action I could think of. I couldn't stomach being who I had become, having done what I did. So, I became a part of nature herself, and of her subliminal decay. I walked into the water, got dragged into the depths, into the waves, tantalized by this shadow. One with his terrible legacy. Beguiled and fooled by his illusions. This dread that promised love but instead gave me an eternity in isolation.

My father's shadow is what saves me and what dooms me at the same time. His shadow and those eyes, those terribly dark eyes that I've known since birth.

Her blood pooling beneath my feet.

I see the regret in his eyes, the forgiving eyes of my father.

My fishtail is sleek and abrasive. My transformation is complete. I've succumbed to the spell that was supposed to bring me love but brought nothing but misery. The cold is insufferable, but I'll live.

He looks so sad, the stars reflecting in his eyes. Always zoetic. I poke my head above water. Wave at him.

He waves back, a sad smile on his lips, a whisper echoing in the waves.

'It wasn't your fault.'

Then his shadow vanishes along with his comforting presence and all that is left is the cold wet sea, the rotten town, and this cursed existence.

He was never the monster. I am. I am nature's wrathful spirit. I am the one who will devour the town and everyone in it, make it rot from the inside out. I am the one who succumbed to the old words.

I am the one who turned to the sea.

EYGLÓ KARLSDÓTTIR

Eygló Karlsdóttir is Icelandic but lives in Sweden with her daughter and her dog. She has published two novellas, ALL THE DARK PLACES and IN HIS MIND, HER SHADOW, as well as the short story collection THINGS THE DEVIL WOULDN'T DREAM OF AND OTHER STORIES. Her newest publication is a short story collection called SEAFOOD & COCKTAILS: THE ZODIAC COLLECTION. Find out more at http://eyglo.info/

BORN OF A BARBED WIRE WOMB

BY KEITH ANTHONY BAIRD

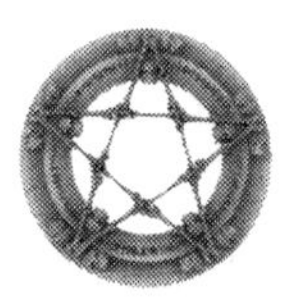

Polish-German border. Winter, January 1945

Each flake drifting down on such a hateful place bore a design of the site's intent. Microscopic pentagrams of a freezing winter's fury laid their white shroud over the train which rattled into the camp. Packed though it was with human cargo, it had carried only emptiness from the ghetto to its clandestine destination. For ten-year-old Zofia, the journey without guardians had been one of fear and merciless cold. A soldier's bullets had taken father away, and mama was perhaps on another carriage, but she did not know for sure. Emptied in minutes, by harsh command and efficient guards, boxcars looked a row of coffins at their final resting place.

Showered en masse, and handed prison uniform, those brought in collected cup, bowl and spoon apiece before being herded into their respective confines. The men were placed in C Block, women in D, and all children taken below ground to an unmarked facility. Many times did she cry, en route and at the end, when the lights were switched off and the concrete space was swallowed by darkness. Up above, a second engine brought in a different cargo altogether. More bodies had arrived, but were merely the shattered remnants of lives spent upon the battlefield. Hundreds of dead Wehrmacht soldiers, fresh from the front, filled each container and only the season's chill preserved them from decomposition.

Prisoners had the grim task of loading corpses onto barrows and wheeling them to storage. Details ran night and day in order to empty the transporter, which would return one week hence with another full load. Suffering heavy losses, in a war on two fronts, the German High Command had needed a work of dark materials to repurpose its beleaguered army. It had long been rumoured a Renaissance castle named Wewelsburg, in the North Rhine-Westphalia region, was the site of Nazi occult practices. And it was there, in the days of growing desperation, that a plan to make the dead keep on fighting for the fatherland had been spawned.

The camp was an enigma, existing only in documentation seen by those at the highest level of the enclave. Underlings who serviced it were sworn to secrecy in the name of the Reich. At its heart, only a select few knew the true nature of what was to occur here. Pioneer of its bio-weaponry programme, which would save the empire from impending doom, was one Franz Grauenstadt. A former researcher at the Institute for Hereditary Biology and Racial Hygiene, he became an SS officer before taking up residence as camp physician. Early trials involving primates had proved successful, and it was time to accelerate those findings in human subjects, before allied forces fractured the might of the Fuhrer's war machine.

The project was built on the findings of the 1934 Greenland Expedition. A Cambrian-era organism had been preserved in number in bacteria-free sedimentary deposits. Stored in ice and brought back to Germany, they'd been subsequently studied and reanimated, and would now serve a more sinister purpose. A refrigerated hive sat at the centre of Grauenstadt's laboratory, and thousands of genetically modified specimens were his to command. Now, with sufficient expendable flesh on site, and with the first wave of broken infantryman in suspension, the process of rebuilding a force to ensure victory for a perceived master race could begin.

In the dark, only sounds could be used by Zofia's mind to draw a picture. Some were distant, others near, and all lent their strokes to the canvas. The things she remembered after arrival: guard dogs, guns, and endless barbed wire, brought a stark finality to the days she would endure. Routines were quickly established. Breakfast, served in bowls passed through hatches, was followed by an hour's exercise in the bitter cold up top. Movements were watched by perimeter patrols and tower sentries. Then more hours in darkness followed, before a second meal late in the day signalled the end of any further activity. On the third day, upon return to the cells, she heard the first distant scream echo throughout complex, and took its fear with her into lockdown.

There'd been no way to tell if her mother was here. She'd seen no sign of adult prisoners anywhere. But the scream... the scream had been that of a man being subjected to something so wrong. It haunted her sleep, which was fitful and void of hope. In a room far from her confinement, his body lay covered by a surgical drape which marked it as a failed example of an outlandish procedure. An attempted graft had left him dead, after host had rejected aggressive organism. Frustrated, Grauenstadt had ordered assistants out of the lab, and simply left the corpse on the dolly as a reminder he must do better the following day. Alone, and in his quarters drowning failure with brandy, his thoughts drifted to the minors in captivity. *Perhaps the key to success lay in more tender flesh?* That option would wait... at least for now.

With the body removed, and all surfaces washed and sterile again, the lab was made ready for another day of surgical horror by mid-morning. A woman in her thirties was next on the operating table. Denied anaesthesia, she was restrained by the apparatus which encased her arms and kept her torso clear of the table. The framework was suspended by chains bolted to steel rafters, and she trembled in its confines. Like a grinning vulture, the physician tested the powered cutting tool which would open up her skull. His assistant injected a drug which would switch off certain neural receptors, but keep her conscious throughout. Withdrawing the needle, he nodded to Grauenstadt and backed away. Another took notes, whilst a third photographed each stage of the process. With the drug deemed to have taken effect, the surgeon leaned in to impart knowledge to the subject.

'Prisoner #659, your pitiful existence is about to come to an end. However, your ascension as a powerful new form for the fatherland shall quickly follow. Any pain you endure will surely die in the surge of affection you will feel for the Fuhrer, and for our noble cause. What you are about to receive is a wondrous gift, and a great honour, so stay with me while I bring you to your glorious reimagining.'

She simply whimpered, but saw nothing as he moved behind, and felt nothing, as he made his incisions with a scalpel. A circular cut, followed by a front-to-back slice across her shaven head allowed the scalp to come away from the bone beneath in two halves. He peeled them off with relish, and placed them in a steel receptacle. Next, the cutter was employed to remove a skullcap to expose the brain. Again, there was no pain, but the tool's vibrations ran down her jaw and rattled tooth against tooth. When he was done, the dome was lifted clear by an assistant so the tissue beneath could accommodate the graft. In a way, feeling nothing was worse for her than experiencing sensation, which heightened her anxiety. But it was only the beginning.

An open-ended glass tube, lowered on its carrier, was set at an angle in front of the subject. A storage box, on a trolley, was opened and residue from the dry ice inside, used to keep the organism dormant, spilled out and down its sides. With tongs, an assistant reached in and removed a container which he placed on a side table. She tried to speak, but whatever substance had switched off her pain had also rendered her tongue immobile. The lid was slowly unscrewed, and again with tongs, the thing inside was removed and her alarm shifted into thrashing revulsion. In the lifting of the organism towards the far end of the tube she had time enough to see all aspects of its form.

It writhed in the grip of the implement, a full six inches in length, with feet like human teeth and branched antennae which looked more antler-like, as they probed the air to sample its surroundings. Its mouth, one of a number of features which had been genetically altered, slowly opened to reveal row upon row of razor-sharp fangs. In order to burrow into the cerebral cortex, it had been so hideously equipped. In another sadistic move, Grauenstadt instructed it be placed upon her lap instead, to provide the assembled their day's entertainment. Regardless of the sedative in her system she found the means to scream, as what to her seemed a fat, prehistoric centipede, began its climb up stomach, chest, and neck towards its goal of the cranial cavity.

Delighting in her abject horror, the team exchanged sideways looks and laughter, and the photographer snapped them several souvenirs. With tears streaking her face, she slipped beneath the trauma of it, just as the symbiote took its first steps onto the brain. The moment killed the mirth, as Grauenstadt focused on the key sequence of the procedure, and called for quiet. It was where everything had gone horribly wrong the day before. Finding its desired entry point, the creature reared up before plunging extended dental saws into the tissue, and began its invasion of the host material. It was like a frenzied feed, though nothing was consumed, only excavated for the necessary space for occupation. Physician and crew stood impassive, merely hoping that after years of experimentation, this day's efforts would yield the result their superiors demanded.

Prisoner #659 did not respond to any stimulus. A battery of tests proved fruitless and so the second human put through the procedure was left in a dormant state, unlike her predecessor who'd simply perished. It gave Grauenstadt a glimmer of hope, in that should he alter some of the life support mechanisms involved, then the outcome might indeed be different. He ordered 'the failure' be gassed and incinerated, updated his notes, and then decided on an afternoon of grouse shooting in nearby woods to take his mind off the whole vexing equation. Disposed of, #659 was wheeled into a small chamber, nullified by a single gas canister, and then left on the processing counter at the furnace facility. By the time the doctor had bagged his fourth bird, the body had left the incineration site, though not by flame and reduction.

Late afternoon brought a blizzard down on the camp, and all activity settled beneath a thickening white blanket. With little to occupy their time, guards relaxed and turned to cards, smuggled drink, and whatever was playing on the radio. Prisoners were given cleaning details, but the mood in general became a more casual affair. Outside, a reduced security presence was confined to just two guards on a perimeter walk-around every two hours. Even then, those on shift were loath to go out given the conditions. In relative seclusion, on the maintenance port floor at the truck yard, prisoner #659 foamed at the mouth as spasms of inner change contorted her body. She twisted all over, as if in the throes of an internal reworking. Blood began to leak from all orifices, before being sprayed on parked-up vehicles and toolboxes, as limbs came away in the roll onto her front.

Teeth spilled out of her head and clattered around like rolling knucklebones. Through a maw of cavities, rows of fangs punched out like a black, dental halo around unearthly moans. Eyes pitched upwards so only the whites were visible, and the writhing torso shuddered as ribs, now powered by re-grafted veins, ligaments, and muscle tissue, ripped through surrounding flesh to give the thing a means to move. Each one increased in length enough to lift the rest of it clear of the ground. The graft was no longer visible in the exposed brain, as the organism had become one all over with its host, and imbued her with a form similar to its own. The gas, used to rid the doctor of his second failure, had proved an unforeseen catalyst for the hellish transformation. In defence mode, the modified creature had purged the cyanide by no longer bonding, but 'becoming as one' with the subject it inhabited.

The last ghastly aspect of what it had evolved into slithered out from the folds in the exposed brain tissue, as its antennae expanded from within to writhe in a probing of its environment. With no reason to stay, it exited the way prisoner #659 had entered, by heading back through the supply tunnel which connected the depot to the main facility. No sentries stood at posts in this section, to put eyes on the outlandish horror which used its mandibles to punch through panelling, before crawling inside. Beyond, a lightless expanse housed the hanging bodies of the fallen soldiers which had been placed in the massive refrigeration unit, awaiting resurrection on a victorious resolution to Grauenstadt's experiments. Hundreds lined the space in preservation, ahead of a proposed conversion... and yet a whole other change was what they were about to receive.

A black maw gripped the ankle of one and pulled the corpse off the suspending meat-hooks which held it aloft. Now suitably horizontal, the mutation crept on top of it and placed its rear end on the dead man's face, for the mouth to receive the eggs it began to deliver in number. Ensuring survival of its kind, it filled the body with a batch of translucent spawn which distended the belly, and leaked a little from the open jaw. With tissue to absorb immediately, offspring began their evolution within, and grew in an accelerated wave before shredding the soldier's skin to birth as smaller carbon-copies of the original. They spilt like innards the corpse no longer possessed across a bloodied floor, and quickly found their way to the hanging flesh throughout the chiller. In the dark, in the cold beneath the cold above, they burrowed into and populated the broken shells of the Fuhrer's fallen.

Hunger, and profound sadness, kept Zofia awake. Unable to cry any more, she sat on her bunk and stared into the darkness. Before lockdown, some of the older children had been talking about the bodies they'd seen that day: a conversation she'd overheard. Life was grey, and hanging by a thread it seemed. She was in shock but did not know it. The whole ordeal had levelled a trauma her young mind could not process. Missing mama so badly, she'd tried to not even think of her father's violent passing. The notion of death had never visited her life until he'd died in the act of protecting her, and now it seemed it would be her fate too. Though confined with others, she felt utterly alone in a world that made no sense. The notion to run when given the chance had already formed, as thoughts of the camp and what she'd seen on arrival, had surfaced through the misery.

Outside of the holding cells, the rest of the camp went into nightfall unaware of what was stirring in the bowels of the site. The snowstorm intensified, to curtail all outer security details. Within, low and high rank alike used the conditions, and their good fortune at being posted away from the front, to take advantage of the down time by drinking and singing empire anthems. The scant few on watches were eventually lured from posts as the disregard for protocol went hand in hand with the consumption of alcohol. The canteen became the hub of activity, while corridors and other ancillary spaces were left unattended. It was a convergence of factors which brought about the inevitable. Spilling from the refrigeration unit via the hole made by the first of their kind, the mutated brood of organism and soldier dispersed in all directions.

The sole child awake in the cell block, Zofia thought she could hear distant screams. It pulled her from introspection, and made the dark come alive with unseen horrors. Anxiety flooded in, but did not sway her from what she'd had planned since the first day of incarceration. The spoon was withdrawn from her pocket, and she rubbed a finger on the end of the handle, to examine by touch the handiwork which had filed it to an angled edge. Whenever alone, or whilst others slept, she'd methodically fashioned a crude screwdriver by scraping it on the walls and floor. From memory, she made her way to the air duct grille at the far end, and set to work on the first of its screws as quietly as she could. In the half hour it took to extract all four fasteners, many times did she hear strange sounds echoing throughout the complex. With the barrier removed, she crawled into the space beyond and felt her way through the pitch black of the air supply system.

I'm so afraid, mama.

Thoughts swirled as she made slow progress through the ducting. The sound of muted gunfire, one source overlapping another, visited the space she navigated.

Where are you, mama?

I've cried so much...

Trembling on a fusion of fears, she found another grille after what seemed an age, which let in diced illumination from the flickering overhead light in the corridor beyond. Its fixtures were on the other side, and so all she could do was use the crude driver she'd made to lever a corner, and then push at the panel. It bent enough to grant escape, giving her access to the network of passages that criss-crossed the complex. Though free of confinement, that very thing was now a protection forfeit in the press for liberty. She had no idea where to go. All routes looked the same in their slate-grey uniformity. The strobe of intermittent lighting, and sounds of distant violence made the choice all the more intimidating. It seemed all options would deliver her to harm. She did a choosing game in her head and it brought small comfort – a trinket from a childhood lost.

I'm going this way, mama... hope I find you.

A DARK SCIENCE was suffering its rebound. Over seven hundred things crept in ravenous annihilation throughout the camp. They broke soldiers in clusters, and in individual confrontations, where training and combat experience served them little in facing down a hybrid terror hell-bent on their destruction, or assimilation. They descended in waves, crawling on ceilings, walls, and the ground on which their targets stood in abject fear for their lives. The canteen had its merriment drowned on screams, and the howls of the horrors which had been twisted into form by Grauenstadt's intent. Some victims had the flesh torn from their bodies, whilst others were enveloped by tendons which lashed out from crawling torsos, to wrap about their cornered quarry. In this way they were absorbed and made similar, to rise as one with an ever-growing hive. A trail of discarded limbs became their calling card.

And it was these Zofia began to find, in every place where ruined corpses of those simply torn to pieces also lay. Always the noise and devastation seemed to be moving away from her position, as if radiating out from a central point. Such scenes traumatised an already broken soul. In shock and on autopilot, she made her way round the carnage amid growing instances of weapons discharge and grenade explosions. Aryan blood was redecorating the grey, and the suffering it took to achieve it was a karmic vengeance. The war child pushed on, affected even more by scenes which made no sense in a world where all hope was gone. It wasn't long before she caught sight of the things born of evil. Time seemed to slow. In a barracks overrun with specimens, a lone soldier, surrounded, torched the room with a flamethrower, knowing his end in fire would be better than one in their clutches. She watched his searing death through an open door, until the raging inferno within spilt its intensity into the corridor, and forced her away.

In his quarters, Grauenstadt pulled his Luger pistol from the holster hanging on a peg near the door, which he opened an inch to peer through. Logic told him the camp had come under enemy assault, and so his first thought ran to locking down the lab and seeking assistance in the defence of secret SS materials.

Slipping out, he made his way there, and once inside, flicked the switch to power up the two-way radio and call for assistance. It took persistence, but eventually someone picked up the handset at the other end... frantic.

'They're everywhere... we cannot stop them,' said the responder.

'Soldier, this is your commander. We cannot allow the work of this facility to fall into the hands of our enemies. Defend your position at all cost, but I must have men joining me at the laboratory when possible. Soldier, acknowledge my order... soldier, do you hear me?'

The sound of intermittent gunfire, screams, and what Grauenstadt took as screeching feedback, were now the only audio at the other end. He tried again, and again, but no further engagement took place. He could only assume back-up would arrive at some point. With that in mind, he set about securing the lab by bolting doors, dropping blast shutters, and placing organism containers on a trolley, ready for transportation via the escape tunnel to the north. In the process of packing his surgical instruments into a case, he became aware of a rising number of footfalls entering the corridor outside. It would seem the unit he'd asked for had arrived. Just as their presence amassed at the door, he unlatched it and barked an order, as it swung open to bring those behind it spilling inside. Only, what he'd expected, and what had arrived, were wholly different in appearance and intent. Gripped with shock, he merely froze as mutation, after mutation, scuttled into the space around him.

Having found the architect of their tormented existence, they fell upon him with a ruin far worse than any he'd inflicted on experimental subjects. Lifted off his feet by their sheer number, he was carried screaming on their backs to the waiting operating table. His gun, out of reach on the nearby bench, would serve little purpose in repelling the onslaught, yet still he reached for it in desperation as they began their reworking of his anatomy. The black maws of four punctured wrists and ankles, and he howled against the pain as they kept him stretched across the table. Two more crawled on top as the multitude in the room began a frenzy of destruction, taking the place apart in a rage he'd planted within them. The one on his chest brought its face to his and slowly revealed the three rows of black fangs it would employ as its own surgical instruments.

The point which felt that penetration was that which housed his enamel clusters. In equal measure, top and bottom row were hit hard with jaws that powered pointed rakes which tore through tissue and bone, as if one were no tougher than the other. It was a spray of white and red, of stifled screams, and of shudders of the body in every rend of him. Teeth were expelled to scatter about, and blood gushed as fountains from the wreck of the opening. But it was only the beginning. Perched on his legs, the other abomination began to drive its ribcage-legs into both of his. Sharp ends of those shards punched in, and it writhed in undulation to drive them deeper in a torturous vein. A murdered mouth issued strangled cries as waves of pain rolled over, before the other horror decided it would have his lower jaw as a toy, and started to snap it free from the rest of him.

It was fraught seconds of mutilation, in which the inevitability of his passing was captured in that moment. There was a split second where the pressure reached its zenith, before the crack and tear of separation curtailed his screams in its brutal release. There was a tide of blood, made all the more swollen by the four creatures pinning hands and feet, which turned restraint to consumption, and began the shred of appendages. It took seconds to strip meat from bone, and rip those inner frames away from their joints. Over in under a minute, the whole termination had been a righteous ending for an agent of suffering such as Grauenstadt. The corpse became a feed trough for the rest, being disassembled in savage pulls from all angles. Each took a piece of him, and each bore the mark his vile experiment had laid upon them. Born of the original hybrid, they carried the same identifier at the nape of the neck. The number 659, the asset tattoo given to the surgeon's second subject, had formed cellular, and crossed over in the genetic splice and secondary cloning sequence.

EMERGING into the snowstorm via the open door of an unattended sentry point, the stinging cold on her face, and biting air in her lungs, were the taste of freedom Zofia experienced before a colossal blast threw her twenty feet away into deep snow. The camp lights, swirling frozen flakes, and apocalyptic illumination drifted from sight as she went under. Sirens, gunfire, and the shouts and screams of German flesh went unheard beforehand, as ruptured eardrums could process none of it. A darkness came, and she felt nothing... happy to drift beneath its cloak. In the open expanse of camp grounds, a giant mushroom cloud reached ever skyward, and hung over its site of origin. At the outer marker of the damage, the main military wings were now rubble and ruin, and at their heart the source of the epic explosion, the armoury, was nothing more than flame and funnelling black smoke.

Six guards had fought desperately in the shadow of the building against overwhelming odds, with the last man to fall bearing a flamethrower, which set the munitions store ablaze on his demise. First a raging fire, the armoury had gone up annihilating everything in a five hundred-metre radius. What still stood was gutted, and prison blocks C and D, protected in part by their siting next to a truck yard full of plated vehicles which bore the brunt, were mostly intact. The compound glowed on a horizon which sat in the viewfinder of the night-vision device employed by the Russian tank corps east of the camp. En route to take up position for the final push onto German soil, their commander ordered encampment, and sent a small reconnaissance unit to investigate.

Mere days operational, the site was now a broken cog of the Nazi war machine. With infrastructure blown apart, its commander taken down by the very horrors he'd inadvertently created, those same terrors overrunning the complex, its troops dead and dying, and the hapless subjects brought there at least safe under lock and key. In the early hours, Zofia woke so cold she could not stop trembling. Emerging from the snow which had cushioned her landing, and concealed her from the chaos in the compound, she wandered aimlessly in a daze amid the destruction. She thought herself dead and touring whatever hell this was. Only when the nightmares of accidental design picked up her scent, and had her cornered, did she realise she'd not escaped the ever grim reality of the compound. They circled her at first, branched antennae raking the air to keep a ravenous focus on their target.

There were no more tears left to come. She simply stood still, and tried to recall the carefree days back home before dark legions came to her town. Different predators now closed in. Theirs was a primal urge to take down prey, not an agenda based on perceived superiority. She knew her end would be brutal and savage, but at least it would be over swiftly. Dropping to her knees in the myriad of snowflakes which had drifted down on evil's lair, she now thought solely of mama, and of the father she'd lost to pure malice. A dozen mutations encircled like a pack of dogs. There'd been no delay in their attacks thus far, so this behaviour was at odds with the unbridled fury they'd displayed in dispatching soldiers. A hive alpha crept forward on clicking bone 'limbs'. Warm breath turned to chill vapour expulsions with each measure of ground it cleared between them.

Crunching snow beneath pointed extremities was a countdown to horrific demise. The thing came within inches. Her lower lip quivered as it slowly leaned in, and retracted the skin around its jaws to extrude the ebony razors that would strip flesh from bone. To a young soul, this creature was the embodiment of dark forces which had torn her world apart. Terror was vice-like, and it pinned her rigid in the final moments before it lunged and... faltered, as if conflicted in its prey's destruction. It went still, save for antennae which snaked forward, and nostrils which sampled the smell of the child. She thought only that it toyed with her, so it seemed the end would be endured the longer. But then the mutation moaned, backed away, and shuddered with an unknown restraint which kept its ferocity in check. Had Zofia not been traumatised, then she might have understood a wave of sorrow was pacifying the beast.

It backed away in hesitant steps, and the others began to scatter and seek out other prey. But the alpha lingered, seemingly torn, and somehow Zofia knew her life was spared. In a last, tormented effort, the thing tore itself away from her presence and went to find other quarry on which to vent its anguish. There she remained, confused, frightened, cold, and all alone. In the distance were the screams of those brought down by the packs. Their last moments, and intermittent gunfire, were the only things which punctured a quiet, eerie backdrop. Until a low rumbling drifted in ahead of the first of the Russian heavy armour advancing on the camp. A lone tank tore through the barbed wire fencing, before others did the same at all quadrants, and mounted machine guns went to work on the horde in the grounds. Zofia stood, watched the further fury unfold, and remained in a daze when a tank loomed up before her and then ground to a standstill.

Life, the threadbare thing it was, went into slow motion. Zofia saw the rage of it all, but ear damage from the blast still crippled the audio. Bullets and flame took mutations to a wasting of flesh, all in a mad ballet which seemed to drift across the eyes. The sole thought in all of this was for mama. *Had she lived, only to be cut down in this endless swirl of violence?* She saw the alpha cornered and riddled with machine gun fire. The gush of blood looked rivulets of a darker hue against the brilliance of snow which stretched everywhere. It seemed peaceful in death, she thought. No longer tormented and tearing at a world which had brought it into being. There came a whisper... a moment where everything fell away and a small breeze, like a sweet caress, kissed her forehead... and then it was gone.

Wearing an officer's overcoat, that which had been draped around her by a Russian tank commander, a ten-year-old Polish girl sat at the rear of the front piece of armour which led the subjects of a liberated camp to life and liberty, beyond the hate of those who had sought to destroy that. All terrors had been slain. All prisoners had been saved by the fact of their own confinement, and all surviving German soldiers were now prisoners themselves. With all experimentation documents extracted, and specimens removed, the site was razed to the ground, and a little-known part of history would be cast into a deep freeze by an unrelenting winter in a time of war. Zofia was never reunited with mama, because prisoner #659 had been one and the same. But in that cruel assembly of human and organism, a mother's love had won through and spared Zofia the true 'horrors of war'.

KEITH ANTHONY BAIRD

Keith Anthony Baird is the author of The Jesus Man: A Post-Apocalyptic Tale of Horror (Novel), Nexilexicon (Novel), And a Dark Horse Dreamt of Nightmares (Book of Shorts), This Will Break Every Bone In Your Heart (Novelette) Snake Charmer Blues (Short) and A Seed in a Soil of Sorrow (Short). His works can be found on Amazon and Audible. He is currently working on a dystopian/cyberpunk novella titled SIN:THETICA and a post-apocalyptic novel titled Wind Rust.

The Diabolica Britannica horror anthology was his brainchild, in which you'll find his own contribution Walked a Pale Horse on Celtic Frost.

2021 sees the release of Diabolica Americana and the European HEX-PERIMENTS anthology projects. The latter being a collaboration with fellow Brit author Ross Jeffery.

When not at his desk writing, you might find him up a mountain, snorkelling on a coral reef with his partner Ann, or having adventures with his grandson. Failing that, it's a good bet he'll be on Twitter (@kabauthor).

THEY CAME FROM THE ROCKS

BY VILLIMEY MIST

The following e-mail exchange comes from contractor Gestur Hilmarsson and Álfaljós's liaison Hörður Bjarnason leading to the events of March 17th and Gestur's subsequent disappearance.

Date: 02/27/2026
Time: 17:15
From: Gestur Hilmarsson <gestur@gverktakar.is>
To: Hörður Bjarnason <hordur@alfaljos.is>
Subject: First drill operation

Good afternoon, Hörður,

I hope you are well.

In accordance with our contract, I am to give you small briefs into the project.

I'm pleased to announce my team managed to put the first drill through the rocks below the glacier. The fumes from the magma have even gone to the top, so it's safe to say we've reached our destination.

It wasn't easy, though. Those rocks are ancient, might be even older than our settlement according to the geologist, and they're sturdier than steel. Hell, it took us quite a while to crack through the ice. Most of our machines came close to malfunctioning the deeper and closer we got to the crust. Unfortunately, two of the three titanium-coated drills that we received from your company dismantled from our machine. We have no idea how it happened, but it seems to have occurred around the same time the first drill broke through the rocks (see attached the link to the cloud server which stores the video footage from the surveillance camera). Geiri, my engineer, and Konráð, my mechanic, tried to fix it but to no avail. I think you mentioned during the orientation that you have specialists that could help? If so, that'd be great.

Other than that slight malfunction, everything is going according to plan.

Between you and me, though? This project is one of the weirdest ones I've done. Not that I disagree with its objective. After the sudden increase in population, we're in dire need of other methods of extracting electricity from what nature can provide for us. Hydroelectric just doesn't cut it anymore. It's why I was intrigued by Álfaljós and their innovative approach to renew geothermal energy. I hope you've been ignoring those protesters parked in front of the company. I know I would, and I'm relieved they're not stupid enough to protest in the middle of the glacier. They're just afraid of change, that's all.

I still want to let you know that not a day goes by that I'm grateful Álfaljós liked the quota from my company. That I'm part of changing the lives of Icelanders for the better makes my heart swell with pride.

I apologise if it sounds like I've been babbling. I have no idea what to put in these briefs.

Anyway, if you could send over your specialist in the next couple of days, we can resume the drilling and advance to the next stage.

Looking forward to hearing from you.

Regards,

Gestur.

[*Cloud Server link: found in folder titled 'Surveillance – drill location 02/25/2026'*]

DATE: 02/28/2026

Time: 14:12

From: Hörður Bjarnason <hordur@alfaljos.is>

To: Gestur Hilmarsson <gestur@gverktakar.is>

Subject: Congrats on the first drill!

GOOD AFTERNOON, Gestur,

I'm delighted to hear that your team has penetrated the first barrier of our initiative. It won't take too long for the second procedure to begin, I presume? I'm unsure if I have contacted the manufacturer in China already about the titanium pipes shipment, but I estimate it will arrive to Iceland in four to six weeks, judging how the weather will fare overseas. I can't wait to relay the first success to our CEO. I'm sure she will be thrilled.

You need not worry about those protesters. Sure, they are pesky and are worried that we are hurting the environment. One such "carer for the environment" even emailed me, saying that nature would pay us back threefold if we were to mess with it. Can you believe that? But it's all right. I pity them, actually. They only worry about the present. They don't care about the future like we at Álfaljós do. Or at least they don't care enough to plan a proper living for their children and their children's children. Because that's what we are doing. Making sure that Iceland will be habitable in places like the highlands without the worry of the forces of nature. I'm glad you see it that way as well, Gestur.

So, you need a specialist? Say no more. I know just the man appropriate for the job. His name is Atli Erlendsson and he's one of the engineers who developed the drills for the project. I'll request a transfer for him later today. I expect he'll reach your destination within the next twenty-four hours or so. He's one of the best, I'm sure you're going to like him.

I do appreciate these briefs from you, Gestur, and I look forward to receiving more of them in the coming weeks.

Have a nice day.

All the best,

Hörður.

Date: 03/03/2026

Time: 18:05

From: Gestur Hilmarsson <gestur@gverktakar.is>

To: Hörður Bjarnason <hordur@alfaljos.is>

Subject: Many thanks

Good evening, Hörður.

I want to thank you for sending over Atli, the specialist, so quickly. The storm last week delayed his arrival, but once the fog cleared up, everything was fine. He immediately detected the problem of the drills' dismantling and set out to work, borrowing both my engineer and mechanic for assistance. I was amazed by his efficiency.

You're not going to keep him forever, right? Because there just might be a position available for him on my team. Atli informed me the repairs would take a day or two, and I told him to take as much time as he'd need since we've been ahead of schedule for a couple of weeks thanks to the lull in weather on the glacier.

He's a good kid and I'm once again grateful for having him here.

I will send you a report of the repairs once he's finished.

Take care.

Gestur.

DATE: 03/04/2026

Time: 08:37

From: Hörður Bjarnason <hordur@alfaljos.is>

To: Gestur Hilmarsson <gestur@gverktakar.is>

Subject: Not for sale ;)

GREETINGS, Gestur,

I told you he's one of the best. And I'm afraid we intend to keep him in our company for a very long time. You can't have him just yet.

But who knows, if he enjoys being in your company, he's free to go over to your side. No hard feelings on our end if that happens.

I look forward to reading your repairs report once I've had

my technical specialist decipher it for me. I hope you won't spread it around that I'm not as tech savvy as the rest of you, lol.

Have a nice day.

Regards,

Hörður.

DATE: 03/04/2026

Time: 18:05

From: Gestur Hilmarsson <gestur@gverktakar.is>

To: Hörður Bjarnason <hordur@alfaljos.is>

Subject: Unfortunate accident

DEAR HÖRÐUR,

I'm sorry to say this, but Atli has been in a terrible accident. You've probably gotten wind of it already since the medic in the helicopter transporting him to Reykjavík hospital requested all his contact information.

I wanted to give you my report of what happened, at least until Atli wakes up from the drug-induced coma...

We were in shortwave radio contact the entire time as the drills are located deep under the glacier. Surveillance cameras are there, as you remember from the footage I sent you last week, but the connection has been crap as of late. No idea why, but we have only been getting very grainy resolutions most of the time. What's important is, I had eyes and ears on him throughout his initial inspection and subsequent repair.

It was around three in the afternoon yesterday when he told my engineer and mechanic to go fetch additional equipment and extra pipes from the small warehouse we keep in the main building above ground. I asked Atli if he was all right working by himself. He just smiled with a silly wave into the camera before turning his back to me and resuming his work.

I can't remember if you went on the tour the day the project began, but the steel lanes are all fastened into the ice itself with a mixture of rods and marine epoxy. It's a weird combo, I know, but it works and hasn't failed us yet.

Until yesterday, that is.

I can´t quite explain it—my eyes must have been playing tricks on me, or I was just too exhausted, but it *seemed* like something crawled *underneath* the lane Atli stood on. It wasn't some animal as there are no animals up on the goddamn glacier.

I radioed Atli to see if he saw anything. He humoured me by looking around but found nothing in the end. It must have been a trick of the atrociously bad lighting down there. I watched Atli work on the drills for about an hour when something completely obscured the camera lens. It wasn't the occasional sleet that slurries down into the cracks. It seemed more solid—I thought for a second it was the palm of someone's hand, which is silly of course.

Then the screams crackled through the shortwave radio.

My heart shot up in panic waves. The surveillance either showed static or darkness. I called for Atli, asking if everything was all right. I received nothing but agonising screams in return.

I contacted Geiri and told him and Konráð to go check on Atli. Something was very much wrong here.

I waited in an anxiety-induced puddle of sweat, staring at the monitor screen, wishing it'd go back online.

As if on cue, the surveillance feed fell back into place.

I wish now it hadn't. I would have been spared the image forever burned in my brain.

The spare rods and pipes Atli had brought with him

pierced his entire body. Some of them bent through the steel grid at different angles, fastening the poor man deeper into the lane. Despite the bad resolution I detected no blood pouring from the multiple wounds. It's as if he had been *merged* with the lane, turning him into this grotesque abstract art display from hell.

It took all my men six hours to cut the rods out of his body. He was conscious the entire time. His screams reached the main building above ground.

I'm so sorry. This is all my fault. If I had been there to supervise in person, this probably wouldn't have happened. I take full responsibility for my carelessness and Álfaljós may direct Atli's hospital bills to me.

God, I hope he pulls through the operation.

No one deserves this much pain.

I'll give a more detailed report when I head back to Reykjavík in the coming weeks after I have re-examined the surveillance footage and conducted a safety procedure on the steel lanes. Please keep me informed on Atli's wellbeing in the meantime.

Regards,
Gestur.

DATE: 03/08/2026
Time: 16:29
From: Hörður Bjarnason <hordur@alfaljos.is>
To: Gestur Hilmarsson <gestur@gverktakar.is>
Subject: Concerning Atli's wellbeing

GREETINGS, Gestur,

I want to inform you that Atli's operation went well. It took over 12 hours, but the doctors managed to pull out the shrapnel from the pipes out of his body without damaging the muscle tissues. He's going to need extensive physical and mental therapy but he's a trooper. I'm certain he will pull through.

The CEO and I went to visit him two days after the operation. He seemed weak, covered from head to toe in bandages and tubes pumping liquid into his body. But he responded well to our gifts, he even managed a raspy chuckle at the grey-coloured éclair his department sent him.

I'm worried about his mental wellbeing, though. After the CEO left, I probed him for answers on the day of the accident. I wanted to know what had really happened below the glacier, since you haven't sent me the report yet (there's no need to rush, of course). However, as soon as I mentioned the steel lane, Atli's eyes bulged out of his sockets, and he gurgled a terrified shriek. His whole body shook violently. I was afraid the tethers that held his legs and arms up would snap. He mouthed something I couldn't hear or understand. The nurses ushered me out of his room before I could lean down and listen to what he had to say.

The doctor explained to me Atli was still in shock after the accident and that his brain was still processing the event and its aftermath. I would have to allow him more rest before I could ask him further questions.

It's frustrating, especially if there's any reason to believe that you and your crew are working in an unsafe environment. Which shouldn't be, given the report you sent me at the start of this year.

I'd appreciate it if you could continue to send me reports—any kind, environmental, weather, morale, whatever you can think of— over the coming days.

It would certainly put my mind at ease as well as the CEO's.

Take care of yourself.

All the best,

Hörður.

DATE: 03/10/2026

Time: 17:38

From: Gestur Hilmarsson <gestur@gverktakar.is>

To: Hörður Bjarnason <hordur@alfaljos.is>

Subject: Requesting new crew

GOOD EVENING, Hörður,

Thank you for keeping me posted about Atli. I'm relieved to hear the operation went well. I really hope he recovers fast from that horrific ordeal. I wish my emails would bring you some good news as well, but sadly no.

I've lost some of my men. I have no idea where they've gone. What I *do* know is they must have left in a hurry because all their belongings are still in their cabins above ground. I suspect they must have been spooked by Konráð's ridiculous story. It's probably nothing, but he claims to have seen some kind of *creatures* climb through the minuscule cracks in both the glacier and the rock behind it. It was only for a second and when he went to check again, they were gone, as if melted into the ice. Like I said, it's ridiculous. I've told Konráð that Álfaljós won't tolerate these kinds of tall tales and that I would dock some of the hours from his wages if he continued to spread them. That seemed to have shut him up.

But it still doesn't explain the absence of my trusty men.

They're like me; old-fashioned, efficient and we take no bullshit at our jobs. We've been away from home for two months, however. Homesickness must have caught up to them. It happens to all of us. I freely admit I miss my children and I've got no one at home to warm my sheets, but I've got a project to supervise, and I won't be able to keep up with the schedule if none of my men will work. The ones who haven't deserted me, Geir and Konráð included, have been taking the snowmobiles and cruised around the camp and its surroundings to see if they stumbled upon a lone straggler, shivering in their boots, but so far, no such luck. I investigated the surveillance footage, but no dice. We bought those cameras a month ago and they're supposed to be state of the art, but the resolution is absolute shit. It's like there's a blizzard within the facilities (see below links to the cloud server).

I hate asking this of you, but I'd appreciate it if you could send over a new crew, one that preferably doesn't believe in superstitious crap. It wouldn't hurt to ship over new surveillance cameras as well.

I'm sure Álfaljós wants us to finish the project as soon as possible but I can't do that unless I get more people over here.

Hope to hear from you soon.

Regards,

Gestur.

[*Cloud Server links: found in folder titled 'Surveillance – crew dorms 03/08/2026'*]

[*Cloud Server links: found in folder titled 'Surveillance – crew dorms 03/09/2026'*]

Date: 03/11/2026
Time: 11:45
From: Hörður Bjarnason <hordur@alfaljos.is>
To: Gestur Hilmarsson <gestur@gverktakar.is>
Subject: Regarding "missing crew"

Greetings, Gestur,

Is everything okay over there?

I tried calling you as soon as I got your email yesterday, but you didn't answer your phone. I understand you've been quite busy since some of your crew seems to have left the facilities.

I looked at the video footage you sent me. You're right, the resolution was really bad, but with the help from the guys at IT, they managed to clear the resolution to a point where I could see obvious shapes of the human kind, if you catch my drift.

So, I did see some of your men leave the dorm premises in the middle of the night. It wasn't like they were tiptoeing towards the cafeteria to swipe beer from the fridge. They were *running* and *screaming*, Gestur. What they were running from, I have no idea. The camera was situated at a place where I couldn't see the intruder.

Did you not hear them screaming that night, Gestur? I realise the storms up on the glacier can get pretty loud at this time of year, but you must have heard *something*, right?

Keep me posted, all right?

All the best,

Hörður.

Date: 03/13/2026
Time: 09:15

From: Hörður Bjarnason <hordur@alfaljos.is>
To: Gestur Hilmarsson <gestur@gverktakar.is>
Subject: Hello?

Gestur,

Why aren't you answering your phone? Why can't I get in touch with the rest of your crew? Did the telephone lines snap during yesterday's blizzard? Do you need Search and Rescue?

Look, I'm getting worried. We haven't heard anything from anyone for the last couple of days. The crew's families have been contacting us, seeking answers and I hate not being able to give them *something*. Anything, really, just a brief hello would suffice.

Please, reply.
All the best,
Hörður.

Date: 03/14/2026
Time: 00:02
From: Gestur Hilmarsson <gestur@gverktakar.is>
To: Hörður Bjarnason <hordur@alfaljos.is>
Subject: She came

I can't believe it...

I must have been seeing things. Too tired from all this weird fucking shit happening here.

I haven't gotten proper sleep since Árný, the cafeteria chef, disappeared. Having no food prepared for you sucks. There was only canned corn, beans and pears left in the pantry and combining that sounds even more horrible than starving yourself to death.

Tension has been high among the few that remain...

No food and no sleep make Gestur something, something...

But why did she come?

She's not supposed to be here. She's not even supposed to be walking on this godforsaken Earth!

She still came. She walked barefoot on the hardened ice, wearing nothing but the dress she was buried in. It had been her favourite dress. *My darling,* out there in the blistering storm.

Her voice called out to me. God, it felt like an arrow pierced my heart to hear it again. She asked me an impossible task: to come join her in the magma. It's where people like us belong, she told me.

I don't know if the veil between the two realms had thinned or if I had simply been hallucinating from inhaling all those toxic fumes from the magma, but I swear to God, she *looked* and *sounded* real to me.

You cannot imagine the terrible grief I went through after losing her from her battle with lung cancer. I almost gave up myself. Wanted to end it and join her. She had been my everything. But I couldn't. Chickened out. Reminded myself I had to take care of the kids.

I'm ashamed to admit I took a few steps outside into the blizzard. If I could have just one more moment with her, I would.

The sleet hitting my face woke me up. She was still there, beckoning me. Her face contorted with taunting glee. Her voice hollowed and sneered, calling me a coward.

I shut the door on her. I've said goodbye to her once. I'm not doing it again.

Her voice bounces on every wall, following me wherever I go...

I can still hear it. Listen...

Don't you hear it?

[*Audio Attachment, 2MB: based on the audio attachment, editor was unable to discern anything aside from white noise*]

DATE: 03/15/2026

Time: 07:30

From: Hörður Bjarnason <hordur@alfaljos.is>

To: Gestur Hilmarsson <gestur@gverktakar.is>

Subject: What is going on over there?

GESTUR,

If this is your idea of a practical joke, it's not funny. If this is something your crew tends to do while away on an assignment, you need to stop it right now.

Were you drinking last night when you sent me that email? If you were, it's highly unprofessional of you. What a load of drivel. There was nothing on that audio clip, except for the wind sweeping across the speaker system. No voice whispering sweet nothings into my ear, whatsoever.

Also, Árný has gone as well?? You should have alerted me of this immediately instead of mentioning her in passing.

This is very unlike you, Gestur. I'm very concerned for your wellbeing as well as the wellbeing of the rest of your crew.

You've left me no choice. I've contacted the police as well as Search and Rescue and requested their help. Once the weather dies down, they'll be on their way to the facilities.

You better be sober when they arrive.

Regards,

Hörður.

DATE: 03/17/2026

Time: 02:00

From: Gestur Hilmarsson <gestur@gverktakar.is>

To: Hörður Bjarnason <hordur@alfaljos.is>

Subject: COME QUICK!!

I'M SORRY, Hörður.

I don't know how else to start...I failed. No, I cracked under pressure. Yeah, I guess you could say that.

Thank you for alerting the police. I'm glad they're coming. They wouldn't have taken me seriously if I had called them myself.

I...did something terrible.

Geiri...Konráð...all of them are dead.

I couldn't help it...

I hadn't gotten any sleep since my wife appeared. She kept me awake with her incessant taunts. No amount of earplugs or heavy metal music at the highest volume could drown her out. I couldn't hear anything else, not even when my crew stood in front of me mouthing something I couldn't understand.

Then somehow, she got inside. I saw her everywhere; she lurked in the main building, danced around the chairs in the cafeteria, slammed the doors in the cabins and even swayed on the steel lanes near the drills down below (see image attachment).

I was going crazy, but I persevered and managed to ignore the ghastly sights till I drank myself unconscious.

The last couple of days are a blur. I remember bits and pieces...

Grabbing an emergency axe from the case in the hallway...

Seeing her wretched face approaching me...the voice I had loved drilling into my ears...

Me, finally having had enough.

A good old-fashioned chase through the hallways. Screaming. Or was it laughter?

Blisters on my hands—muscles feeling taut from over-exertion—blood obscuring my vision—laughter.

So much laughter...It didn't sound human at all. At least I had gotten rid of her face.

When I came to, I was standing in the warehouse. Mangled bodies, in various stages of decomposition, littered the concrete. Maggots writhed through puss-festered wounds. It was my missing crew.

I remember screaming till my throat grew hoarse and raw. Bile rushing from my oesophagus and exiting violently on the floor. I scrambled out of the slaughterhouse and went searching for the others.

Security cameras told me they were down below where the drills were. Their cut-up bodies greeted me when I stepped on the narrow lane. Blood dripped through the grid, sizzling from the extensive heat.

I barely recognised Geiri and Konráð among the mutilated corpses. My hands still held on to the bloody axe. I hadn't noticed it till now.

Then something moved underneath the severed body limbs. Child sized and drenched in dark crimson they appeared obsidian. An oily hue slicked their narrowed eyes. Jagged rows of teeth chomped into the dead flesh. Sharp claws pierced through the limbs like clay. Scratches reverberated from the rocks. Tiny stones toppled from the cracks as more shapes grew bigger and more prominent, eager to join the feast.

LOOK, YOU HAVE TO HURRY!

I've locked myself in my office, but I know they're coming.

No, wait...

WAS THAT BANGING ON THE DOOR??

I HEAR SCRATCHES!

FUCK, THOSE SHRIEKS!

IT'S THEM!!

HOLY FUCK, KONRÁÐ WAS RIGHT ALL ALONG! WE THOUGHT THEY WERE MYTHS, A TALL TALE TO WARD OFF PEOPLE SEEKING TO HARM OUR NATURE. BUT SHIT, WE WERE WRONG!

THE TRUE INHABITANTS OF THE MOUNTAIN HAVE COME TO CLAIM THEIR LAST INTRUDERS.

OH GOD, THEY'RE HE

[*Image Attachment, 25MB: Due to the grainy resolution, editor was unable to discern any kind of human shape in the image*]

VILLIMEY MIST

Villimey has always been fascinated by vampires and horror, ever since she watched Bram Stoker's Dracula when she was a little, curious girl.

She loves to read and create stories that pop into her head unannounced.

She lives in Iceland with her husband and two cats, Skuggi and RoboCop, and is often busy drawing or watching the latest shows on Netflix.

Villimey is the author of the Nocturnal series which currently comprises 3 books; *Nocturnal Blood*, *Nocturnal Farm* and *Nocturnal Salvation.*

Villimey's work has previously appeared in *Campfire Macabre,* edited by Joe Sullivan and John Brhel, *The One That Got Away: Women of Horror Anthology Vol.3*, edited by Jill Girardi, *Of Cottages and Cauldrons: An Autumn Anthology,* edited by Tiffany Putetis, *Krampus Tales: A Killer Anthology,* edited by Alexandra Rose, *Far From Home: Anthology of Adventure Horror,* edited by Sam Kolesnik, *Were-Tales: A Shapeshifter Anthology,* edited by S. D. Vassallo.

THE GREAT WITHERING

BY ROSS JEFFERY

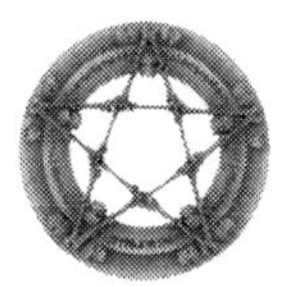

The boy was flung into the restroom wearing nothing but a dirty loincloth. He tripped due to his uncoordinated, tired legs, landing awkwardly on the ground. The tanned skin of his back crisscrossed with reddish welts, wounds which were healing in aggravated pink scar tissue.

He remained on the floor, breathing heavily, his back expanding and contracting, his ribs showed with each laboured breath, he was seriously malnourished. The scarred skin of his back rippled like a fish's scales in the harsh, clinical lighting of the bathroom. He scanned his surroundings quickly, looking for some place to hide, his eyes huge with fear, they were desperately trying to locate a place he'd be safe and hidden.

The door to the restroom flung open again and the boy turned his head; his long, brown and matted hair hung over his face like a dirty veil. His bright, green eyes peered through the follicle curtain and alighted on the figure skulking towards him, a tormentor with vengeful determination in their stride. The young boy braced himself for what was to come – he gritted his teeth and prepared for the stinging taste of the ASP on his skin.

The hulking figure stood before him, his shadow loomed over like a tower. In a well-practiced routine he flicked his wrist and the telescopic baton appeared from thin air, as if he were a magician and this act of torture his sadistic sleight of hand. The sound of the baton forming made the boy flinch before it had even touched his skin, but touch his skin it would, there were guarantees in life; birth, death were two of them and the third was the sharp sting of the ASP. The man raised the baton and brought it down with a whip across the boy's already scarred back. The force of the blow drove all the air from his lungs, he collapsed onto the cold tiles with a guttural moan. The floor, snow-cold against his skin, and the frigidness of it made him feel alive, albeit for a second, but he hugged the tiles because he needed to feel something, anything to remind him that he *was* still alive, that they hadn't killed him – yet.

The boy placed his slender hands on the floor and began to lift his skeletal frame from his prone position; he knew from experience that if he'd stayed down, if he gave up, it would only earn him more lashes with the baton. And so with trembling, weak arms and a few ragged breaths he began to rise. He breathed through the burning pain that shot across his back, he'd been burnt by them during their experiments so he knew the feeling intimately, but he'd also suffered much worse at their hands. There was always a chance the situation could spiral out of control and match those torturous beatings if he remained apathetic to his plight, and so he continued to rise from his grounded position.

A boot soon connected with his stomach which lifted the boy from the ground. He was momentarily weightless before he fell back down to the cold tiles. From this new position he reached out his arms, gripped the water pipes from the hand basin and pulled his way under the porcelain shield of the sink, narrowly missing another attempted swipe from the ASP. Once under cover, he pulled his legs up to his chest, going foetal in an effort to protect the soft and delicate parts of his body from the beating that was to come.

'You dirty piece of shit!' the man spat as he charged toward the boy. He swiped the baton down again and again, the sound the ASP made as it cut through the air was a sharp whistle, each swipe ended in sickening, dull thumps as it connected with the boys arms, legs, side and back. The man was furious in his desire to destroy the boy; the keychain at his hip jangled a merry tune throughout.

The blows rained down until the man grew breathless and red-faced, his uniform now marked by dark rings of damp under the arms and his shirt had become untucked around his rotund gut. He stowed the baton on his belt next to his gun and keys. He tucked himself in and straightened his uniform before he stared down at the wounded boy on the ground, raised welts and thin cuts decorated the boy's already puckered back in a latticework of torment.

The man stared at the fresh carnage he'd caused, a mirthless grin peeled across his blotchy and sweat-riddled face before he raised a hand to his mouth and wiped the creamy spittle that had formed in the corner with the back of his hand. He hawked a chunk of phlegm from his throat, and spat it at the child before him, the marble of green and yellow catarrh landed on the boy's back with a splat before it began its slow descent, trickling over raised cuts and welts.

'That'll teach you for pissing in your pen, you disgusting little pig. We should have left you in that shit-shack of a village to starve like the rest of mankind. You got ten minutes - piss, shit, tidy yourself up and then I'm taking you to dispatch – it's almost time for transport!'

The guard checked himself in the mirror and ran a hand through his thinning hair. After he ensured his comb-over covered his bald patch, the hulking man turned away from the bloodied and broken boy at his feet. His rubber-soled shoes squeaked on the floor as he turned and departed, not before he shot one final glance over his shoulder at the specimen that quivered on the floor, he was making sure he'd not killed the pathetic child, *Riddick* and *the project* would not be pleased if he had. The boy squirmed and with a sigh of relief the guard shook his head at the thing before him and left, leaving the boy to lick his wounds. The door closed and trapped the boy within a new prison.

The child took a moment. A long pause to ensure the man wouldn't return and beat him down again, which was often the case. When he was sure the guard wasn't coming back, he rolled over and got onto his knees. With shaking, skeletal arms he reached out and clutched the edge of the basin. Pain coursed through his body, he winced as the cuts on his back opened wide with the sudden movement. He pulled himself up, placed both hands on the rim of the sink and paused. He lifted his gaze; his green eyes peered through his sweat-dampened fringe at his reflection in the mirror. He turned away from the mirror to observe the deep cut on his upper arm.

The child watched intently as tiny tendrils, green and vine-like in texture wriggled free from within the bloody laceration. Vines climbed out of the gore like weeds desperately struggling towards the light. His eyes darted to the wall, when he noticed the shadow that was cast by his body. Tendrils danced in the shadow, and he realised that his back was alive with the roving fronds that twirled out of his sliced dermis like naked branches in a winter sky. He shuddered as they moved independently around his body, as they tickled his flesh with their fussing.

His eyes returned to the deep gash on his shoulder. Green shoots reached across the wound and embedded themselves into the healthy untainted tissue, before they burrowed into his flesh like a needle and thread. He looked on fascinated, as his skin was pulled closed from within, as it knitted back together; all that remained was the pink scar tissue of fresh growth.

A clear secretion oozed from the wound on closure. He reached his hand up and dipped his fingers in the substance. It was tacky, honey-like as he rubbed his coated fingers together. He lifted it to his nose, sniffed, it smelt sweet. He poked the tip of his tongue out and lapped at the resin, he needed to be sure that it was the same as last time. His face screwed up with the flavour in his mouth, there was no denying that it was sap. It tasted of honeysuckle. The boy peered into the mirror before he turned, desperate to see his back, although he knew what he'd discover but he had to be sure, after contorting his body he saw the fresh wounds across his back had been sealed, the skin also coated in the same syrupy secretion.

What have they turned me into? he thought, as he peered at his haunted face in the mirror again and wished he was back home in his village, back before the bad men came to take him away and experiment on him.

BACK TO WHEN he was a boy – before they made him a bomb.

THE BOY COULD SMELL a strong odour of mould. It filled the room with a thick choking miasma. He tore his gaze away from the mirror and padded around the room in search of the stench. The fragrance was cloying, as if unseen hands were intent on pulling him towards its source. He tasted the earthy mushroom notes in his mouth. He staggered towards one of the closed toilet cubicles. He pushed it open and the stench smacked him in the face as he wheeled back as if struck. He ventured forwards, glanced inside the toilet bowl, nothing. He scanned the floor, again nothing. His eyes slowly rose to a tiny window near the ceiling, where he noticed the moon. *How long has it been since I've seen the moon?* the boy wondered, as he edged further into the cubicle.

The smell was thick, his mouth watered. He felt something ripple under his skin, as if the vines that had crept out were maggots that burrowed beneath his dermis, where they feasted and festered in darkness and blood. He glanced down as the sensation pulsed through his arms and noticed the veins on his forearms had grown engorged; the vines or was it sap pulsated towards his hands in rippling waves. His hand raised all of its own volition, his fingers splayed as if he were trying to stop something charging towards him. His fingers tingled as his hand trembled in the air, pressure building in every digit.

He soon noticed the mould. Dark splotches had accumulated in the corner of the rotting wood of the window frame. It was the source of the stench. With his hand outstretched, directed at the mould he watched as the small cluster of fungus began to spread like ink on blotting paper. It feasted on the wood in moments, the timber splintered and ruptured in the frame. Fungus bloomed, and then withered, as if a whole season had happened in the blinking of an eye. Fresh growth again blossomed from the mulch left behind. Plant growth soon manifested from the loam, small shoots appeared first then they quickly morphed into thick, thorny vines which pressed and scratched against the glass. Suddenly there was a crack; the pane of glass shattered but each jagged piece was caught by the green hands of flora that appeared.

The boy felt the cold night air for the first time in years, as it settled on his skin, he felt both lost and found, and with a sinking feeling in his stomach he also felt terribly alone.

This was the moment he'd been dreaming of, the chance to escape the *bad men* and their experiments, he could be free at last – but what was left of the world he'd been torn from all those years ago? What was left of his village in India? He'd heard the other children that came after him talk about the fall of the world; the riots, the pollution, rising tides, and global warming. But what pained him most was the talk of mass deforestation to ensure the cities didn't fall. But the cities did fall, but not to lack of fossil fuels (although they were now in short demand), they'd become the birthplace of pestilence and the epicentres around the world for the *Great Withering* as the guards often referred to it. The boy wondered if his village would still be standing or if it had gone the way of the *Great Withering* too; the hope that filled his heart wounded him gravely and tears fell from his eyes, carving clean tracks through the grime on his face.

He tore himself away from reverie as he noticed that the vines had formed a hedge ladder from the window to the ground, steps that he could ascend and escape. He peered once over his shoulder at the door, half expecting his tormentor to rip him from this sweetest of moments and return him back to the labs and the tyrannical and vicious perversions of Riddick, the *very* bad man. But no one came.

He turned back to the cubicle, and stared up at freedom in the shape of a broken window. He could fit through that gap now; the vines had removed some of the bricks and the hole now tailor-made for him, and him alone. The boy stepped tentatively forwards. He climbed the ladder quickly, and then jumped down from the hole in the wall, finally he was outside. He choked as he breathed the outside air, it tasted foul, it was thick with smoke and choking fumes. He peered up and in the distance he noticed fires raged in what he imagined were once cities and towns and woodland.

He pulled himself up and lent against the brick wall. He leaned into the shadow as searchlights roved the concrete wasteland he now found himself in. Sheltered in the dark, away from the cruel eyes of the guards in their kill towers, the tendrils appeared again. This time they emerged from his mouth and nose, his teeth shifted in their moorings, his nose tickled and he thought he would sneeze as vines crept up and out of his nasal cavity. The green barbs pierced through his gums, anchored themselves to his lips and nose, where they formed a lattice-work of foliage. It soon began to restrict his breathing. The boy panicked, his hands gripped at his throat and then his mouth, as he attempted to tear the fibrous growths away. He feared choking and suffocation, but he feared most making it this far only to fall by his own enhanced mutation. But as he struggled with the vines he soon realised he could breathe, that the mesh over his mouth wasn't choking him but filtering the smog-filled air he breathed. Taking a deep breath of clean air he closed his eyes and imagined he was far away from here, back in his village, back with his family.

He was torn from his thoughts by the sound that emanated from the bathroom window; he craned his neck and lifted his ear to the broken window above. He could hear the slow, squeaking footsteps of his tormentor. The guard was back in the room stalking his prey. *'Your prey's long gone'* the boy thought with a smirk, before the deep baritone voice from his nightmares ripped any joy from the moment, and the boy soon realised that getting out of that room was only the start of his escape.

'Come out, come out wherever you are?'

There was a bang as the cubicle door was kicked open and clattered against the wall, the sound echoed into the night like a gunshot. The boy stood still, his naked back pressed up against the brick wall.

'What the actual fuck.' The guard's voice rang out into the night.

The boy didn't move. From his position he scanned the concrete jungle that had replaced the actual jungle he was used to, a chain-linked fence about three hundred metres circled the camp. The ground between the fence and his position was lit up every few moments by searchlights; the boy didn't have time to study their pattern, to find a way through the puzzle of beams. It suddenly dawned on him that although he was outside, he was a long way from free.

He flinched as the booming voice hit him again, his panicked eyes returned to the window, but he knew the guard would never be able to fit through that hole, and when he'd climbed down the ropes of vegetation had crumbled to dust once he'd made his exit. But he still needed to stay out of sight in case the guard peered out.

'Riddick, come in Riddick,' followed by a hiss from the guard's radio, 'We've a situation with London, come in Riddick.'

London? The boy thought. Memories of the pens invaded his mind; he could see the other children in their glass boxes, their scared faces stared back at him. Each pen had a name above it; Rome, Helsinki, New York, Istanbul. They were some of the places that had succumbed to the Great Withering, there were more, and the boy knew this. He'd heard hushed conversations, seen diagrams and maps in the laboratory too, each showing a city that needed to be *re-pollinated* with life - *I must be London?* The boy mused.

'This is Riddick, what is the situation with London?'

'He's escaped, sir.'

'Escaped? How the hell did he manage that?'

'There's a hole in the lavatory window, sir, seems the boy climbed out, there's.... there's signs that his mutation is active, sir.'

'Of course it's active, he's due to be detonated – need I

remind you that our investors are expecting delivery of London today?'

'Sir... no, sir. I'll find him. He couldn't have gotten far.'

'Good, because if you don't find him... well let's just say the joint council won't be happy, the investors will be baying for blood, they'll make an example of you, do you understand?'

'I understand, sir. I'll trigger the alarm.'

'The fuck you will, soldier. I don't think you understand, we've got the eyes of the world on us right now and I don't want to raise a panic on the eve of our maiden voyage. The walls are now closed around London. The chosen are in place, *everyone* in the London Ark has paid a great deal to be there for the first re-pollination. And you, losing London on the eve of that great spectacle, when the world is watching and praying for an end to the Withering... shit. The investors will not be happy GODDAMNIT! Find London and whatever you do don't raise the alarm, we want to project the sense of calm here, do you understand?!'

'Yes sir. Sorry, sir.'

'I haven't got time for apologies, just action, now find him, or it's all our heads on the block.'

London heard the guard grunt in anger then a fist slammed into the cubicle door. London flinched again, imagined that hand finding his flesh as it had so often. He listened intently and heard the man's feet squeak away from the window. London glanced around the camp, he was still pressed up against the wall in the shadows; he'd observed the area ahead before making his escape, as he pondered which route he'd take, London heard the radio crackle to life again.

'The pens? Are the pens secured?' It was Riddick again, his voice tinged with worry.

'Yes, sir. I believe they are?'

'Make sure London doesn't get to the pens soldier, he may

try to free the others. We, and when I say we, I mean you, soldier, need to ensure that we secure the other assets. If London escapes and you better pray that he doesn't, we don't want him leading those vessels away with him and detonating all over the wastelands; it'll make a mockery of the programme, this programme is for the chosen, it's not for those that live on the fringes of society in those withered shit-stinking places, do I make myself clear?'

'Crystal, sir.'

'But if he does escape, we'll need to spin it as an exercise gone wrong. But if he should become nullified in his escape, we'll just supplement him with another; we can't keep the chosen waiting. The other children might not be ripe yet, but their extinction event should bloom new life nevertheless, just on a less grander scale. So make sure you lock down the assets first, before you fuck anything else up.'

'Roger. I'll check the pens and ensure the resources are locked down.'

'Don't fail me, soldier.'

London listened intently to the silence that followed. He could hear the soldier's harried breathing which was replaced with a cry of rage as he slammed the door to the restroom and left. London knew that now was the time for action. He steadied himself against the rough brick and breathed through his mask of moss, the filtered air became somewhat of a tonic to his addled mind, thoughts tumbled like a rockslide; *should I run and get as far away from this place as possible, would I make it, how far would I get before a searchlight found me and a bullet tore me down.* It was the pens that kept him rooted to the spot; the children, most of them younger than him, and their eyes, haunted orbs that pleaded for help. Their innocent faces pained him gravely. He needed to do something to make this right, and in a moment of clarity he realised he needed to fight.

London's arm prickled as he surrendered himself to rescuing the children in the pens; he glanced down and discovered his forearm was crowned in purple thorns that ran along its edge, each barb emerged from his dermis through a slit of flesh that glistened with the sap that coursed through his blood. The thorns hardened in place, each one thirsty for the taste of revenge. He noticed that his fist had changed colour, it was now purple and white, his knuckles bloomed into a gristly club, but organic in nature, prickly barbs appeared and he realised it wasn't a club but the head of a mighty thistle. Armed with the weapons that nature provided, London strode in the direction of the pens, he had no option other than to fight. Someone had to free the children from the experiments and the evil intentions of man and money.

Nature was fighting back and London would be its willing soldier.

THE GUARD WAS DISPATCHED with ease. Blood dribbled down London's arm; each thorny barb coated in ichor and flayed skin which had peeled away from the guard's throat in stringy ropes like pulled pork. London hadn't wanted to resort to violence, but something deep within propelled him to take a life, as if the Earth's vengeance needed fulfilling and he was the vessel chosen to release its wrath upon those that wanted to harness its ways for the few.

With the guard's key card in hand, London let himself into the pens. An eerie quiet met him as he made his way through vacant tunnels and experimentation rooms. News of his escape yet to have been passed down the line, but they'd be aware soon enough; and so he quickened his pace. He peered over his shoulder as he approached the bulkhead door leading to the pens; he paused, peering into the darkness. When nothing appeared, he swiped the card. The panel on the wall turned from red to green, the doors hissed open. London half expected to find soldiers on the other side, guns and batons raised ready for attack, but there was nobody there, only glass pods and the haunted faces of children that had been subjected to the unthinkable and the unimaginable.

London stood before the child whose destination, and new name he assumed, was Helsinki. She sat at the back of her cell, cloaked in darkness, her pale arms wrapped tightly around her legs; she rocked, lost in her own torment. He tapped on the glass. Helsinki raised her head, the fear in her eyes soon dissipated to what he assumed was hope as she crawled from the darkness on hands and knees, towards the glass that separated them. London placed his hand flat against the pane, Helsinki reciprocated and there was a connection, not with their hands, but in their plight as they studied each other. She smiled at him.

They were one and the same and their mutations made them brothers and sisters in a new age. London watched on as Helsinki's smile stretched further and further, her mouth splitting and peeling back at the corners, her skin fraying like a torn plastic bag as the top of her head fell backwards. Glistening white shards sprouted from her bottom jaw and as her head flipped back, more of the barbs sprouted from the other half of her mouth. As the two halves of her head yawned open they swayed like two large petals; the gore it revealed glistened wetly and invitingly – it was horrifically beautiful and London couldn't look away. Her head had become a humanoid Venus Flytrap.

Her head quickly snapped back, the shards of tusks slipped back into their moorings and London watched as tendrils of green began the work of affixing her mouth back in place. He smiled, gesticulated that he would be back. Helsinki pleaded for him to stay but he needed to check on the other children before it was too late.

Rome stood before London, his mutation was visible unlike Helsinki's and his own, they could hide their gift but the sight of the boy pained London greatly as he knew there was nowhere in the world Rome could hide without the corporation finding him again. Rome's eyes were deeply set in a dark pillow of flesh, masked in soft fuzz. London watched as the boy shook his head vigorously; the fine fuzz drifted away from his face and floated around the cell. Rome's naked head was a blackened bulb; two white orbs stared out from a slab of darkened skin. London watched as new seeds sprouted from his skin. Within moments the boy's head was covered again in dandelion seeds. London knew the seed pods that drifted in this boy's cell showed the exact reason the corporation had him captive and were prepping him for detonation, each seed a kernel of hope and the promise of regeneration, or as Riddick had delicately put it, re-pollination.

London checked the other cells; there were seven children. Eight cities including him had been highlighted as the first to receive re-pollination, but he knew it would never end there, especially when the world witnessed London's detonation and re-pollination in action, they'd clamour to be next. He knew they'd hunt down more special children, they'd subject them to tests and torture, tearing them away from all they'd ever known for the ongoing quest of money and the survival of the rich and those deemed worthy. The poor weren't allowed to thrive, they'd been left to fend for themselves in the hinterlands after the *Great Withering* – the only purpose they served was a neck for the chosen to rest their aching feet.

London reached for the key card and brought it up to the terminal. He flinched as something stung his neck. Suddenly his moss mask started to deteriorate; it turned to dust and crumbled away to the ground. He lifted his hand to his neck, his fingers feeling for the source of the pain. He pulled the object he'd discovered from his neck and held it between his fingers. His vision grew cloudy, he shook his head to clear the befuddlement, when it swam back into focus he realised he held a dart. Glancing up he noticed a wall of human shapes in the distance, one stepped forward and even though his vision was impaired he knew it was him, his tormentor, back to inflict one last atrocity.

London prepared himself to fight, but soon staggered on legs that didn't feel quite his own. He placed a hand out to the cell next to him, steadied himself before he succumbed to the tranquiliser and collapsed to his knees. The figure loomed over London as it often did before it crouched down and pressed the tip of his ASP to London's already aching chest, he pinned London to the floor and ended his feeble struggles. London knew it was over.

'Riddick. Come in, Riddick.'

'Yes. Do you have an update on London?'

'The payload has been secured and nullified. He is ready for transportation.'

'Get him in a pod and start the preparations, we've a timeline to keep and we're already behind thanks to your stupidity. Don't fail me again.'

'Affirmative, sir.'

London was lifted from the floor by two guards. His head lolled back and through the haze of his failing vision he noticed the children of Mother Nature screaming from their cells, each of their mutations bloomed and reset as they mourned the fall of their would-be saviour. Unceremoniously, the guards dropped London into a waiting pod, as he fell into the cushioned interior he couldn't help but think it was his coffin. The soldiers closed the transportation pod, as London stared out of the glass. As they sealed him inside, they also sealed his fate, and with an aching feeling of dread he knew that there would be no coming back from this.

London was in a new prison, scared for what was to pass as they took him for transportation and later detonation. Deep within his core London felt oddly at peace, although he was scared he knew that nature would find a way to survive, it always had. The children and London were a testament to that. As the freezing fog filled his chamber for transportation, and just before he gave into the drug-induced sleep, he closed his eyes and prayed he'd live long enough to find out if that old adage was true. If nature would indeed find a way.

ROSS JEFFERY

Ross Jeffery is the Bram Stoker Award and Splatterpunk Award-nominated author of Tome, Juniper, Only The Stains Remain, Milk Kisses & Other Stories and Tethered.

Ross has a number of projects in the pipeline including the third book in the Juniper series 'Scorched' publishing through Stygian Sky Media, a novel 'The Devil's Pocketbook' plus a debut horror collection 'Beautiful Atrocities' all of which are slated for a 2022 release.

Ross' fiction has appeared in various print anthologies and his short stories and flash fiction have been published in many online magazines.

Ross lives in Bristol with his wife (Anna) and two children (Eva and Sophie). You can follow him on Twitter at @RossJeffery_

THE DUMB SUPPER

BY TRACY FAHEY

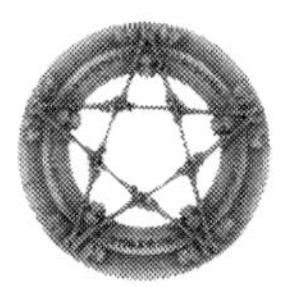

You came back from New York in February with gifts and a persistent sore throat. In the mornings I could hear you gargle, the noise amplified by a cold bathroom echo. I thought nothing of it at first; you were always coming down with bugs after your long-haul flights. It wasn't until the news started to leak through from the US that we started to worry. And by then it was too late. You were in quarantine, and so was I.

Now I lie awake at night and wish you'd never come back.

It's the fourth week of isolation and silence lies thick and charged between us.

The first week we binged the news channels. They beamed into our apartment; a relentless parade of images. We watched the scenes in New York; the hospital tents, the Manhattan streets, gleaming and silent. The Valentine Virus, they called it. An apt term; it was identified on the 14th February and transmitted by physical contact.

'Nice work on the name,' I said drily. 'The up-side is that it might kill off that whole commercial romance industry for good.'

'Cynic,' you croaked from your nest of blankets on the sofa. 'I love my red roses.' I looked at the wilting bouquet from Tim, leaves beginning to crisp and curl. He'd delivered the late gift in true Romeo and Juliet fashion, throwing them upwards to our balcony. Lovely Tim.

'We'll except Tim from the rule,' I allowed.

'Thanks, o mighty one.'

'No problem, Lori,' I said graciously. 'I refuse to let my sour grapes cast shade on Love's Young Dream.'

'Bella...' Your laughter caught in a cough; but it wasn't making that raw, tearing sound anymore. Your case was confirmed as mild. No one yet knew what the risk factors were that could push the virus from a mild case to a deadly infection, but you were one of the lucky ones. Already your voice sounded less ragged, your breathing more even. It was easy then to think this was all just a temporary nuisance.

'I'll make some more tea.'

'Thanks.' Your eyes were still streaming.

On the way to the kitchen I touched the drooping roses briefly, imagining for a brief, ashamed moment that they were for me.

I CALLED AUNT VERA, my closest relative, to break the news about our quarantine. I'd been putting it off, but it was inevitable. She'd know when I didn't show up for my monthly visit home to the country. In all, she reacted reasonably calmly, just mildly annoyed.

'Ach,' she sniffed. 'That Lori. I might have known she'd be up to all sorts, flying here and there.'

'It's not her fault.' As usual I was defending you. 'It's a pandemic, Vera.'

'That's as may be.' Her voice was brisk. 'Now mind yourself, you hear? I read your cards yesterday. They say there's troublesome times ahead.'

'Thanks for the warning,' I rolled my eyes. 'I'll be fine.'

And yes, we were fine that week. The worst part was that so few people in Ireland were quarantined—just the ones who'd returned recently from New York. Outside was the constant reminder that life was going on without us. When we sat out on the balcony we could see the pavement thronged with people, spilling out of shops and restaurants. Their voices and laughter drifted upwards, tantalising.

Apart from that, there was a vague sense of holiday that permeated. We'd opted to quarantine together, and me to work from home. That was OK. We hadn't spent that much time together since school—I won't deny that part of me was slightly happy at the idea of hibernating together.

'It'll be fun,' you said. 'As soon as the last of this cough goes.'

It didn't seem real. We pretended it wasn't happening. *We'll be going for drinks this time next week and laughing about it.*

But we didn't.

THE SECOND WEEK was more tense. We watched the TV screens as the red stain spread out of New York and into neighbouring states. Little red dots started to appear elsewhere; across Europe, even in Ireland.

'That's us,' you said, and coughed, pointing at the Irish dot in Dublin.

'The pariahs,' I said solemnly.

We clinked glasses. 'To the pariahs of Dublin 8!'

But as the week went on, alarm grew. The government met constantly and made no decisions. Flights from the US continued; the Irish map became blistered with red spots. Official statements talked about the 'special relationship' with the US and the need to allow citizens back in. Message boards were peppered with angry comments about the returnees, so by unspoken consensus we stopped going on social media. Outside, the world seemed more subdued. People stayed in more, and some of those who passed under our balcony were wearing surgical masks.

So instead we ignored it. The days I wasn't working we slept late. We made popcorn and watched old movies as the sun sank outside. Your cough waned, but you still lay around on the sofa, snoozing; a clutter of snack wrappings building slowly beside you.

One evening there was a sharp rap on the window. I glanced over at you, fast asleep, one hand wedged in a tube of Pringles. I belted my blue kimono and slid the French doors open.

'Tim.'

He looked up at the balcony and smiled, a lock of hair falling over his face, pale under the streetlight.

'How are you girls doing? I brought some supplies.' He held up two plastic bags. *Lovely Tim.* 'Oh thank you! I'll open the front door, shall I? You can leave them there.'

'Sure.' He hesitated. 'Where's Lori?'

'Oh, she's sleeping,' I said in a hushed voice. 'Don't worry, I'll run down to you.'

When I opened the door, he stood there, awkwardly twisting the bag handles. 'Hey,' he said, raising his chin in a nod of salutation. 'Just making sure you had the necessities.' He placed the bags down carefully and stepped back.

I picked up one, feeling the tell-tale weight of wine bottles. 'You're an angel,' I said, and meant it.

'No problem. Good to see you. I like the kimono, by the way. Very chic.'

I flushed, absurdly pleased. 'Thanks.'

He smiled. 'Sure. Tell Lori I called by.'

'I will,' I called after him. But I padded upstairs silently and unpacked the bags, gloating over the contents, his thoughtfulness. I didn't wake you. *I'm letting you sleep, you need it.*

That's what I told myself.

THAT WAS THE SECOND WEEK. The third week was grimmer. TV maps blazed red with the Valentine Virus; a grim ticker-tape of fatalities ribboning across the bottom of the screen. Inbound flights shut down, but too late. Ireland was a ruby island, awash in the blue sea. Our quarantine was still ongoing —a month—but we were all locked down, confined to a five kilometre radius. Neither of us wanted to watch movies. We huddled down in our separate rooms, phones in hand.

I bumped into you late one night in the kitchen. You were sitting there in the dark, drinking wine. A half-empty bottle puddled a red stain on the counter.

'I'm scared,' you said. 'What if this is the end?' Your eyes reflected the gleam of the muted TV.

'It's not,' I said shortly. 'Look at you, you're fine.'

'Yeah.' You took another swig of wine. 'But millions aren't.'

I sighed. 'We need some fresh air.'

I opened the French doors to the balcony. The streets below me lay empty. A lone crisp packet fluttered and drifted in the breeze.

Now it's the fourth week. Everyone's been asked not to leave home, unless there's an emergency. Our government, indecisive too long, scrambles to contain us now. The apartment seems smaller and stuffier each day. We circle each other like wary cats. You leave crumbs on the countertops; I wipe them down, trembling with unspoken rage. You dump teabags in the sink that I pick up and fling into the overflowing bin. You leave your bedroom door open during long, noisy phone calls to Tim.

Me? I'm a saint. A martyr. Until you tell me in a low steady voice that if I don't stop humming under my breath you'll take your chances on the street. I start laughing, and with that, the tension is broken.

'C'mere, you eejit.' You extend your arms. I pretend to flinch away. 'I've washed my hands,' you add in mock-seductive tones and I giggle. For a moment, as your warm body crushes against mine, we're reconciled.

'Seriously though, Lori.' I break free. 'We need to find something to do.'

'Do what? Read? TV? Movies?'

I scowl and pick at the front of the kimono I've worn like a uniform for the last four days. There's a coffee-stain hardened like concrete on the right lapel. 'Can't focus enough to read, the stupid virus is everywhere on the TV. Plus we've watched everything. Told you we should've gotten Netflix.'

'Yeah, yeah.' You've stopped listening. Then you grin, that magic-flash grin. 'I know, why don't you read our cards.'

I could have said no. I wish I'd said no.

But instead I shrug. 'Why not?'

I CAN'T EVEN REMEMBER LEARNING how to read Tarot. The dog-eared, worn cards were always there on my aunt's dresser, tucked behind *Old Moore's Almanac* and ragged cookery books. In the evenings, when the chores were done, she'd take them out and smile at me.

'What will the cards tell us tonight, my love?'

You look at me, pleading. 'Go on. Tim hasn't texted me today.' You frown at your phone. 'Just want to make sure he hasn't shacked up with some virus-free neighbour.'

'Tim wouldn't do that. You're one of the lucky ones.' I hide my warm face behind the card deck. 'But OK.'

I shuffle the worn cards expertly. 'Now if we're doing a relationship spread, the first card is you, the second, Tim, the third, the relationship.' I cut the cards into three piles. 'Choose one from each and lay them face down.'

You do it, and look up at me expectantly.

'Turn over the first one.'

The Lovers. You smile, confident. I clear my throat. 'This is a relationship card. It means choices and potentially some sacrifice.' *And temptation, and uncertainty about a partner.*

'Pick Tim's card now. It'll be clearer as we go along.'

Death. I frown. Yes, it doesn't mean physical death, but it's never a good start.

'Oh no.' Your front tooth dents your bottom lip.

'Don't worry. Death often signifies some kind of...' I pause. *Ending.* 'New beginnings and changes.' I ignore the fact that it's reversed. In my head I see Vera, head tilted to one side, hear her sharp voice. *Oh, reversed this card isn't good news. It can mean a lack of awareness, delayed change, and even a long illness.*

'And now the third, your relationship.'

The Tower. You look at me anxiously. 'Even I know it's not a good one.'

'Well,' I say, 'as you can see it's a tower struck by lightning. This means change also, potential danger, but also liberation.'

'Liberation!' You grin then. 'Freedom, Bella. Freedom!'

I don't tell you the card is reversed. Vera's voice rises again in my head. *Illness again. Loss. Volatile situation.* I've learned from reading your cards before to filter negativity as much as possible.

'Now yours!'

'OK.' I shuffle them again.

'Let's see if there's any romance brewing for you.' Your smile is impish. 'Do it the same way; you, the mystery person, the relationship.'

I shrug and choose three cards. 'Go on,' I tell you. 'Turn them over.'

Two of Cups. 'OK, this is actually a love card.' I can't keep the surprise out of my voice. 'It generally signifies a relationship, monogamy, bonding.'

I turn the next one. *The Lovers.* I flush slightly. 'Well, you know this one, I don't need to tell you what it means.' Hastily, I pick up the final card.

The Tower. Surely you'll notice the similarity. I laugh; a forced sound. 'I guess I didn't shuffle them properly. Sorry!'

'Don't be silly. Right, the omens are good. Change and freedom. Let's think about who it could be...'

I stop collecting the cards, heart thudding. 'No...I mean...'

Your phone chirps the double-bleep of a WhatsApp message.

'It's Tim.' You smile at me. 'Aw, the cards sorted it.'

I stow the deck back in the drawer.

'Mind you,' you say, thumbs already flicking, writing a text, 'this is to be continued. We need to find out who the mystery lover is.'

'GoodNIGHT, Lori,' I say pointedly. You laugh and dip your head back over your phone. As I see you there, golden hair perfect and lustrous under the lamplight, I feel a twinge of something sour; a bitter aftertaste.

If only we'd stopped at that.

Images jumble and slur; I'm adrift in a haze of half-seen buildings, running down looping corridors on marshmallow legs. An alarm sounds; blaring through rooms that melt like smoke.

I blink. I'm awake, it's Saturday morning, and the phone is shrilling beside my bed.

'Yes?'

'Bella. It's me, Vera.' She always says that, as if I can't see the caller display.

'Mmm. Hello.' I sit up and push the untidy hair out of my eyes.

'Are you all right?' Her voice is tense.

''Course I am. Told you yesterday. We're fine. Lori's feeling lots better.'

'I just...' She pauses. 'I had a dream,' she says slowly. 'Things were not as they should be. I felt danger. So I drew a card for you this morning, and it was the Tower.'

I swallow. A coincidence, nothing more. 'Honestly, everything's OK.'

'Isabella.' She only calls me that when she's serious. 'You'll forgive an old woman for caring. You're all that I have, since your parents passed.' *Well done Vera, that's the guilt trigger.* 'Call me later.'

'K. Bye.' I lie back and groan. Rain splatters thick on the windowpane. 'Coffee, Lori! Stat!'

THAT MORNING we don't turn on the TV. I've already seen the news on my phone and the situation is worsening. The Valentine Virus has spread its dark wings all across the country now. I know before I look out the windows that the city has frozen to a standstill. The absence of traffic noise beats loud as a sound. The apartment building reverberates with footsteps, music; bottled, restless energy of the inhabitants.

You sigh and drink coffee on the sofa, huddled in the fleecy pyjamas that make you look like a beautiful sheep.

'Imagine it, Bella. If it was a normal Saturday we'd be out in the city; brunch on Camden Street, wandering into town via Georges Street market.'

I open my mouth to contradict you, and then shut it again, feeling foolish. You mean you and Tim, of course. We never hung out on weekends. I think of my own Saturdays, trawling round second-hand book shops, coming home to silence, Chinese takeaway and a box-set of Scandinavian crime.

That day we spend watching *Pride and Prejudice*, the five-hour BBC adaptation. We know it by heart, so from time to time one of us dozes off, lulled by the thick heat from the radiators, and the dull rain driving against the windows.

I don't know it at the time but it's the last of these tedious days—if only I could turn time back and recapture that precious, stifling, boredom.

THAT EVENING, you're restless. You flip endlessly between apps on your phone, checking, checking; WhatsApp, Facebook, Twitter, Instagram. The screen sounds are on, so as I'm trying to read, I hear a succession of quiet bleeps as you tap in your status, over and over. I grit my teeth.

'So, the cards...' You look at me expectantly.

'We just did them,' I say shortly. After yesterday's session I don't want to read them again.

'Nah. I was just thinking about yours. We need to find out Your Destiny.' You capitalise the words, dragging them out. I feel a vague surge of irritation. It's all right for you. You have Tim.

'Come on,' you say, and look at me beguilingly. 'I just want you to be happy.'

My irritation subsides, and I feel a pang of guilt. I'm a bad friend.

'Doesn't your aunt have any other tricks?'

I think about it. 'Well there's the apple peeling? You cut a strip from an apple and throw it on the ground and see if it spells an initial.'

You consider it. 'No apples.'

'Fair enough.' I consider it. 'I really don't know any other spells. Now if you wanted to hex your neighbour or stop their cows from giving milk, I'm your woman. Or rather, Vera is.' I get up.

'Where are you going?'

'Oh I don't know, a little stroll, some dinner, maybe a taxi to the airport and a trip to...where d'you think? I'm going to have a bath. And switch the news off. I've had my fill of the Valentine virus.'

And that's why I don't answer my phone. I hear it buzzing

in the next room, but I'm lying back in lazy, sudsy heaven of a steamy bathroom. I hear your voice, uplifted in a question and wait for the knock on the door. But you don't disturb me, and I relax, lift one foot and rest it on the tap, admiring my painted nails.

I come back out, towelling my pink face, rubbing at my hair. You smile at me, smugly.

'Problem solved.'

'What problem?'

'That was Vera. I asked her about love spells. She said there was one called the Dumb Supper, but it was'—she drops her voice to a deep, hushed tone—'*too dangerous.*'

'Wow.' I sit down, towel on my lap. 'I haven't heard that one in a long time.'

'What is it?'

'It's like Vera says. It was thought to be a very powerful charm, but if you were caught doing it, you could get excommunicated back in the day.'

'No way!' Your face is flushed with excitement. 'Why?'

I raise my shoulders in a shrug. 'Dunno exactly. I think it was just a pagan ritual that the Church of today was trying to stamp out.'

'So what is it?'

I pause, remembering. 'Well, you cleanse the room...sage or salt. Then on the stroke of midnight, you switch off all electrical devices, light candles, then bake the bread, eat it, think 'Come to me,' and a figure will appear, your true love. That's about it. Oh and the reason it's called the Dumb Supper is that it has to take place in silence. That's the most important bit.'

You get up and go into the kitchen. 'I reckon we have everything we need.' Your voice is muffled as you open the cupboards. 'We have lots of candles, and salt, and remember that first week we got all the flour and stuff for baking?'

I laugh. 'Yeah, we never did sink to that level of boredom, did we?'

You reappear. 'So we're doing it?'

'Why not?' I twist the towel round my head. 'It's only a game, after all.'

A GAME? Vera might contradict that. She always had a healthy respect for her rituals. When I went to live with her as a child I'd become aware that she had a special status in our village. People consulted her as seriously as a doctor. They called her a healing woman, a cunning woman, a wise woman. It was mostly women who came to her. Sometimes they arrived at the house tear-stained, talking of medical difficulties in hushed tones and veiled terms. Sometimes they brought children in tow, pulling back their clothes to show her a mystery rash, a festering cut. And sometimes—these visitors generally came late at night—they came to ask her about darker matters. I never liked those women; their frantic air, their wild looks frightened me, even as a child, before I understood what they came for, what reassurance they sought.

Even Vera was wary of these women. She opened her door to everyone, no matter how late they called. It was a question of responsibility, she told me, and I nodded gravely, even though I was too young to really understand what she was saying. But one night, I woke up to hear the sound of raised voices, and loud sobbing.

I crept out of bed and sat at the top of the stairs. Through an acoustic trick, I knew I could hear everything from there, unobserved.

'Why won't you help me?' A strange voice, strained and hoarse.

'Because some things we're not meant to meddle with.' Vera, calm and firm.

'But I need him! Why won't you listen to me!' A burst of crying, loud and uninhibited, childlike. It had a frantic quality that made me shiver.

'Three things I won't do. Conjure the dead. Risk my soul. Perform black rituals.' Vera's voice is louder. 'What you're asking me to do breaks all three of these rules.' She paused. 'I'm sorry for you, Maura, sorrier than I can say. But on this you can't persuade me. I need to ask you to leave now.'

There was the thump of footsteps, more sobbing, and Maura Byrne from the post office stamped into the hall, pulling on her coat in short, vicious jerks.

'Bad luck to you, Vera, and your precious rules. I hope some day you're in the same boat. See how you like it!'

The door slammed with a force that reverberated through the wooden stair beneath me. Vera went to the front door, put a hand on it, and sighed. Without turning, she said 'Go to bed, Isabella.'

'How did you know?' I don't know why I was surprised. Vera could always tell where I was, what I was doing.

She turned to face me. Her face was exhausted, the lines on her forehead dark grooves. 'Let this be a lesson to you. Don't let anyone make you do something that isn't right.'

'Come on Bella!' You stand there, eager. All the ingredients are set out neatly on the table; flour, buttermilk, bicarbonate of soda, porridge oats and salt. Oh well. I guess we're doing this.

I sigh and check my watch. Eleven-thirty. 'We can't bake it yet. It starts at midnight. But we can prepare. Here.' I slide the salt over the counter to you. 'Pour it out in a circle around us.' This is the old lore Vera taught me; protective lore, witch lore.

You open the top of the shaker and spill the salt out in a looping circle. 'And you're cleaning that up tomorrow, too. This is your idea.'

'Fair enough.' You finish and brandish the salt. 'Now what?'

'Remember we won't be talking when it turns midnight. So we'll set out the candles on the countertop, and when it turns midnight we light them and switch off the lights. And then I'll bake the bread. You can help me, but don't say anything. Then we wait for it to cook, take it out and I'll eat a bit. Oh and as I do it, I concentrate and think *Come to me*. And that's it, really.'

Your eyes gleam. 'Excellent. Let's get ready.'

MIDNIGHT. I click off the lights, and unplug the TV. The streets outside are empty. I've already switched my phone off and told you to do the same. The apartment is transformed by the tea lights on the table, the tall Yankee candle on the countertop; the walls flame in a mass of flickering shadows. A deep amber glow from the oven signals that the temperature is rising steadily to the required two hundred degrees.

I sprinkle the baking sheet with flour, and pour the dry ingredients into the mixing bowl. The last to go in is the butter. It's hard to see in the low light, but I rub the butter in, feeling the mixture thicken and coagulate under my fingertips. You pass me the buttermilk, silently, and I tip in the carton, stirring it in with a spoon. A final kneading, and the dough is ready.

I take a deep breath and shape the loaf in a rough circle, then take up the knife and press it into the top to mark a cross. I've watched Vera do this a thousand times.

'It lets the fairies out,' she'd say, and smile.

I open the oven door; a rush of hot air blasts out, and I place the weighted baking sheet on the tray. This part is done now.

Your eyes look at me, an unspoken question. I nod and point at the clock. Time to wait.

IT'S A LONG THIRTY MINUTES. There's no phone, no TV to pass the time. I try and read a book but the candlelight is too muted; my eyes ache. You pace about restlessly. I want to tell you to stop, but it's too complicated to explain that in sign language. The vanilla scent of the Yankee candle on the counter mingles with the hot aroma of baking.

Finally the time is up. I switch off the oven, put on the oven gloves and slide out the hot tray, careful not to let the metal touch me. I turn over the loaf and tap the bottom, as Vera always did. The tone is resonant, hollow. It's done. I put it on the wire rack and cover it with a tea towel. You look at me, impatient. I shake my head and mime being burnt, waving my hands and popping my eyes. *We need to wait for it to cool.* You nod and roll your eyes. You've never been good at waiting, Lori.

I touch the cloth again. It's warm now, rather than steaming hot. I cut the loaf in quarters and break off a little piece. A sudden draught of air blows; candle flames flicker, shadows jump and dance. That's odd. The windows are all closed. I pause, uncertain, then shrug and pop the hot fragment of bread in my mouth. I focus myself and think—*Come to me.* I bite in.

And that's when the Yankee candle sputters and goes out.

My heart thumps hard in my chest. I grab your hand, hard. The bones move beneath your skin as your grip tightens on mine.

On the perimeter of my vision, a shadow lengthens, detaches from the wall. The outlines waver. I see it then. My pulses beat a wild tattoo. Darkness melts into the form of a tall figure; there's a flash of pale skin, dark untidy hair that falls over an indistinct face—*him!*

'No!' The word is out of me before I'm aware of it. I plunge for the light switch beside me. We blink, dazzled, in the harsh light that spills over the scattered ingredient on the countertop. Steam rises slowly from the cut loaf. We're still holding hands.

There's nothing else there. And as we look at each other, your phone starts to ring. You pull your hand out of mine and pick it up.

'Yes? Tim?'

That's when your face changes.

That's when everything changes.

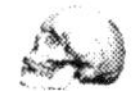

I LIE IN BED, and cover my face. From the next room I can hear you crying, a desperate keening sound that tears my heart. I writhe in a tangle of sheets.

This is your fault. I hear Vera's voice beat a steady metronome in my head. *You should have known better.*

She's right. And now Tim lies in a hospital, enmeshed in a web of plastic tubing and bleeping machines. He was hit by a car, you see, as we were playing our stupid games. A quick-thinking passer-by picked up his phone and rang the last number dialled.

Lori. I can't even bear to think about how you feel. I put my hands to my hot cheeks. *This is your fault.*

I switch off the bedside lamp, but the darkness presses hard on me; thick, charged. My breath comes quick and shallow in my throat. I click the switch again, and the lamp radiates a circular glow of yellow light.

What should I do? I lie on my back, tears leaking hot down

my face. Your sobbing continues; muffled now. I ache to go to you, to comfort you, but guilt plugs my head. *This is your fault.*

Did you see what I saw? Did you see what I saw in that moment before the world changed?

I close my eyes, feeling the tears cool on my cheeks. There's the whisper of a breeze from the open window, the faint sound of the blinds stirring and rattling against the sill. There's a feather-light touch on my face. I jerk upwards in bed. There's a shadow growing over me. It wavers, then comes into focus. Pale face, dark hair. *Tim.* And as I stare, skin prickling in ice terror, his eyes widen, his mouth opens. Behind him...

I try to scream but only a rush of air comes out. Closing my eyes, I blunder to the door, tripping over a chair on the way.

I spend the rest of the night in the living room, every light blazed on. My leg throbs where I've smashed it against the chair. Lying awake I see him, over and over. The desperation on his white face. And the shadows behind him.

It's never the same between us. How could it be? We're trapped in this box of an apartment; you, me, my guilt. You can't even go to the hospital, thanks to the Valentine Virus. We keep the news on all the time; the grim news of the virus fatalities, the government warnings, all these help distract us. I stay in my room as much as possible. Sometimes I catch you looking at me, and I don't know what to say. But your expression says it all. *This is your fault.*

It is my fault. I was the one who envied you. I was the one who performed the ritual. I was the one who thought the words —*Come to me.* I sleep in tiny snatches under the electric lights, to the soundtrack of your weeping in the next room.

You move home to be with your parents. It's allowed, even

in a pandemic. I understand. You need people around you, people who'll look after you in ways I can't. I'm frozen, incapable. So you go, and a small, treacherous part of me is relieved. I don't even worry about how I'm going to pay the rent. There are bigger things to worry about now.

I have what I wanted. Tim. He visits me every night now. Sometimes he looks terrified, sometimes angry. He's trapped in the limbo of a coma, and I'm trapped there with him. I ring the hospital every day, hoping, but there's always the same response. 'No change yet.'

Days drag by, and nights are filled with shadows. There are others now. I still see Tim the most, but there's also a woman and a man that I recognise from old photographs. They just stand and look at me sadly. Once the woman reached out for me, but the blurred figure beside her put a hand on her arm, forcing it down.

It's just me now. Me and them.

'VERA?' After ignoring my phone for weeks, I finally have the courage to call her.

'Isabella.' Her voice is timorous. For the first time she sounds like the old woman she is.

'Aunty Vera.' The old childish name bursts out of me. I can't help it, I start to cry. 'I did it. The Dumb Supper.' I cry harder. She waits for my sobs to subside.

'I told you, Isabella. I told you.' I can't bear the disappointment in her voice.

'Can't you help me? Can you undo it. I see him every night, I see him—I see them...' I break down again.

'Oh Bella. I can't help you now. No one can. That's why it's a forbidden ritual.' She's crying too now. 'It's a portal, you see. You've opened it, and now it can't be shut.'

'Can I come home?' It's all I've been able to think about.

She pauses. 'No,' she says softly. 'I can't have you back now. They'll follow you.'

'But I want to come home!'

'Oh my Bella.' I hear the love and sorrow in her voice. 'You can't.'

THE COLDNESS of spring melts into summer. There's no end in sight for the lockdown. What began as weeks is now months. Running in a babbling stream from the TV that's always on, there's a stream of edicts, waves of dissent. I watch the bodies on trolleys, piled in makeshift hospitals. It all feels so removed now, so far away.

I wait. There's nothing else I can do. But I'm not alone. For every night they come and wait with me.

There's more and more of them now.

The light is starting to fail outside. A bird flits by the window. I get up and look outside at the empty world. Somewhere in the distance I hear the sound of crying.

Behind me, my shadow guests assemble for an eternal Dumb Supper.

TRACY FAHEY

Tracy Fahey is an Irish fiction writer. In 2017, her debut collection *The Unheimlich Manoeuvre* was shortlisted for a British Fantasy Award for Best Collection. She has published two further collections; *New Music For Old Rituals* (2018, Black Shuck Books) and *I Spit Myself Out* (2021, Sinister Horror Company) and one novel, *The Girl in the Fort* (2017, Fox Spirit Books).

Fahey's short fiction is published in over thirty American, British, Australian and Irish anthologies including Stephen Jones' *Best New Horror, Nightscript V,* and *Uncertainties III*, and her work has been reviewed in the *TLS* and *Black Static*. Nine of her stories have appeared on Ellen Datlow's Recommended Reading Lists from 2016-2020. Fahey holds a PhD on the Gothic in visual arts, and her non-fiction writing on the Gothic and folklore has appeared in Irish, English, Italian, Dutch and Australian edited collections. She has been awarded residencies in Ireland and Greece.

CEREBRAL SALVAGE

BY KEV HARRISON

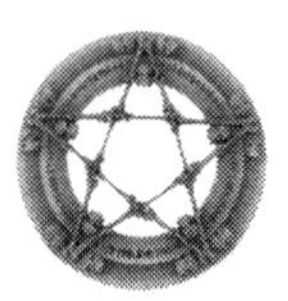

The rabbit gingerly crept forward, its jaws grinding as it chewed the fine strands of grass. Beady eyes, obsidian-dark in the green palette of the night vision lens, darted right to left as any hint of a sound reached its long, slender ears.

The wolf advanced, unseen, from the top left of the picture, droplets of saliva visible around its hungry lips. Doctor Czarna leaned over the console, delicate fingers caressing the button for the inhibitor device, waiting for the right moment.

The silvery beast leaned back, so slightly as to be almost undetectable, then burst toward the hapless bunny with explosive pace.

Czarna pressed the button. The wolf froze.

The rabbit slinked off into the bushes which skirted the unmarked, grey walls of the facility.

'Test complete,' said Czarna into the system mic, and a meaty slab of compensation spilled into a trough several metres from the wolf. Freed from its temporary paralysis, the beast lunged forward and sunk its teeth into the flesh.

Czarna scribbled furiously in her notebook, noting the

classic signs of hunger you might expect from an adult wolf who'd been starved for nigh on five days. Despite all that, the inhibitor had worked. A smile played across her lips as she wrote, before it was wiped away by a blinding flash on the screen. Then another.

The soupy green of the night vision filter transformed into a brilliant white and back again in mere fragments of a second. Unblinking, Czarna tapped at the keys on her console, switching between external cameras until she saw the phosphorescent glow of something burning to the east.

Pressing the button for the intercom, she spoke.

'Yevgeny. Fetch the flatbed. Something's come down.'

SHE BOBBED in the passenger seat of the small truck as Yevgeny's huge form expertly leaned across the steering wheel, keeping the ancient vehicle free of deep ruts and potholes which littered the even more ancient landscape.

It was five years ago now that Czarna had left her post in cerebral biotech at Oxford University and opened her own lab in Siberia. One hundred and sixty kilometres north-east of Omsk, this was rugged, antediluvian land and she still didn't trust herself to drive across country. Less so at night, when a darkness so thick you could almost take a bite out of it descended, twisting trees and animals alike into monsters from one's most vivid nightmares.

Flames raged at the crash site, now only a few hundred metres ahead, but—whether or not it was a trick of the light—Czarna could make out no smoke.

'Stop here,' she said, unclipping her seatbelt and swinging the door open. She stepped down to the ground and gestured. 'With me, Yevgeny.'

He turned to face her, lips parted, eyes like saucers, as if considering the request before mouthing a silent '*Da, da*,' and climbing down to the frozen earth. Despite his size, he hung back as Czarna led the way to the first of the two objects.

The heat emanating from the crash site was intense, sweat beading on Czarna's forehead even in the chilly night air. She held up an arm to shield her face from the blazing warmth and approached the object. It was cracked open like an egg, most of its contents charred cinders. The curious, smokeless flames centred around an object that was all angles, about a metre tall. It nestled beside a carbonized bipedal shape that looked almost human on the far side.

She stepped backward, certain there was nothing salvageable.

No survivors.

'Let's check the other one,' she said and stalked across the frigid earth toward the second burning object.

The shell was fractured along one side, but much closer to intact than the first. Czarna squeezed her head and shoulders into the gap created by the impact and assessed the damage. To her left, there was another of the angular objects, shrouded in flames, the blackened corpse of one of the human-like beings beside it. To her right, a panel had collapsed from the ceiling, obscuring her view.

She reached into the shell with one hand to move the panel aside and screamed as the heat of the surface scorched her palm. Forcing first her torso, then her legs, through the gap into the burning room, she pulled her coat sleeve over her hand and shoved the panel to one side. Behind it, there was another chamber which seemed to mirror the first. Here though, there was no fire.

The angular object was silver, with a pearlescent effect which made it shimmer in the flickering light from the flames.

Beside it, on the ground, lay another of the bipedal creatures. Its skin was a translucent blue, its naked body apparently devoid of any markings or details, beyond black lines of what looked like veins running like a roadmap beneath the surface. The head was a near-perfect oval, with no visible eyes or mouth. From around the lower half of the head and part of the neck, fine tendrils, seemingly made from the same gelatinous material as the thing's semi-opaque skin stretched out and plugged into the angular object.

'Yevgeny, we need to ...' Czarna turned back to see she was alone. 'Where is he?'

Using her sleeve to shield her skin once more, she pried open the crack in the outer shell of what she now supposed was a vehicle and stepped into the cold night. Yevgeny stood metres away, visibly quaking.

'There's a body and an artifact in there. We need to get them both back to the lab.'

He remained frozen to the spot.

'Preferably *before* they're consumed by the fire.'

'In my village, Okunevo, we see these things in the sky. Many times.'

'Many times? And you never wondered what they were?'

The burly man swallowed loudly, then: 'We know what they are.' He crossed himself twice.

Czarna rolled her eyes.

'It's not *Satan*!'

Yevgeny crossed himself again.

'Not *everything* is bloody Satan, Christ! Look, I can't carry it all to the truck by myself, so I need you to help me. Need I remind you who pays for your food? Or what you were doing *before* I took you on as my lab assistant?'

Yevgeny's quiet demeanour and limited capacity for speech had labelled him as 'broken' in his rural village community.

He'd been shovelling dung for a living for the best part of two years when Czarna had offered him the job.

He rubbed his heavily-stubbled chin, then stepped forward, taking thick working gloves from the pockets of his overalls and using them to widen the makeshift doorway in the wall of the vehicle. Czarna followed him inside and, together, they managed to free the shimmering device from the floor of the vessel.

It was surprisingly light, and cool to the touch. As Czarna held it in both hands, it gave off an almost undetectable humming sound. Yevgeny leant forward and lifted the motionless body, its tendrils still bound to the device.

Carefully, they moved their quarry to the flatbed, then began the drive back across country to the lab.

For days she ran scan after scan of both the object and the body, trying her best to determine composition, provenance, radioactive properties and more besides. Running out of ideas and no closer to discovering anything of note, she decided to perform an autopsy.

Cutting through the body, she discovered the 'meat,' for want of a better word, was of a consistent texture throughout, with spaces seemingly carved out for what were probably organs, connected with the thin, black veins visible from the outside.

Then she arrived at the head.

The entire head and neck were filled with dozens of nodes. The tendrils which fed into the device linked into each of them with a fine ivory thread, which reminded Czarna of spider silk. She sat forward in her chair and lifted her goggles to her forehead to get a better look.

Struck by a sudden flash of inspiration, she equipped an electrode with a small charge and pressed it to one of the nodes.

The body spasmed wildly, before a shockwave threw Czarna to the floor, shrouding the facility in darkness.

When she came to, Yevgeny stood in the doorway of the cold room. Emergency lighting pulsed behind him, his shadow expanding and contracting on the ground in front.

'You okay?' he asked. 'I tell you. This ... very not good.'

Czarna sat up and rubbed the back of her head where it had hit the tiles. She scrambled to her feet and dusted herself down.

'Did you see what this thing did? How much *power* it has? Whatever distant corner of the cosmos it came from, it's really something special.' She turned away from Yevgeny and placed her hands around one of the angular limbs of the object, felt the vibrations as they resonated through her fingertips and into her bones. 'How to control it though? These nodes ... like, neurons. Maybe if I reverse the data flow on the inhibitors I used on the wolf ... hook it up to someone's brain ...'

Yevgeny stifled a cough and Czarna spun to face him.

'Not *your* brain. I'm not a *monster*.' She brought a hand up to her chin and gazed off into the distance as she thought.

'I know,' she said at last. 'We'll take one of the kids from the orphanage in Okunevo.' Yevgeny's eyes widened.

'One of the ugly ones. The ones who won't get adopted anyway. Let's get the main power back on. We'll find our subject in the morning.'

A DENSE MIST drifted low to the ground as they pulled up on a side road nestled along the bank of the Tara River. The orphanage was located in an old, converted farmhouse, just north of the main settlement. Czarna knew they had to be quick—Okunevo had begun to attract a raft of spiritual tourists, looking for a place to soak up the smell of cow dung while crossing themselves profusely until struck by some sort of enlightenment.

'Now Yevgeny, stick to the plan, all right?'

'*Da, da. Ya znayu.* Ask Sister Uliana for help with truck. You find ugly boy.'

'You don't have to make it sound quite so heroic.'

Yevgeny shrugged and ambled up the steps to the front door of the orphanage, while Czarna crept around to the rear of the barn, which served as a makeshift canteen and classroom for the children.

Hugging the weathered wooden wall, she watched as Sister Uliana, still wearing her apron from breakfast service, was beckoned from the barn by the loud peal of the brass bell at the door. The moment the old woman slammed the screen door at the back of the main building closed, Czarna scurried to the entrance of the barn and knocked on the open door theatrically.

The four orphans' lively conversations halted immediately; all eyes trained on the doctor. As she prepared for the next stage of the plan, she cursed the relative uniformity of the children. No standout ugly kids to abduct.

'Who likes chocolate?' she said in her thickly accented Russian, clutching a clandestine slab of Cadbury's.

Four hands shot up.

'Who wants to come and help me with a tiny science experiment?'

Hands down.

'All the chocolate you can eat for my willing volunteer.'

Hands back up.

'Who was first...' she stretched out the suspense for as long as she could without risking Sister Uliana returning, then settled on the blond boy at the left of the class. 'You. What's your name?'

'Maxim, miss.'

'Perfect. You're my guy. Come on.' She beckoned and the boy left his chair, walking cautiously toward her.

'What about Sister Uliana?' The girl with red hair in the middle piped up.

'Ah, yes. This is a secret from Sister Uliana. If she asks, Maxim went to the toilet, okay? If you agree, you'll get chocolate, too.'

'*Kruto!*' the remaining kids cheered in unison.

Forcing a smile, Czarna threw the chocolate bar to the girl. 'Share with your friends, okay?' Then, turning to Maxim: 'You, with me, this way.'

She half-dragged Maxim around the side of the squat farmhouse and held him to the wall. "What's this *science* experiment?" the boy asked, his voice already thick with teenage cynicism at age eight or whatever he was.

'Alien mind control. From space.'

He snorted a laugh, and Czarna stared him down. His smirk vanished. She heard Yevgeny's loud "*spasibo*," and knew it was time. She grabbed the boy's collar roughly and dragged him toward the road.

'Come on.'

Back at the lab, after insisting on scoffing half of his cocoa allocation before the surgery, Maxim lay out cold on the operating table. A good thing really, as Czarna was wielding the circular saw directly above his newly-shaven head. Yevgeny stood ready beside the fridge in case blood bags were required.

Even after so many years' work on cerebral implants,

Czarna's stomach never failed to lurch when the teeth of the whirring blade bit into the flesh around the cranium. First there was the shredding of that thin layer of meat and the pooling of blood. Then there was the ear-piercing vibration, squealing as it sliced into the skull—like a dentist's drill only infinitely worse.

Within a few moments, Czarna had the cap of the boy's skull on the stainless steel table beside her and, after a quick glance at his vital signs, she ran a practiced, gloved finger across the numerous cortices of his comatose brain.

Finding the primary motor cortex, she implanted several reverse-calibrated versions of the transmitter she'd been using with the wolves in the gelatinous strip of pink-grey matter and tested the connection. The receiver in her hand gave a satisfying bleep, lights blinking in several colours, so she re-affixed the cap of the skull with glue, stapling the cut closed and applying anti-scarring ointment liberally to the wound.

She allowed herself another look at the boy's heart monitor, before heading out of the operating room and into the functional lab to install receivers in the alien device. As she finished the work, she noticed Yevgeny in the doorway, wringing his hands.

'Haven't you got blood to mop up? Or goats to butcher for when we get back to our lupine project?'

'Is not what you think, Czarna. The boy... his soul.'

'When this is all over, you can teach me the Russian equivalent of hail Marys and I'll come and do a few with you, okay?'

The huge man muttered something unintelligible and scuttled away from the doorway.

Czarna's watch buzzed, waking her. She was about to look at the time, when the system notification burned itself into her retinas:

Patient Y: conscious.

She climbed from bed, tugged on a t-shirt, and hurried down the steely grey corridor to the operating room. Masking up and pulling a lab coat over her nightwear, she stepped inside and looked lazily into young Maxim's eyes.

'How do you feel?'

'What happened? What did you do?' He sounded drowsy, as if he were drunk.

'Installed the alien mind-controlled device. I told you. Can you move?'

He clenched his teeth and squeezed his eyes shut for a moment, then stopped, panting. 'I don't think so.'

'It's to be expected. The anaesthetic dulls you. Give it a couple of hours. Can I bring you anything? Water?'

'Please,' he croaked.

Czarna fetched a glass of distilled water from the sink and held it to the boy's lips. He drank, slowly but with a definite thirst.

I'll come back and see you in the morning, and then our work will really begin.'

Czarna was so close now that she knew she wouldn't be able to sleep. Instead, she went to the room with the device, poring over her photos of the dissected alien body, and the position of the neuron-like particles within that brain-matter head.

After a couple of hours of sketching connections and scrawling hypotheses on her tablet, she decided it was time. She called Yevgeny on the intercom and summoned him to the primary lab. Together they wheeled the strange, pearlescent device into the operating room.

'What the hell is that?' Maxim was certainly a little

spunkier than when he'd woken up. Nevertheless, he remained on his back, seemingly unable to move.

'This is what I've hooked up to the motor cortex of your brain. You're going to control it. Help me channel its power,' Czarna said breathlessly as she lowered the device to the ground. 'I'm going to ask you to make some movements for me. But you need to follow my instructions precisely, okay?'

'Okay.'

'All right. First of all, I want you to ball your right hand into a fist. Slowly.'

Maxim's face tensed, eyes scrunched half-shut. 'I... can't...'

'Keep trying.'

A tear welled at the corner of his left eye, front teeth biting down into his bottom lip.

The device began to hum, something akin to the sound of a bassy woodwind instrument, before falling silent as Maxim was exhausted, breath quick and heart pounding in his chest.

'Sorry.'

Czarna hurried to his side, mopping sweat from his scarred forehead.

'No, no. You did brilliantly. Yevgeny, bring some more water.'

Her assistant barrelled to the sink and filled a glass.

'A few moments' rest and we'll try again.'

'But I'm tired.'

'Oh hush, don't be a baby. We're on the verge of a breakthrough.' She took the glass from Yevgeny and held it to the boy's lips.

As he leaned forward to drink, the air around the device became hazy, blurred. Startled, Maxim dropped his head back, eyes wide. 'Did you see that?'

'Do it again.'

'I don't think–'

'Stop whining! *Again.* Or no more water.'

Maxim strained, the muscles in his neck visibly tightening as he lifted his head higher from the pillow this time. The air around the device took on the same fuzzy quality but, as he stretched further, it spread outward, obscuring the health monitoring machines at the boy's bedside.

With a groan, he collapsed backward onto the pillow. The distortion in the air subsided. Czarna scrutinised his features and realised he was not acting out or being weak. The boy was spent. She turned to Yevgeny.

'Watch him. Let him sleep, but if his vitals drop, buzz me.'

CZARNA WAS TYPING up notes on the last three wolf observation sessions when the phoned thrummed on her desk.

'What is it?'

'He's awake. Moving.'

She hung up the phone and sprinted the length of the corridor between the control room and the operating area.

Maxim sat upright in bed, mouth agape as clouds of nothing swirled around the room, rendering furniture and even parts of the structure of the room invisible. Yevgeny cowered beside the sink in the far corner.

'Leave the room, but don't go too far,' Czarna spat, and the big man fled the way she'd just entered.

'I'm scared, Doctor,' the boy said, visibly trembling.

'Take my hand,' Czarna said, reaching out.

Maxim extended his arm to its fullest extent, fingers reaching for hers. Sparks sliced into the air at jagged angles in vivid shades of pink and purple.

'Just a little further. Come on, boy.'

He grimaced as he lunged towards her, the skin on his forehead strained against the staples keeping it together. Blood beaded and trickled in three narrow fingers down his cherubic face. The sparks extended, binding together into what looked like a localised lightning storm. A smell like burning sulphur filled the air before there was a deafening boom and Maxim was gone.

As the haze in the room dispersed, Czarna dashed to the other side of the bed where the boy had been lying. The device, too, had vanished. All that remained was the bed, the life-support machines and that lingering, sulphuric scent.

Czarna screamed for Yevgeny and was pacing the room, agitated when he appeared in the doorway.

'Ugly boy is gone,' he said, startled.

'It's a good thing I didn't hire you for your skills of observation, isn't it? Now, tell me what happened earlier, when Maxim began moving. Did you see any of the sparks before I arrived?'

'Sparks?'

'Lightning. Bits of pink and purple fire?'

Yevgeny shook his head vigorously.

Czarna buried her face in her hands. 'I don't believe this,' she said, her voice muffled.

Her phone buzzed in the pocket of her lab coat. She fished it out and swiped the screen awake.

'It's the proximity alarm. There's something outside.'

She barged past Yevgeny and down the corridor, into the control room. After powering up the monitors and navigating to the external cams, she froze. Hovering in the air at the western side of the building was an object, small and out of focus. Turbulent air swirled around it, vivid streaks of light pulsing periodically through the mist.

'It can't be.'

Czarna bolted from the room, Yevgeny's thumping feet close behind. Bursting from the side door, Maxim—or a version of Maxim at least—hovered in the air in a cloud of haze. He was naked, his body riven with raw scar tissue, some sections seeming patterned while others were more like the random slashes of an abstract artist. Beside him, the device floated, its angular protrusions extending and retracting. The lighting effects Czarna had witnessed in the recovery room had now expanded into pinkish forks of lightning which cracked the air around the floating boy.

'Maxim! You figured it out?'

'Of course.' His lips remained still as he spoke, his voice a monstrously multiphonic impersonation of how he'd sounded hours before, transmitted directly into Czarna's brain. 'They showed me. In the other place.'

Yevgeny appeared at Czarna's side, knelt. '*Ad*,' he whispered.

'Hell is such a simple word.' The boy's corrupted voice again. 'Likewise inferno, hades. All crude approximations fashioned by your defective species.'

'But you've only been gone a few minutes.'

'Here, perhaps.'

'But the objects, they came from the sky,' Czarna protested. 'From another–'

'Dimension.' The boy-that-was finished her sentence for her. 'And what now, I wonder? You were so keen to understand, doctor. So resolute in your desire to harness this power. Do you still thirst for it?'

Czarna scrutinised Maxim's hovering form, his lips turned up to a grin which revealed blackened gums, absent of teeth. The whites of his eyes were yellowed, veins starkly cutting lines from the shrivelled iris and outwards. Then there was his skin, patterns scored deeply into the feeble muscle tissue clinging to his bones.

She shook her head. 'No. Please. No.'

The boy raised his left hand, palm open, floating closer toward her.

'Please. I didn't know what it was. Where it came from.'

'Run, Yevgeny,' the boy's voice again.

'Stay with me, Yevgeny. Protect me.'

The huge man stood from his kneeling position and began to back away, arms outstretched in front of him. He gave a nod toward his employer, before turning and sprinting into the forest at the edge of the facility.

'Come with me. See where the power comes from. What it can do.' The boy and the device swooped downward, the bolts of light intensifying, the cloud of turbulent air expanding.

Czarna dropped to her knees and, for the first time in decades, tears ran down her cheeks. She looked up and into the vortex, into the hard, almost animal eyes of the approaching thing that had been Maxim, until she was absorbed.

KEV HARRISON

Kev Harrison is a British writer of horror and dark fiction, living on the outskirts of Lisbon, Portugal. His most recent novella, *Below*, is out now from Silver Shamrock Publishing, while his debut collection, *Paths Best Left Untrodden* is available now from Northern Republic. His debut novella, The *Balance*, a reimagining of the Slavic folk tale of Baba Yaga set in cold war Poland, is also available. He has two novelettes, *Curfew* and *Cinders of a Blind Man Who Could See*, both part of the Short Sharp Shocks range. When he's not writing dark tales, Kev can be found running, sampling too many craft beers for his own good, singing bizarre songs to his cats and travelling to far flung places with his better half, Ana. You can find him at www.kevharrisonfiction.com or on Twitter as @LisboetaIngles

WHAT THE WAVES RETURN

BY DEMI-LOUISE BLACKBURN

Waves battered the coastline, depths of the water as grey as the sky above, promise of winter heavy in the ocean's spray. Even the seabirds were too cold to scream. Flocks huddled along the rocks, loose feathers clogging brine with more debris, leaving the birds colder still. They blinked back salt and sunk into themselves.

Daniel, too, sunk deeper into his coat, wrinkled hands fishing through a small rock pool. Fingers skimmed layers of seaweed, swirled snakelocks, brushed the leathery shell of a mermaid's purse. Settled at the bottom, camouflaged against pebbles and sand, the tapered head of a sea scorpion blinked up. Daniel cupped it with one numb hand.

The longer he stared into the rippling surface, the stranger the fish became. Dark stripe on its back a misplaced mouth, defensive spines formed wayward teeth, slime dripped like drool and the creature wriggled away.

Daniel straightened to survey the bleak coastline. Opposite the water's lip, home rose from a landscape thick with heather, matching cottages dotting the hills like sheep. A steady patter of rain urged him back to Joanne. But, even well into retirement, work habits remained, a calling so deep it plucked at his nerves.

Inside the man's backpack lay a tub for specimens, a rusted wallpaper scraper, a journal littered with murky recollections from his time working on the Cerulean Project. From the bottom, he retrieved a metal cylinder, not dissimilar to an oversized syringe, and a sieve.

He tapped the beach with his foot, pressed the device deep into the ground, and lifted. Sand pulled hungrily until, with a slurp, it released. He pushed the cross section into the mesh frame, lower half of the grit dark as tar, and moved the filter in circles.

Creatures emerged. Pasty spiral shells shuddered, muscles reaching out and quivering in the open air before retreating. Crustaceans woke, beady eyes flicking away particles, their skeletal legs navigating unfamiliar terrain. A bloodworm broke through, writhed like a wayward vein.

Daniel mouthed species' names as though evoking spirits. A ghost of a smile drifted over his face, recalling years past where he'd spent months cataloguing the infinitesimal network hiding within their coastlines, hoping to find something remarkable. He couldn't quite remember if he ever found it.

Thoughts wandered. Drifted to the biting, chemical stench of the Cerulean's laboratory. The smile faded.

A large clump of particles remained in the centre of the sieve. He squeezed it, flinched, and watched as red welled on the tip of his thumb, popped the appendage inside his mouth to suck away the taste of copper. Grit crunched between his teeth.

The sand unfurled.

Within, the brown, segmented shell of a woodlouse. Body marbled with tendrils, thin and pale as parasites, exoskeleton slick and oozing despite the silt clotting its casing. Antennae waved mid-air, patted the mesh as though moving under the cover of night. The isopod hobbled about the netting, seemingly injured.

'Poor sod.' Daniel grasped it between finger and blood-streaked thumb to inspect its legs and frowned.

Embedded in the isopod's stomach, a large, milky-grey cluster set like gems in a ring, sizes mismatched and vying for space. Daniel tilted it, mouth slack and eyes narrowed, until, at last, he understood. They were not clumps of sand, or pebbles, or a collection of smooth moonstones.

They were eyes.

Daniel flicked his thumb across the creature's belly. One socket burst, secreting a pale liquid, and ten dark, compound orbs glared at him. He imagined fresh optics bubbling from the gore, replacing the one he damaged, gurgling as they opened.

'Now, then...' Daniel muttered. Where the eyes should have been, crowning its insectile mouth, there were only vacant, scar-stitched holes.

Thunder rumbled, dragged Daniel out of his head and back to the shoreline where cold settled in the atmosphere, thick as fog. An ache, bone deep, pulsed in his arms and legs. He glanced towards home, as though he might find Joanne's glare lit up as strong as a lighthouse beam. A blurred silhouette of the house greeted him instead.

There was little to do about the creature. Report it to his old co-worker if the man still worked with the Cerulean, tirelessly picking away at the unseen seams of jellyfish and amphipods. Daniel's own retirement had been an abrupt, premature thing, but chances were Arthur continued in the field.

He grabbed a tub from his bag, dropped the creature inside with a fistful of sand, and made his way up the coastline.

Above, a storm roared from cloud to cloud. Seabirds rose from their perches, screaming their last into the sky, and the water drew Daniel's gaze again. Waves galloped up the beach to catch him, easing long, supple fingers into the rock pools, dragging the life within far, far out to sea.

Daniel wondered what else it might leave in its wake.

Morning brought with it sunlight, spilling in from a gap in the bedroom curtains, and the sound of Joanne bent double over the toilet, sobbing. Daniel's dreams fled. Their many-legged shadows long gone by the time Joanne called out his name.

Soon, he joined his wife on the bathroom floor, pushing thin, greying hair behind her ears. He ignored the warm press of saliva against the side of his neck, soothed circles across her back, and willed the rapid-fire beat of his own heart to slow.

'You're all right, Jo,' he whispered. 'Come on.'

'I've had enough of this, Dan. Sick to death of it all.'

Daniel pressed his face into Joanne's hair, focused on the scent of shampoo rather than the stale, telltale odour seeping from her pores. Body emitting its own silent warning, a whisper in the sunrise silence of their home: *not long now*.

Half an hour passed before Daniel coaxed her back to bed, Joanne off-white and shaking, Daniel with burning eyes and thunder inside his brain. The sun warmed their crumpled sheets but did not warm them. Sheep bleated in the fields outside and seabirds woke with their shrill alarms. Above, a clock matched Joanne's quiet rattle, muscles working to swallow and struggling.

Daniel brushed his knuckles down his wife's thin arm and she hummed, as close to *thank you* as she could manage. His throat tightened. 'Always ruining my lie-ins, you are. Right pest.'

Joanne laughed. 'You're not allowed to sleep in if I can't. Should know that by now.'

Silence fell between them, and rest found Joanne once more. Daniel listened to the steady rhythm of her breaths, to distant waves lapping at the shoreline, matching the pull of Joanne's lungs. He inhaled deep, squeezed his eyes shut tight, and with his exhale came the fear at last, tears muffled into the pillows.

The cold morning light gave way to a gold-hazed noon. Daniel laid awake, restless, counting each inhalation and thinking, all the while, of that strange isopod resting in a tank inside his old office, its many eyes blinking at the shadow of itself. Eyes it should no longer have.

Most of all, he thought of Arthur. Of the laboratory inside the Cerulean, sterile and silver, glimmering beneath industrial lamps. Smelling, all the while, of death and the sharp, metallic stench of things made anew.

Daniel stared at the paper on his desk, smudged letters so thin they were indistinguishable, and debated throwing it away. It was his third attempt of the afternoon. The ideas swam, muddled and vague within his head, fighting to get out. It hit him, with a pang of shame, that this was his first attempt to contact Arthur since he left the project. Daniel pushed the thought aside before looking at the page again.

Arthur,

I imagine you'll be surprised to hear from me. But there's much I'd like to tell you. To ask. I suppose I should have found a number. But I remember things far better when I write them down these days. I'm a bit of an old git now, you see.

Have the years treated you well? What became of our work

at the Cerulean, or did you move on? I'm not sure I blame you if you went on to do better things. That place never deserved your heart.

But, I admit, a selfish part of me prays you're still there.

The thing is, Arthur, I've come across quite the oddity. I know it would've caught your inter-

Joanne's voice rocketed down the hallway.

'Yes, love?' Daniel replied.

'Didn't you hear me before? Your dinner's ready.'

'I thought I said I was sorting dinner out? You need a rest, Jo.'

A pause. Daniel looked from his letter to the open door. In the hall, light spilled out from the kitchen, Joanne's shadow moving back and forth beyond the threshold, the tail of a cornflower blue smock flitting past.

'And I told you I can still look after myself. Stop nattering, will you, and come get your dinner.'

Daniel could hear, rather than see, the irritated scrunch of her face from the tone of Joanne's voice, and bit back a fond smile. 'All right. I'll be two minutes.'

Pots and plates rattled in response. Daniel read over his words, felt a telltale flip in his stomach again, urging him to forget about contacting Arthur altogether.

But the tank, tucked atop a dresser along the far wall of the office, gave him pause. Sand lined the bottom along with a rock Daniel picked up from the garden. Beneath it the isopod stirred, feelers flicking, tasting the air. Tasting *him*.

Daniel moved over to the tank and grasped the crustacean. Even without its honeycomb of a stomach, the parasitic form of the isopod set his nerves on edge, a fear borne with the Earth, ancient and primal. It squirmed, tried to curl up and hide. Daniel adjusted his grip and realised, too late, he'd crushed one leg beneath shaking fingers.

In his head, the phantom of a voice emerged, murmuring through the folds of his brain. *Will it grow back?* Daniel swallowed. Debated. Ran his thumb over the snapped, cartilaginous appendage, and the question grew louder. Deafening.

The legs came off easily enough.

Daniel laid the isopod back in the tank. He imagined the eyes, trapped beneath the weight of its own body, rolling. Discomfort rose within him. He wrung his hands together then wiped them on his trousers. Though he knew it to be impossible, Daniel swore he was being watched as he resumed the letter.

I know it would've caught your interest.

An isopod. I assumed it to be ligia oceanica, only it's far too big. Coloration is off, too. We used to bring specimens of them in all the time when we were fresh on the project, do you remember?

Only this is different. Its eyes are missing. But when you flip it over onto its belly, they're there. Ten or more. It's regrown them, Arthur, like crabs amputating their own injured claws, just to grow a replacement. But in such numbers?

It has me wondering. Can it regrow all injured parts in such quantities, too, or just the optics? I wonder if you know of the species already. Perhaps, right now, you're working on a round of drug trials derived from it for the Cerulean, as we tried with turritopsis dohrnii.

Admittedly, this isn't quite as neat a regeneration as the immortal jellyfish. No earlier life states, no reverting to polyps, no starting afresh. But to regrow what is damaged... as good enough a treatment as any, no?

Or, most likely, I'm a senile old git who hasn't taken to retirement as much as I thought. But it tugs at me. As though I left something buried out there under the sand and must unearth it again.

We got close before, didn't we? Fulfilling the Cerulean's promise of unearthing that mythical cure-all.

I think that's why I can't let it go. All I have are fractured recollections through the years. I can't even recall why I left the project so suddenly. All I know for sure is seeing that creature brought so much to the surface again. Was this what we were missing?

Then again, reality is, it's probably nothing at all, is it? A deformity. Pollution. My mind running away. Interesting though.

Get in touch if you can. All the best.

'Daniel?' Joanne's voice came sharp as a gunshot.

'What's the matter, love?'

'Your tea's getting bloody cold, that's what.'

Daniel sighed, folded the letter, and placed it inside an envelope. 'What are you on about, love? Told you I'd sort us both out tonight, you need some rest.'

He looked towards the hall, where Joanne's shadow stilled in the kitchen doorway.

TENSION LAY thick across the house.

Joanne sat in the living room, fingers toying with her wedding ring, face pale and expressionless bar the crease of her brow. Warm afternoon sun failed to hide the hollow of her cheeks. Clad in a suffocatingly large nightgown, the furniture formed like oversized props against her slender frame. Behind, in the kitchen, a washing machine whirred its last, struggling to deafen Joanne's silence.

Daniel hovered in the doorway, throat clogged with consolations, tongue bitter from them. He longed for her to speak, to erupt into a blinding flare of anger, if only to prove some fight remained. But none came, and Daniel's fright darkened another shade.

'Bedding's sorted,' he finally said. 'I'll help you back into bed and make some lunch for us in a bit.'

Joanne a deadweight against his side, they hobbled towards the bedroom and sat on the bed, quietly ignoring the change of sheets. Daniel's heart throbbed, slow and painful, while Joanne's cheeks flushed red and furious. He gripped her icy hand, kissed it, then her temple. She hardly moved.

Daniel stood. 'Get settled. I'll make you a cuppa once I've tidied up the office.'

'Sorry,' Joanne rasped.

Daniel shook his head. 'Don't start with that. Nothing to be sorry about. You've sorted me out in worse states.'

'That's not the point.' Joanne's eyes settled on the doorway to their bathroom as though the sight infuriated her. 'Never wanted to get like this. Shouldn't have to look after me, especially not with *that*.'

A lump formed in Daniel's throat. 'Give over. It's what you married me for. Wasn't for my cooking now, was it?'

'Daft sod.'

The air lifted, if only an inch, and Daniel let his words go unheard in the hallway as he left: 'I've got you, Jo. Don't you worry.'

In the office, Daniel tried not to let his eyes wander over to the tank, kept his gaze set on a pile of half-written letters to Arthur. A needling sense of curiosity gnawed at his skull. He looked at the paper, words smeared into a Rorschach test, and, at last, looked at the container.

It sat empty.

Daniel lurched forwards, found a divot in the sand where the isopod once rested, and examined the stone, expecting the crustacean to be glued to it like a scorpion hiding from the heat of midday sun. Heavy in the crook of his neck, Daniel's pulse thrummed, lightning fast. *Where is it?*

Behind: a noise.

Cartilage shifted. Bones cracked into place like wood popping inside the mouth of a fireplace. The sound dragged Daniel to nights, long-since passed, spent in paralysed agony as a child, where night rested heavy and oppressive. Tree limbs brushing against the windows, tapping with bark-ridden fingertips, knowing the safety of his parent's room lay at the end of an infinitely expanding hallway. Innocent noises nurturing horrible nightmares.

But he was not a child.

He was a man well into his years, in his own home, listening to the sound of small, chitinous legs scuttle across hardwood floors, just out of sight.

The movements slowed, stiff limbs dragging against the ground, aware of being watched. Daniel crouched, eyes pinned on the dark lip at the bottom of his desk, sure the moment his gaze aligned it would emerge, fast as a bullet, towards him.

Ticticticticic.

Daniel's head snapped towards the sound, quick enough to catch one long, insectile leg slipping past the open door. He followed.

In the hallway, all was still.

A wounded noise escaped Daniel's mouth. He stemmed the flow of it with his fist, turning back into the office where the empty tank gave no solace from its vacancy. Fog rolled inshore, mind dark and blurred. Questions and angry, familiar voices rang, loud as church bells, in his head. *It's the stress*, he reasoned, *everything going on with Joanne.*

Joanne.

Minutes passed. A frightened voice in Daniel's head urged him to search for the isopod lest Joanne find it. Or *it* find *her*.

Yet, all he could do was rest against the doorway, shock receding with each steady rush of blood, replacing itself, again, with haunting curiosity. A tide dragging him towards the horizon. He ignored his wife's voice calling for him and picked up a pen.

Arthur,

My heart sinks to write it, but the isopod escaped. I can only pray I'll find it again or come across another specimen. I assumed right. It can regenerate other parts. Other limbs. At such an accelerated rate, it's near-frightening.

But more than the fear, I'm hopeful. What would it take to use this creature? Restore what is ill or injured in the body? No other species we studied ever recovered at such a rapid rate. And we know, now, it isn't limited to what it can repair, either. We could use it. Wield it. My only fear is how long it would take to unravel this creature.

It's funny. I realise, now, I never told you about Joanne, did I?

Arthur, I know I'm old. Me and Joanne both. But I'm not ready to let go of her. Every week since her diagnosis, I've scoured that beach. I think, subconsciously, I've always been searching for that one piece we missed all those years ago. To finish things. I can't help but believe this is it.

Could this help Joanne? Keep her with me for a while longer.

Please write back. If only to tell me I'm a fool making connections where there aren't any. Or, Lord willing, if I'm onto something.

I'll return to the beach. Dig up as many specimens as I can. They're yours. If you'll help me.

Please.

Your friend,

Daniel.

Waves roared towards the shore, spray flying like spittle, as though the maw of a rabid dog snapped at the rocks. Only the wind spoke. Seabirds roosted, eyes narrowed and reproachful. A short stretch of the beach lay pockmarked.

Daniel's teeth squeaked together, features stretched into a painful grin as he slipped across the rocks, trousers sodden, wallpaper scraper in hand. His gaze roamed over obsidian shells, clinging onto the rock face in clusters of unopened black lilies. One by one, he peeled away the fibrous membrane holding them steady, examined the mollusks with watering eyes, found no insectile bodies hiding snug within their threads. Scrape, rip, peel until, eventually, an anomaly.

Attached to the rocks by knotted string, Daniel discovered a blossom. Shell split, orange-cream flesh spread wide, dripping slime and ocean brine. But the pasty, solid muscle used to drag itself through silt and sand, was no longer singular. A tightly clustered anemone burst wide open, extending out to Daniel, beckoning.

He followed it and, like a newborn clutching the finger of its mother, the creature's appendages swarmed Daniel's own. He tore at it, swore the flowered form twitched in surprise, and stowed it away inside his pocket. It writhed, wet and soft, against his thigh as he scrambled off the rocks, mind whirring. *It's not just the isopod. Why?*

The ocean heard Daniel's inner words. Waves rushed inland, spat out sun-starved, twisted creatures. Eye stalks crowded with pitch black optics. Fish struggling to swim, backs split into bloody, gaping holes, lined with needle teeth. Moon jellyfish bloated and immobile, bulging at the weight of their new-found organs.

Mist seeped into Daniel's ears, stomach twisting as he took

in each mutated creature, glancing away only to find the houses skewed, roofs bent, doorways slanted, everything foreign and *off*. Drums beat a heavy rhythm against his temples.

A seagull chuckled, its low, rumbling tones spilling into the sky, pulling Daniel outside of his own mind, steadying the beat of his heart. He looked up.

Atop the rocks, a lone bird stood, unmoving, not so much as swaying in the rising winds. Its beak formed a thin, morose line. The seagull cocked its head, one eye glaring, the other a smooth stitch of skin and downy feathers–and opened its beak. A long, soaring wail cut through the air.

The eyes within its gullet winked, flinching at the vibration of its own vocal cords.

At Daniel's scream, the seagull fell silent, but its mouth remained agape. Rogue sockets blinked from the shadow of its throat and multiplied. Lids opened, the bird's neck retracting, jerking, attempting to swallow the cluster of pupils. They kept coming. Popping into existence, liquid thick and dark as oil dripping from the sides of its beak, staining pale feathers crimson.

Daniel's bowels contracted as the beak split ever wider. Forced apart, until all that remained were those yellow, red-rimmed orbs bursting from within. The seagull chuckled, choked, collapsed into a heap and called no more. Just a thin, reedy gurgle, deep within its chest, organs fighting to replicate themselves. What remained defied all form. Offal and optics fused to the rocks, water drawing the blood away in a thin, dark stream.

The hope, nestled warm and safe in Daniel's chest, shrivelled, and turned arctic. He reached into his pocket, where the familiar, malformed mussel lay immobile, and threw it into the sea. Feet sunk into sand as he turned, tried to flee the realisation washing inland.

Blinding light smothered the coastline.

Daniel covered his eyes. Salt in the air faded, the stench of sulphur and copper rolling in. Each muscle vibrated, strained, electricity roaring within his ears, chest rising in shallow jolts. Water seeped through his clothes as he dropped to his knees and, finally, Daniel opened his internal eyes. Forced himself to remember.

The Cerulean greeted him-but not entirely as he remembered.

The form remained the same, silhouettes of the laboratory counters and cabinets as clear as the day he first saw them. But he did not remember the furniture to be forged by pearlescent shells, floor swathes of ocean grit, walls algae-thick and dripping. Here, fog-filled tanks hummed and hid away monsters. Here, the world was hazy and green and refracted.

From the shadows, Arthur's back crystalised into view, hunched and strained over a counter. On the surface before him, tentacles slipped from his hands, each grasp revealing more limbs in its stead until Arthur's body stood framed by a writhing, leaking mass of flesh.

'We can't let them just take it over, Dan. It's our work.' Arthur's voice came clogged with water.

Daniel's tongue formed words of its own accord. 'It's our work, yes, but not our project. We wouldn't have come this far without the Cerulean funding it. They can terminate it, reap it, whenever they please.'

Arthur turned, his eyes spirals of lamprey teeth, mouth a yawning chasm of coral teeth, clicking as he spoke. 'It can only do harm with the state it's in now. Look at what it did to the isopods. What could they possibly want with it?'

Daniel's gaze moved down to the waterlogged floor where crippled creatures drifted across the tiles. Arthur's calcified neck fractured as it cocked to one side.

'Dan? You know, don't you?'

'It won't be any of our concern. We'll get paid off, that's all that matters.'

'What will they do with it?'

Daniel knew better than to deny him again. Droplets gushed from the ceiling tiles, the water in the laboratory creeping up to his knees and so, too, crept the answer, clawing its way from his throat.

'Euthanise the sick.' Through the veil of his calcareous visage, Daniel watched the pain blossom in Arthur's face. 'We've been swimming against this tide for years... aren't you tired of it? Each step we make, another strain appears out of nowhere. But with a purge...'

Above, the ceiling collapsed, and with the rushing water came the mangled debris of their test subjects, floating upon the surface in clouds of crimson gore.

'You can't be serious? We wanted to eradicate illness, Daniel, not eliminate those suffering. You'd have them kill us all for the greater good? For hush money?'

'It would be out of our lifetime. Years after we've gone.'

'We're handing them a weapon, for Christ's sake. Think of how many people will die.'

'It'll be of no concern to us by then.'

The room shrank. Walls bowed inwards as though a great pressure built beyond their sight. Coral cracked and flaked off into the rising water, the rush of it deafening, the press of it like ice. Arthur's malformed features grated together, the tentacles behind him quivering anxiously.

'Think for a minute,' he pleaded. 'This isn't you at all, Dan. Neither of us signed up for this.'

Daniel's silence roared again.

'Don't tell me you always knew?' Arthur's face erupted with the words, coughing up a swarm of feelers and chittering

mandibles. The tentacled monstrosity behind him grew, wrapped around his limbs, and squeezed. Ringlets of flesh bulged, pulsed, room filling, vision fading to a smear of off-white light, further still to grey, to black.

Water lapped at Daniel's temples.

He rolled onto his back, chest rattling, watching as the sky cut itself open in streaks of washed pink. Sand crunched next to his ears. An isopod crawled up his face, over one eyelid, and rested there. A shock of pain rocketed through Daniel's skull as the creature bit down on his pupil. He sat up with a yell, dislodging the infected creature, and caught the blurred, blood-streaked outline of home.

Joanne's name tore his throat apart.

Wind whispered through the bay window, lace curtains billowing like the soft, translucent hood of a jellyfish. Daniel stood in the doorway, a wet trail of footprints behind him, gnarled shadows closing in. He watched their creeping forms, unable to convince his trembling legs to push on further into the house. The silence swam, thick and choking as smoke, Joanne's name long-since dead in his mouth. He dared not speak.

Outside, a silhouette fluttered by, cutting through the dim glow of the living room lamp. No call came. Daniel heard the beating of wings, webbed feet scraping across the roof tiles before settling. He imagined one too many amber eyes staring out into the twilight gloom, waiting for him to move, waiting to speak. Wondered, distantly, how prematurely the Cerulean had released his tainted remedy, how far the agent spread now it was airborne.

Bed springs creaked.

The mouth of the hallway yawned at Daniel, and he let the shadows of it swallow him. Photographs of himself and Joanne stared out of the darkness. Walls bulged out, too close, brushing Daniel's shoulders as he staggered towards the bedroom where Joanne slept, unaware of the monster he'd brought inside. Oblivious to the danger she might be in. Between his own foot-falls he expected to hear, too, the chitinous clatter of the isopod's footsteps.

Where is it? Hiding in the dusty corners of their family home, a hundred limbs crouched, poised, ready to jump at but a tremor across its stolen spiderweb. He prayed it didn't survive long outside of the tank. Segmented shell punctured from rogue legs, curled up somewhere in the dark, extremities wrapped around its dead eyes, turning sour and soft.

He arrived at the closed door of their bedroom, vision quiv-ering, temples pulsing with a deep, age-old ache, a haunting of his skull.

'Joanne?' he called, waiting for the croak of her voice to come back. Weak, but there.

No reply.

He willed the door to open, to see her form cut through the shadows, thin frame emerging, haggard and ghostly, but there. Alive. The wood of the door felt cold beneath his palms. He pressed his ear to it and listened. Waited. Longed for his pulse to slow. Pushed the handle and opened the door.

Joanne was not there.

But *something* was.

At the foot of the bed, the remnants of a vacant wasp's nest, dry as autumn leaves, pale as the moon. From it, a hundred sprouts. It reminded Daniel of insects infected with fungi. Thin white tendrils bursting forth until the creature's silhouette projected like white noise. The isopod lay, half-concealed by the bed frame, dead.

Atop the bed, a form Daniel couldn't decipher.

His brain gnawed and ground and chewed at the sight. Unable to devour it, unable to understand. A haze of sensations filled his head, lower jaw shuddering, eyes watering, his body reacting despite his brain's insistence there was nothing to make sense of inside the room. His mouth filled with spittle.

He smelled the acid of Joanne's stomach, heavy and acrid. Questioned how he registered such a scent over the blood. The last, weak remnants of daylight shone through a gore-slick window, flooded the place scarlet like the stained glass of a cathedral, flushed Joanne's drained features pink.

Daniel looked upon the flesh of her and remembered the mussel. Meat doubled, tripled, bloodless fingers squeezed out of the shell. Only this was so very red. A wet rose unfurling. A blossom so intense in its flowering that the doubling organs degloved the skin of her fingers, covering pulled tight enough to rip. Joanne's wedding ring glinted at him, resting flush against the webbing of her hand, bone brighter than the diamond set into it.

The world tipped onto its side.

Daniel's throat flexed, mouth open, but the scream did not come. He dropped to his knees, brittle bones cracking, and pounded at the floor, as though he need only make a noise, need only wake her. If she heard, the flower of her organs would retract, eyes would lose their milky glaze and roll back to him, bloodshot and tired, but twinkling.

Sobs suffocated Daniel's apologies.

So, too, did the eyes.

DEMI-LOUISE BLACKBURN

Demi-Louise Blackburn is a dark fiction author from a small town in West Yorkshire, England.

Her work often explores the external and internal challenges of mental health, whilst also indulging in her soft spot for the horror genre, ensuring many of her protagonists fight dual monsters.

With support from friends and family, Demi began sending work out for publication in 2020. Since then, some of her short stories have found homes with *Kandisha Press*, *All Worlds Wayfarer,* and *Ghost Orchid Press*. She continues to chip away at numerous projects.

If not writing, you can most likely find Demi painting or playing video games. She enjoys watching wildlife documentaries, listening to podcasts, and collects taxidermy insects to decorate her writing office with.

Keep up to date with Demi's work here: demi-louise.com/social-media

BREAKING THE MOLD

BY PAUL KANE

E*ntry 1:*

BEGIN RECORDING:

I... hello.

I don't know who'll be listening to this, I'm not even sure what I'll do with it once it's finished. Upload it, I guess. But I thought it best to start a fresh journal to document what's occurred. Not a company one, or a personal one; I don't really go in for that anyway, or didn't. I just feel like it's important that there be some record of what's been happening, here at least. Of what *will* happen...

Jesus, give me a moment. I'm still trying to wrap my head around everything.

[*Sighs*]

Oh, I should probably start with who I am, shouldn't I? My

name is Dr Andrea Strauss, and not to toot my own horn – well, maybe a little – I'm pretty damned smart. I was a bit of a child prodigy don'tya know, which surprised the hell out of my parents on the farm, I can tell you! They didn't know what to do with me, or how to relate to me, so they packed me off to a school for the gifted. Not in an X-Men way, you understand – okay, I'm raising my hand now, genuine card-carrying geek here – but so I wouldn't feel out of place when I graduated from university at the ridiculous age of just nine, then went on to become an MD by the time I was 14.

I've got a few specialisms, including biology, urology and microbiology, and in the past have consulted for the likes of WHO – the World Health Organisation, not the Doctor; I wish! – and the CDC, before being headhunted by an organisation that's so top secret I don't even know the name of it.

[*Laughs*]

Which is how I came to be here, at this facility. Again, I can't really tell you where that is – because for one thing I don't know myself exactly. We were all drugged, voluntarily I should add, before being deposited here. We've each of us spent time in places like this before, though... Okay, maybe not places exactly like this one but close enough. What I do know for sure is that it's in the arse end of nowhere, and it's underground; full of corridors and labs. Bet you thought those kinds of facilities were only in bad horror movies, designed to cook up viruses that turned us all into zombies or lunatics?

Sadly the lunatics are all out there in the world it seems, above ground. And, much as it pains me to admit it, this might be one of the safest locations to be right now.

We are, or were, conducting experiments, I have to confess. Medical mainly, as you'd expect. Working on cures for various things, the different forms of dementia for one. And yes, the work includes breaking down certain viruses, studying them.

I'd be lying if I said the potential wasn't there to splice, to manufacture. To weaponise. But, like most scientists I guess, I try not to think about that. The trade-off is worth it, if we can do some good.

I've been using that collective word 'we', haven't I? That's because there's a team of us here. A select team, I grant you, but a team nonetheless. Sort of. I knew a couple of the members by reputation, but not others. Dr Hina Matsui for example, I was familiar with her work on the Greenberg Incident. A quiet lady, with the tiniest feet you've ever seen and such penetrating eyes. You can tell she's weighing you up just by looking at you... and probably getting it right, too.

Then we have Professor Byron Flood. Another person I'd heard of because, well, who hasn't? Okay, you might not have done out there in whereverland, but take my word for it he's brilliant! I've been reading his articles in *New Scientist* for years, never thought I'd be privileged enough to meet him. Silver-haired, with bushy eyebrows, he's the very definition of a gentleman. Next we have Dr Charlotte Driver, or Lotte as I've come to know her. She's very much like an older version of myself, some ten years down the line. We get on really well. Then there's Jerry Lachlan. The exact opposite of Professor Flood. I still don't know if that man's a doctor, professor or whatever the hell he is. He seems to only have a passing interest in science altogether. To be honest with you, I think he's a company man just here to keep an eye on us. He definitely keeps an eye on me, in fact I get the impression he hates my guts. He's as quiet as Hina, but I don't feel like it's shyness, just that he's good at keeping secrets. Jerry's more at home with the animals they have here. You know, dogs, pigs, chimps... Those especially; he even looks like one!

[*Laughs*]

I know, I know, animal rights. But I promise they're all well cared for and we have to run our tests on something. Hey, I grew up on a farm; sue me. None of us are budding Dr Frankensteins, we don't do the whole human guinea pig thing...

Which leaves us with Sukru. Dr Sukru Adem, to give him his full title. I'm... He's another person I wasn't familiar with before coming here, who I got to know a little at the welcome party-type affair we had on the first night. Nothing fancy, just a bit of music, some wine in plastic cups. Breaking the ice kind of business.

Sukru has piercing eyes too, but in a different way. He's... Oh Christ, you can't see my face right now, but take my word for it I'm blushing. We're not supposed to form romantic attachments doing this kind of work, but sometimes you— I don't suppose it matters now, does it? What can I say? All right, I *like* him. There I've admitted it. Are you happy? And I'm telling you because it might help you understand some of my actions.

Now, I'm not saying he's the man of my dreams or anything. I'm not the type of girl to wait for a Prince Charming to come along, to whisk me off my feet or wake me up with a kiss. But sometimes it just hits you, doesn't it? There's a connection and you think to yourself 'oh, *there* you are!' Or even 'where the fuck have you been?' because let me tell you, it's been no joyride in that department.

I'm rambling, aren't I? I do that. When I'm nervous. When I'm not nervous. And when I'm...

[*Sound of crying*]

Just give me a second, will you.

Recording Terminated.

Entry 2:

Begin Recording:

Right, okay, got my head together a little bit. With a little help.

Took some pills because I've got a migraine building. I've suffered from them all my life. My price for, as my dear old mum used to say, 'thinking too much.' Like I can help that... Ironic really, because when the headaches hit I can barely think straight at all.

So, pills to stave it off. Because I really need to be able to think right now, to try and fix this. Physician heal thyself, right? Heal thyself and...

Where did all this begin? I hear you ask. Or imagine you asking. Maybe you're asking what the fuck I'm waffling on about, but if you're out there somewhere chances are you probably know already.

The first we were aware of it was when Hina came rushing from the rec room on her break. 'Have you seen the news!' she was virtually screaming. It was the most she'd said in a month, and infinitely more loudly. 'Have you *seen* it!'

'Wait, wait. Slow down,' I said to her as she almost collided with myself and Lotte in the corridor. But she took it to mean slow down with what she was saying, because she sucked in a breath then.

'It's all over the news,' Hina said, stringing out the words.

'What is?' asked Lotte.

'About... about what's happening.'

'What *is* happening?' I prodded, still not understanding. It was then that she gestured for us both to follow her, back to the TV where she'd seen whatever shocking thing it was that had animated her so. My eyes were drawn immediately to the crowds depicted on screen.

Another riot, I assumed. We were getting used to those of late, people up in arms about some slight or another. But there was something wrong with the way these folk were acting. Not banded together, the crowds versus the authorities or what have you. No, this was more of a free-for-all, with bodies climbing over bodies, scratching and clawing. Some were using weaponry, don't get me wrong – I spotted someone with a hammer just laying into skulls, the end covered in grey matter; another person stabbing with a pair of scissors – but a lot of the others were just punching and kicking, headbutting. The camera panned away from one assault, where a middle-aged man in a suit and tie, who looked like he'd be more at home working in an office, was ripping the throat out of some teenage girl, vampire-style.

I'd read a horror book once where the adults all turned on the kids, can't for the life of me remember what it was called, but it was about blood or something. Blood making them crazy, forcing them to kill. It wasn't just a generational thing on this occasion, though, as the reporter was saying, and I'm paraphrasing here: 'We're seeing this in so many locations now, Trisha. Men and women, even children... There's something the matter with all of them, it's like they're... I don't really know how to describe it...'

[*Draws a breath*]

Hell. That's what it looked like to me.

Some kind of strange depiction of Hell from the Middle Ages, with people stripping off as well, just tearing their clothes off. The camera was panning around again, and this time inadvertently catching a couple on the ground. No, a woman being violated by *two* men, just rutting away there – and nobody was trying to stop them. Indeed, one of the men still had part of his policeman's uniform on. The very people we rely on to protect us from such behaviour.

Thankfully, the camera fell away. Fell to the ground actually, as the guy who'd been holding it suddenly went for the reporter with the microphone. All we could see was their feet and legs as they wrestled with each other, then the reporter's bloody face as he collapsed next to the lens.

It cut back to the anchorwoman in the studio, whose mouth was just agape. She touched her ear, then said: 'It appears we've lost the feed... But...' She just shook her head, and I can't say I blamed her.

'What the...' began Lotte.

'I know, right?' This was Hina again.

I'd backed off from the screen until my calves connected with the edge of the sofa, then I simply flopped backwards onto it.

Things would only get worse. After a while news stations stopped broadcasting altogether; I mean *all* news stations, everywhere. We had to rely on satellite feeds then, access to company technology which Jerry seemed to know his way around a little too well.

The same thing was happening all over, people just going nuts and pulverising each other. When they weren't talking complete nonsense. You think I ramble, you should have heard some of the shit coming out of their mouths.

'So, what are we thinking?' Lotte asked eventually, broaching what had been on all our minds. 'Some kind of chemical weapon?'

'But who used it on whom?' I replied. There seemed to be no rhyme nor reason to it, no boundaries. 'Was it something that just got out of hand? Mutated?' An artificial virus we'd created, or something more natural? Unnatural? Could be fucking black magic that cooked it up for all we knew!

[*Sighs*]

Every now and again you'd see someone who appeared to be okay, but it was few and far between. At one point I spotted this guy, almost looked like he was shimmering. Jerry was leaning forward, pushing me out of the way to get a better look. Then he tapped the screen. 'That's a S.K.I.N, that is,' he informed us.

When we looked puzzled he explained it was something the company had been developing for exploration of other worlds. 'Survivor's Kinetic Integrated System. Recycles everything. He'll be all right.' Protected, but for how long? He was still being chased by the crazies out there, still in danger.

Having said that, we could have used some of those S.K.I.N. things as all this developed. For our guys who were outside the facility. For Byron. For Sukru.

But I'm getting ahead of myself again. I...

[*Sound of crying*]

Recording Terminated.

Entry 3:

Begin Recording:

I'm back.

Okay, so, here's the deal. Byron and Sukru were already up there when everything went to pot. They were gathering samples, various flora and fauna. Oh, one of Sukru's specialisms is botany, the use of plants against diseases, herbal science. Not sure how that could be used against this particular... But, anyway, they'd been on a field trip – literally – with Byron going with him to 'stretch his legs' as he put it.

Both suited up, standard environ-gear, complete with helmets, going through the motions when they got down to this level in the lift, which opens out into a decon-cubicle with a toughened glass-front. Logging their samples in the box-chute on the wall provided. Sprayed with chemicals as they entered, regulation quarantine procedures. You never know what you might be bringing back into the facility, and this place is scarily clean... They have bots that sterilise everything; Mini-Scutters I call them. Geek, remember?

[*Laughs*]

I'll be honest, I was relieved when they returned. But of course by that time, we'd come to understand what we were dealing with. Had seen pictures of it growing everywhere, eating away at flesh and bone. Buildings, vehicles. All at different rates. Those black patches, starting off tiny but inevitably growing in size. Creating not zombies, but something else, because the people out there weren't dead – when it killed them, they just decayed. Were decaying *before* they died, inside and out. Nobody was rising from the grave to bite anyone anyway, thank Christ! What we were dealing with was horrifying enough.

'Some kind of rot,' said Hina, 'but it's not like anything I've ever seen before.'

'Mold,' I whispered, reminded of my childhood and the patch of blackness in the corner of my bedroom wall on the farm. The blackness that spread out, with fingers like tentacles. The kind that my parents could never get rid of, even though they washed it with bleach and even bought some special stuff from Korea that was meant to do the trick. It's one of the reasons I had asthma until I was in my late teens, all that time in there as a kid.

'What's the difference?' Jerry had asked. See what I mean? Not much of a head for science.

'Well, they're both fungi, I'll give you that,' Hina informed him. Since she'd started speaking, you couldn't shut her up. 'But there are many different kinds of each, for example Common genera of molds include Acremonium, Trichophyton, Cladosporium—'

Jerry held up his hand. 'I didn't ask for a bloody lecture.'

Hina folded her hands over her chest. 'Okay, but what I do know is that it's been scientifically connected to depression, insomnia, anxiety. Breathing in spores like that.'

Not too much of a stretch to think it was causing the mayhem out there. Chemically altering brains, like the dementia we were trying to cure... or reverse. The body, the brain, is just an organic machine when all's said and done. When one part fails...

'Dr Adem, he'd be the one to ask about it all,' Hina finished, then clamped up again.

I wished we could, but he was still a way off returning at that point. When he did, I was waiting at the clear doors to greet him with a smile. Him and Professor Flood. 'Did you see anything... I don't know, unusual out there?' I asked.

'How do you mean?' replied the professor. So, I had to explain what was happening out there in the world. Hardest thing I've ever had to tell anybody, and now here I am going through it again.

[*Sighs*]

'You didn't see any examples of that out there? Affecting the plants, trees?' There wouldn't have been any people around, so no point asking about that. This place was too remote. Both men shook their heads. 'If we could take a proper look at a sample, maybe we could do something about it.'

'No, I don't think—' The professor stopped talking then, and lunged at Sukru, hands around his throat through the suit. Trying to strangle him, bringing him to his knees.

'God almighty!' I shouted, hand reaching for the door release. That was when I felt someone grab my wrist, hard. I turned briefly to see Jerry there, preventing me. Then I turned back to see Sukru breaking the professor's hold on him, standing and shoving the man backwards with some force. He was his junior after all, stronger, fitter. Byron hit the corner of the decon-cube and slid down it.

'You want a sample?' Jerry hissed in my ear, then finally let go of me and pointed at the crumpled figure of the man. And suddenly I spotted it, the black patch on his environ-suit. That had eaten *through* his suit to get to the man himself, like cracking open a coconut to get to the flesh, the milk.

Sukru stared at this himself, then back over at me. And I've never seen anyone look so...

[*Sound of crying*]

I'm sorry, that's enough for... I can't. I just can't.

Recording Terminated.

Entry 4:

Begin Recording:

. . .

I'M SORRY.

Sorry for not getting back to this sooner, I've just been busy. Working on the problem at hand, working on trying to find a solution. And when I wasn't, just spending time with Sukru, sitting against that glass, holding my hand up so that our fingers would be touching if it wasn't in the way. Oh, he took off his suit a while ago. Figured it hadn't done Byron any good anyway. Wasn't like it was a S.K.I.N. protecting him... No, we're feeding Sukru through the box chute. Food and drink that's sealed. And we incinerated the plant samples they'd brought back with them, just in case. The professor's doped up to his eyeballs, using the tranq-gun we slipped Sukru with his meals. It's been keeping Byron under control for the time being, and maybe even slowing the infection... Because, Jesus, it's really taken hold of the man. That blackness all the way up his arm now, spreading out in the corner of the bedroom...

[*Sighs*]

Decon-cube, I meant to say. Christ, this headache...

The work. Right. I was talking about the work. It's been all hands on deck, really. Using the scans of the mold from Byron's suit – we couldn't risk bringing it inside here for fear of contamination, bad enough I'd almost exposed us all to that crap – we've been studying it, trying to break it down. Trying to figure out a way to break it down *for good*. Even reverse what it's doing. Treating it like we would do any other virus.

I still can't tell if this was down to us, and by us I mean the collective... Whether we made this and it escaped from somewhere, or whether it's natural. Some kind of revenge of nature thing. You could hardly blame the planet after the way we've treated it.

But, anyway, I just wanted to explain what I was doing – so you didn't think I was just sitting on my arse twiddling my thumbs. We're making progress, I think. We should be, the collective IQ in here is staggering.

I just hope we find the solution soon.

Recording Terminated.

Entry 5:

Begin Recording:

Oh God.

Oh God-oh-god-oh-god...

[*Sound of crying*]

How did we – how did *I* – not see this coming? How? Fucking how? Okay, I need to slow down, get all this on record. It didn't happen that long ago, but—

What am I talking about? Jerry... *Fucking* Jerry!

The pig... Not Jerry, although he is... But... That was the first I was aware of what was happening. A pig running through the corridor, barging past me. It had been let out, but it was also leaving a trail of prints behind it. Red prints.

Blood.

Tentatively, I followed them. Back up in the direction the animal had come from. There was more blood, in fact it was everywhere. And then I saw the body, Lotte's body, just lying there in a pool of the stuff.

I let out a howl, calling out her name and bending to try and help her. But it was too late, obviously too late. Her throat had been torn out, and even now the wetness was still spilling onto the shiny floor of what had once been the scarily clean corridor. Scarily...scary...

There was a growling sound coming from not far away, and I looked up to see one of the dogs there ahead of me; snarling, mouth bloody, cocking its head. That had been freed too. It was obvious what had happened to Lotte. A very different kind of revenge of nature. For all the things we'd been doing to them here.

'I couldn't just leave 'em in those cages,' said a voice. And now I saw Jerry, stepping out from a room on the right, holding a chimp's hand and brandishing another tranq-gun. 'They deserve better. They're more loyal than any of you fuckers!'

And, as he stepped even further into the corridor, I saw more blood. A pair of tiny feet beyond him. Hina's feet.

'Especially you!' he shouted at me. 'You with that... I mean, how *could* you? You knew how I felt about you. I made it pretty obvious!'

'What?'

'You and *him*! You whore! Don't even try to deny it. You think there aren't monitors in all the quarters. You think I don't have access!' The dog growled again at the level and intensity of its master's voice. 'We could have had something special, y'know? I could have let you in...'

'Let me—'

'You stuck-up bitches are all the same!'

'You're... You're insane!' I shouted back.

Jerry paused to think about that for a second. 'Am I? *Am* I?' Then he raised the tranq-gun and pointed it at me. I couldn't let him do it, knock me out and do whatever the hell he wanted to do with me. To me. So I started towards him, but as I did so the dog started towards me – leapt up to go for my throat as it had done with Lotte.

Without even thinking, I grabbed it and used the animal as a shield – putting it between myself and the tranq-dart. It was what they were intended for anyway, those guns. To use on the animals. In seconds, the thing was on the floor and twitching.

'*Bitch!*' Jerry screamed again, pulling back the pin in an effort to reload and fire. He'd let go of the chimp, but that had wandered off in the other direction. The gun was up and facing me again when something struck Jerry's leg and he looked down.

It was one of the mini-Scutters, racing to try and clean up this mess. To make the place scarily clean again... scarily...

That was all the distraction I needed to reach Jerry and tackle him, shove him backwards past Hina's prone body and into the wall of the corridor. He let go of the gun, which clattered to the ground. But that just meant he had two hands free to tackle me. He grabbed both my wrists this time, and I felt the strength from before when I'd nearly freed Sukru without thinking. He yanked them sideways, almost wrenching my arms out of their sockets and I let out an almighty cry.

Then he headbutted me, letting go at the same time so I could fall backwards. I was just getting used to the pain on the bridge of my nose when he kicked me, hard, in the side. 'Whore!' he said again, in case I hadn't got the message. 'Fucking—'

Jerry stopped, eyes wide. I looked up through my own watery eyes to see what had happened. A tranq-dart was sticking out of the man's chest. I traced its trajectory back down to Hina, who was still on the floor, but had raised herself up enough to aim the discarded weapon. She was also priming it again, shooting again, even though Jerry was already falling.

She put two more darts into him even after that. An overdose that would have killed an elephant.

Ignoring the pain I was in, I crawled over to where the

woman was. My quiet-loud friend. Hina hadn't been bitten, but rather stabbed repeatedly; the scalpel was still sticking out of her side. She let the gun drop, her head dropping with it. 'I-I never liked that guy,' she whispered as I got close enough to hear.

I've just come from the med-bay, where I've been operating. Attempting to patch her up. She was in such a mess. I just hope I was able to do enough. And that I was in time.

Painkillers. That's what I need... My nose. My head, it's...

[*Sound of crying*]

I just wanted to record this, tell someone about what happened.

Just wanted to...

Recording Terminated.

Entry 6:

Begin Recording:

[*Sound of crying*]

I lost her. Hina.

The internal bleeding was just...

[*Sound of crying*]

I owe her so much. Not just because of Jerry, but what she was doing when he attacked her. Making that final leap, working from what Lotte and I had done. Breaking the... I just need to test it now, which I'm going to do on...

Oh, that's right. I haven't told you yet, have I? The dog. The animals. All of them, actually. I found out when I examined them, after I'd rounded up the pig, the chimp, putting them back again. They were all infected, had been when they were brought in here. It was just slow to take hold. Certainly the dog was; should have realised from the neck biting thing.

Couldn't find a sign of it anywhere on Jerry, though that doesn't mean a thing. He could just have been nuts, obviously, but... Should have known, should have realised from the way he looked at me. Not hatred; quite the reverse. Stupid! Stupid!

Turns out not all the lunatics were above ground, after all.

Who knows whether he was infected? Who cares? The mini-Scutters can incinerate the bastard!

So, I'm just working up a serum to test on the infected animals. I can't wait to tell Sukru. Let him out of that damned...

[*Sighs*]

It's been a long couple of weeks.

Recording Terminated.

Entry 7:

Begin Recording:

[*Sound of crying, then wailing*]

Gone... He's... Even before the black, spreading... S-Suk... he overdosed... tranqued... Byron is long gone, long gone... nothing left of...

I had it! The cure! The... Break. We'd broken... The dog... the dog woke up, he was...

Jesus, my head!

[*Sound of wailing*]

I wasn't in time. Wasn't soon enough. I know what Sukru would say, I can help others now. Help people by letting... Letting them know what... that... I need to upload all this, in the hopes that someone can—

I need to work up enough to dose myself and this... Need to stop it in this place, in the... the world, but takes time... need to work up enough and the mini-Scut...they've started breaking...

Breaking down.

The whole... the facility is my bed...room now. The mold... how scarily... scary is that? Blackness, stretching out. In the cube. The corri...

And, fuck. On me. It's—

I can see the dark...

I can—

Recording Terminated.

Entry 8:

Begin Recording:

[*Sound of heavy breathing*]

Need to do... I was going to... Whar...what was...

[*Laughs hysterically*]

I'm ranblink again, aren... I does thaat when... when... Where is I? What was I... Asking...the fuck... waffling...

[*Draws a breath*]

I'm... It's my r-rooom... bed... The... in the corner... black... black spreading... no break. Broken...

I'm... What was I—

What was—

B-Blackness. Brake!

[*Laughs*]

B-Broken...

Broke.

Recording Terminated.

PAUL KANE

Paul Kane is the award-winning, bestselling author and editor of over a hundred books – including the *Arrowhead* trilogy (gathered together in the sellout *Hooded Man* omnibus, revolving around a post-apocalyptic version of Robin Hood), *The Butterfly Man and Other Stories*, *Hellbound Hearts*, *Wonderland* (a Shirley Jackson Award finalist) and *Pain Cages* (an Amazon #1 bestseller). His non-fiction books include *The Hellraiser Films and Their Legacy* and *Voices in the Dark*, and his genre journalism has appeared in the likes of *SFX*, *Rue Morgue* and *DeathRay*. He has been a guest at Alt.Fiction five times, was a guest at the first SFX Weekender, at Thought Bubble in 2011, Derbyshire Literary Festival and Off the Shelf in 2012, Monster Mash and Event Horizon in 2013, Edge-Lit in 2014 and 2018, HorrorCon, HorrorFest and Grimm Up North in 2015, The Dublin Ghost Story Festival and Sledge-Lit in 2016, IMATS Olympia and Celluloid Screams in 2017, Black Library Live and the UK Ghost Story Festival in 2019, plus the WordCrafter virtual event 2021 – where he delivered the keynote speech – as well as being a panellist at FantasyCon and the World Fantasy Convention, and a fiction judge at the Sci-Fi London festival. A former British Fantasy Society Special Publications Editor, he is currently serving as co-chair for the UK chapter of The Horror Writers Association. His work has been optioned and adapted for the big and small screen, including for US network primetime television, and his novelette 'Men of the Cloth' has just been turned into a feature by Loose Canon/Hydra Films, starring Barbara Crampton (*Re-Animator, You're Next*): *Sacrifice*, released by Epic Pictures. His audio work includes the full cast drama adaptation of *The Hellbound Heart* for Bafflegab, starring Tom Meeten (*The Ghoul*), Neve McIntosh (*Doctor Who*) and Alice Lowe (*Prevenge*), and the *Robin of Sherwood* adventure *The Red Lord* for Spiteful Puppet/ITV narrated by Ian Ogilvy (*Return of the Saint*). He has also contributed to the Warhammer 40k universe for Games Workshop. Paul's latest novels are *Lunar* (set to be turned into a feature film), the Y.A. story *The Rainbow Man* (as P.B. Kane), the sequels to *RED – Blood RED & Deep RED* – the award-winning hit *Sherlock Holmes & the Servants of Hell*, *Before* (an Amazon Top 5 dark fantasy bestseller) and *Arcana*. In addition he writes thrillers for HQ/HarperCollins as PL Kane, the first of which, *Her Last Secret* and *Her Husband's Grave* (a recent sellout on both Amazon and Waterstones), came out in 2020. Paul lives in Derbyshire, UK, with his wife Marie O'Regan and his family. Find out more at his site **www.shadow-writer.co.uk** which has featured guest writers such as Stephen King, Neil Gaiman, Charlaine Harris, Robert Kirkman, Dean Koontz and Guillermo del Toro.

VESSEL

BY DAVE JEFFERY

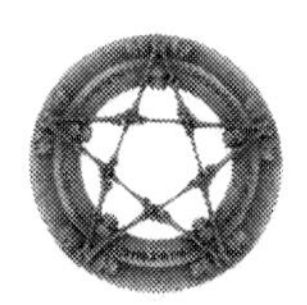

'Yes, what is it?'

'Professor Cooke?'

'You dialled my number, Dr Ritter. Who else could it be?'

Jason Ritter's voice was hushed, his ability to breathe impeded by fear. The cell phone creaked in his ear, the glass facia slick with the sweat on his cheek. 'Yes, sorry. Sir, we have a problem.'

In the receiver, the response came as cold and stark as an Arctic landscape. '*You* have the problem, Dr Ritter. I suggest you fix it. And fast. Before I make my employers aware.'

'You don't understand, Professor. I can't. Not without help.'

There was the briefest of pauses; the only indicator that Cooke was perplexed. 'Then you're in trouble. And such a thing will incur consequences.'

Jason took another breath, trying to retain some composure as desperation weakly rallied against his fear. 'Not if you agree to a request, sir.'

'For what?'

'Sanction. To call in an outsider.'

'Out of the question.'

'They're the only person who can get this thing done.'

Cooke's tone turned bitter. 'We are paying *you* to 'get this thing done'. Did you not approach us as an expert in this matter?'

'Yes. But ...'

'But what?'

'He's *better*.' The admission added extra weight to Jason's quandary.

'Maybe I should consider terminating your contract with immediate effect? Go to this person who is 'better' instead. What do you think, Dr Ritter?'

Jason pawed at his messy mop of brown-grey hair. His hand came away damp. 'He won't come on board without me asking him. He trusts me.'

Cooke's response came back, whiplash sharp. 'The way we trusted you?'

'More. Like family. Like a brother.'

This time, Jason could sense Cooke taking his time, dragging out his own discomfort. The doctor was a sprat on a hook in the hands of a seasoned fisherman.

'You have two days. Make it happen. Or expect repercussions.'

'I can guarantee this matter will be resolved, Professor.' Jason almost believed his own lie.

'Just get it done.'

'Yes, sir.'

But Cooke had already ended the call. Jason tossed his phone onto his workstation where it knocked over a desk-tidy, scattering stationery across the silver surface. Ignoring the mess, he leaned forward, placing his elbows on the aluminium, his face seeking solace in his palms.

There, he screamed his frustration against the meat of his hands.

The doorbell rang out again, its insistence gnawing into Richard White's concentration, forcing him to accept that whoever was standing on his doorstep had no intention of leaving him in peace. He placed his copy of *A Brief History of Time* on the small, glass coffee table and got to his feet. Part of him held reservations, very few people knew where he lived, and that was deliberate.

Had it really been ten years ago, all that mess? All that guilt? All that love?

The doorbell again. Longer this time, bringing with it the visitor's impatience. Richard made it to the hallway. 'Give me just a minute, damn it!'

Mercifully the doorbell ended its tirade. The cottage door was fashioned from heavy oak, stained ebony. Framed by the small oval pane of frosted glass, Richard could see the haphazard shape of his unwelcome visitor. Cautiously, he unbolted the black deadlocks but slipped the chain into its bracket before drawing the door open.

'Whatever you're selling I've already got it. Piss off.'

Jason stood on the doorstep. The coastal wind came in from the northwest and made any attempt to tame his unruly hair completely fruitless. Richard had always known his ex-colleague to be an awkward soul. Today the doctor's demeanour was made even more gawkish by his relentless fidgeting as the hiss and sigh of the Atlantic Ocean danced on the air.

Still, Richard had no intention of making things easy. 'Don't I know you?'

'It's Jason.'

Nonchalance slipped from Richard's face, revealing a mask of contempt. 'Yeah. Never forget a face. Especially that of the low-life bastard who fucked off and then stole my work.'

Placating hands came up as though they'd have the same effect as fending off blows. 'I just needed to know what happened that night. I needed to find *it* again.'

Richard's eyes narrowed. 'If you'd have stuck around, you'd have known exactly what happened.'

'You shut me out of the ritual, remember? I'd no idea what I was getting into, Richard. I still don't. Not without you.'

'You're so full of shit, and just as delusional. Bye, Jason. Enjoy whatever rock you've been living under.'

'Richard, wait. Please!'

He took a step forward, but the door thumped shut. Desperation joined in a moment later. Like a sinner seeking redemption, he fell to his knees and jabbed open the letterbox. He peered through and saw the shadow on the sandstone tiles of the hallway. 'Richard, please listen to me. It's back! Do you hear me? And I have it!'

Seconds stretched out like warm toffee.

The rattle of a chain was the only indicator that the door was about to open. Jason stood up so quickly he got giddy and planted his hands upon the doorframe.

Richard stood aside and jabbed a thumb down the hallway. 'You want some coffee?'

THEY SAT across from each other, Richard on the sofa, Jason on the matching armchair; separated by the coffee table and years of mistrust. It hadn't always been this way. Science was meant to be the vehicle for great discovery but, as it turned out, they'd lost so much along the way.

Jason nursed a mug of coffee in his lap. About him, the chalk-white walls were undulated; interspersed with crooked, brown beams and the shimmering gold frames of seascapes. Against the windows, the ocean and the wind still made themselves known.

'When did you get so tidy?' He took a sip of his coffee. It was tepid and bitter, just like the attitude of the man on the sofa.

'Are you writing for *Good Housekeeping* now?'

'Let's just say my current job pays better.' He set his mug down on the coffee table.

'You always were a slave to the buck, Jason. Wished I'd seen that earlier. Before I got to trust you.'

Jason shook his head. 'You seriously think I set out believing what we were doing could ever make money? Most of the time I thought the only thing we'd get out of it was a Section Three.'

Richard's smile held no warmth. 'You needed more faith. I told you that at the start.'

'What can I say, you're right.'

'You could've said that over the phone. Why are you here?'

'I need your help.'

'Now that's a doozy. What're you after? Forgiveness?'

'No. I need you to come to my lab. We're working on something. Something big.'

'Who's 'we'?'

'Phoenix Industries.'

Richard laughed but it was humourless. 'That bunch of charlatans? Good to see your moral standards remain as poor as ever.'

'They invest in a future for all.'

'They're an amoral conglomerate who have no other interest than getting fat on the woes of others.'

'Yeah? Well thanks to them I was able to find the vessel.'

Richard shifted in his seat. 'So you've said. And I don't believe you. It was lost after the ritual. I made sure of it.'

'It's sitting in my lab as we speak. Believe it or not, but it is a fact.'

There was a creak from the next room and Jason paused, eyes on the hallway. 'Are we alone?'

'Yes. Old houses complain sometimes. Just like people.'

The silence became another entity in the room until Jason sighed. 'We've come a long way, you and I.'

'We're not at Oxford anymore, if that's what you mean?'

'They were simpler times.'

'We can't undo what was done. We can only atone.'

The wind and ocean fed the silence for a short time until Richard sighed.

'I'm sorry I ran, Richard. I truly am. I was scared, okay. You kicked me out of the room, and all I heard were the screams. But we were there that night because of you and no one else. It was your obsession – your intuition – that led us to the ritual.'

Richard sipped his coffee, his eyes closing for a moment. 'I accept my part in it. That's why I choose to be away from others.'

'But we can make sure we finally learn from what happened.' Jason's tone was cautious, but the conversation was too raw not to ignite Richard's ire.

'You mean to Lesley and Beth? They were interns in our employ, they trusted us. I promised them it would be okay. But it wasn't.'

'Now we have another chance.'

'To get others killed?'

'To fix it. Have you ever thought that maybe this time we can get them back?'

Richard shook his head slowly just in case it would help Jason get the message. 'There's no getting them back. That's why I made sure it was lost.'

'Yet here we are now, today. We share this burden. It affects us in different ways but share it we do. There's no denying it. We have a second chance.'

'You're serious?'

'Yes. As are you when it comes to the vessel. There is an opportunity to put things right. Are you not prepared to help me do that?'

Richard considered his visitor. His brow was a ploughed field, as though this very act would give him the power to see through reason and unearth the deceit beneath. After several moments he sat back in his seat, his hands latticed across his stomach by a hashtag of fingers.

'I'll think about it. Call me tomorrow morning.'

Jason nodded and stood to leave. 'Thank you, Richard.'

'I'm not doing this for you.'

'I understand.'

Richard didn't look up from his mug. 'I guess there's a first time for everything.'

ALMA SAT at the kitchen table, her delicate fingers drumming the surface. Where skin met mahogany, a dust of brilliant light danced on the air. She heard the front door close on the squeal of the wind and the footfalls that came up the hallway were heavy as though their owner carried a great burden. She knew that this was not far from the truth.

Richard lingered in the doorway, his left hand on the jamb as though he'd topple without its support. 'He's gone.'

She hooked a strand of blonde hair over her left ear. 'You always were a good actor.'

Richard pulled out a chair next to her. 'With my upbringing it's no surprise.'

It was all too easy to go back to thoughts of his father. They came with images of spittle flying from sanctimonious lips, and balled-up fists ready to pummel. In the White's family home, love and hate had often worn the same face.

Alma scrutinised Richard's troubled expression. 'Pain at the hands of those whom we love makes us special,' she said. 'We have both endured it. And our ills gave the universe the means to bring us together. We exist to heal each other.'

'Yet our love was born from great tragedy. Two people died.'

'And we must bear their pain every day. As we should.' She paused as her eyes became a sparkling rainbow. 'Do you regret answering my call?'

He took hold of her fidgeting hands. 'You are my world, Alma. My first and last thought every damn day.'

Her iridescent eyes held genuine fear. 'But does this event change things?'

'No. Balance is everything. The universe needs it to exist.'

'How did they find it? We wished it lost forever.'

'It doesn't want to be lost anymore. That much is clear.'

'Then we must redress what was done in the name of liberty.'

'So, I must accept their offer?'

'Yes. Yes, *we* must.'

The car journey was unremarkable; a thirty-mile trip inland, through B-roads cutting open yellowed fields of rape, and bypassing small villages of white, thatched cottages.

Richard watched as Alma stared at the road ahead, her pale slender fingers light on the leathered wheel of the Audi. The sunlight played tricks with her complexion, first dark and sullen, the next bringing brightness to his heart. Her place in his life had come about so suddenly, and at such cost, there were times when he thought his perpetual fear of losing her was to be his ultimate penance.

Lesley and Beth had left this world without their faces. And Richard knew that Jason's accusation was right, it *was* his fault. He had found out about the existence of an incredible item through incredible means, and then it became an obsession, a passion. A curse.

He became aware of Alma's voice. 'There's a turning up ahead.'

'Leading to where?'

'I guess we'll find out soon enough.'

She steered the car left, where the hedgerow gave way to a dirt track that seriously tested the A4's suspension. Through the windscreen, the horizon bucked and jigged as the car snaked another mile until the access route opened into a wide driveway made of tarmac so fresh, it glistened like a leather coat in the rain.

The house at the end of the drive was old. It was neither a mansion nor a stately home, but it was big enough to have the tranquility of both.

Alma chewed her lip. 'Nice place.'

'Perfect for a ruse.'

'Oh, I agree. I suspect James Bond, secret bunkers and the whole shebang.'

'It's kind of obvious given this company's reputation. There are bad people on its payroll.'

'Then why hasn't it been shut down?'

'No accusation of scientific maleficence has ever stuck. Bad money buys good lawyers and makes witnesses rich enough to forget. It's no coincidence the vessel is here.'

The satnav wasn't quite done as it guided them past the grey brick and black windows of the house, and north, for another half a mile until they came to a lodge surrounded by dense woodland.

Alma turned off the engine. 'Not so grand after all.'

The lodge was a green, prefabricated oblong, where a short run of steps led to a portico. No sooner had they alighted from the Audi, Jason was descending the steps. Despite his excitable gait, the lines on his face were drawn with deep concern. Another man followed him out. He was tall and wore both a lab coat and a dour expression.

Jason approached, his face a blend of relief and uncertainty as his eyes flitted to Alma. 'So glad you made it.'

The tall man stepped up, his ice-blue eyes were behind black-framed glasses, his reedy frame making him look like a cadaver on the run from the next med-school experiment.

In the man's presence, Richard watched as Jason's stature diminished, his shoulders stooping as though in reverence. Or was it fear?

'Who is this woman?' The challenge was brisk and without refinery.

'Her name is Alma and she's a condition of me being here,' Richard said coldly. 'You don't like it then we'll just turn around and leave you to go and fuck yourself.'

There was no sign of reproach on the man's face. He stuck out a hand. 'I'm Professor Cooke. Welcome, Dr White.' He nodded once to Alma. 'Miss.'

Alma shuffled under the professor's steely gaze and slipped her hand into Richard's as Cooke continued. 'You know why you are here. We know why you're here. So, shall we proceed?'

Richard nodded. 'It's your madhouse.'

Cooke's tight smile seemed genuine. 'Quite.'

The professor moved towards the lodge and Jason sidled up to the couple. 'You never said how you two met.'

Richard met Jason's perplexed gaze. 'No. I didn't.'

THERE WAS an ambiguity attached to the interior of the cabin and the reason for its existence. The open plan area of beige walls and grey kitchen appliances oozed conservative rural retreat. A man and a woman occupied the space, both with dark hair and warm smiles, the epitome of a couple on a weekend break. But there was a limit to the air of calm they gave out, and when they stood, Richard glimpsed the butt of a handgun beneath the man's tan jacket. Like the building, these people were for display purposes only.

'The male is Jenkins, the female – Howells. They're here for protection.'

Richard and Alma nodded a greeting to the security staff. They smiled back, but their eyes remained shrewd, analytical. Neither guest was under any illusion as to where their loyalties lay.

Cooke moved things along. 'Okay, Jenkins. Let us through.'

Jenkins took a smartphone from his jacket pocket and touched the screen several times. There was a thud, and remarkably the sofa lifted from the floor for a few inches then slid aside, revealing a stairway of stainless steel.

Alma gave Richard a wink. 'See? James Bond.'

'And the whole shebang. Smart lady.'

'Don't you ever forget it.'

'Like I ever could.'

THEY DESCENDED into a long corridor that had the smell and feel of an emergency department. The air was cool and came to them as a low hiss from horizontal vents in the ceiling. White walls were interspersed with silver-framed, oval lights, and plain doors without windows or handles. However, to the right of each jamb, a retinal scanner with a blue screen and blinking green lights stood as a bastion of the high-tech security afforded to the contents of each room.

Richard walked with Alma at his side. Ahead, Cooke had his two security personnel in tow. *Everyone needs to feel safe somehow*, Richard mused.

He spoke as Cooke walked on. 'As I'm sure Jason's explained, the vessel could have come from any point in history. Other than low-level environmental erosion, there are no indicative markings, and it has no historical record.'

'The question that no one seems capable of answering is how come you found out about it?' said Cooke without looking back.

'A dream.'

Cooke stopped and turned. 'A what?'

Although he tried to hold it in check, there was no hiding the petulance in Richard's voice. 'You heard me. I had a dream. The same dream, for over a year. The vessel and its resting place. Hiding in plain sight. No hint to its past or its purpose.'

'A dream?' Cooke repeated, the corners of his mouth were taut as he thought this over.

'It's not something I expect you to understand but the evidence is conclusive. An artefact that does not exist is here in this place because I saw it and where it was kept hidden from the world.'

'And why would it do that? Why did it choose *you*, Dr White?'

'Who can say? Perhaps it wanted to be set free from the storage crate at the museum? Maybe it knew my old reputation for repatriation of lost artefacts.'

'How can you repatriate what doesn't exist?'

'How can a facility such as this exist? Playing catch up is the very nature of science, isn't it?'

'Interesting.' Cooke continued down the corridor and they all followed, children behind the piper.

Fifty feet later, they stopped at another unremarkable door. The professor stooped and presented his left eye to the retinal scanner. The door slid soundlessly open as Cooke stood upright. He extended a long arm to invite entry.

'Shall we?'

THE ROOM WAS a stark contrast to the sterile corridor. Banks of workstations and computer consoles were butted up against three of the four featureless walls. At the workstations, two women in blue coveralls flitted, making further notes on tablets with white e-pencils. From time to time they would look at the fourth wall, a rectangular stadium, its area made of inky black Perspex. Neither scientist acknowledged the newcomers in the room, their focus was only on the data.

Richard stared at the dark Perspex. 'May we see it?'

'Of course,' the professor said and indicated a workstation nearby.

Jason went to it. With a few taps on a silver keyboard, the

blackness of the viewing portal dropped in tones until it was so clear, it gave the impression that there was no glass at all.

Richard looked at the window, at the bland, steel pedestal upon which sat the object that had come to him in the most implausible and brutal manner possible. He saw the familiar outline: the grey, stone urn with its pock-marked surface making its shape irregular. He hadn't seen this object for many years and, as he scanned its image, he felt both exhilaration and fear. He sensed Alma's hand sliding into his, this was a shared experience, this object was the beginning of their time together. Something beatific to rise from the tragedy.

'It's been a long time,' Richard whispered.

Cooke's voice was loud in the room. 'And now you must do what you have agreed, Doctor. You must open the vessel so that we can begin to understand its history.'

Richard shook his head. 'It requires more than I'm prepared to give.'

Cooke sniffed with nonchalance. 'We'll see.'

Alma was dragged backwards so quickly; Richard could imagine he was still holding her hand. He wheeled around and saw her with Jenkins' beefy left forearm about her throat, and the handgun from his jacket now pressed to her temple.

Cooke's tone was deadpan. 'You will help us further the knowledge of mankind. Or Jenkins will demonstrate how far we *haven't* come as a species.'

Richard looked at Alma. She didn't struggle with her captor; she made no attempt to deter her fate.

Jason's voice was at his side. 'Please, Richard. Do as we ask.'

Richard rounded on him. 'You'll always be a hack, Jason. Open the fucking door.'

Hands held up in platitude, Jason backed off and went to the door alongside the viewing screen. This time he used a retinal scan followed by a code over ten digits long. The door clicked and began an opening arc as gyros hummed. When it met the adjacent wall, it locked into place.

'Off you go, Doctor,' Cooke chided. 'Time is now a commodity. And your assistant is on the meter.'

Nodding in concession, Richard turned and addressed Cooke. 'I need a small amount of blood. It can't be mine, and it can't be hers.'

'Explain.'

'It serves as a conductor, connecting this world to that of the vessel.'

'For what purpose?'

'Equilibrium. The way deep sea workers have to decompress between jobs.'

Cooke's voice was hushed. 'Fascinating. Howells?'

The security operative stepped forward. 'Yes, Professor?'

'Please execute the agreed dismissal protocol for Dr Ritter.'

Without pause, Howells brought up her handgun and shot Jason in the head. The discharge was loud, the result as spectacular as it was shocking. The doctor's head changed shape as the bullet struck his forehead, his left eye rolled back into its socket while the right spasmed as though he was trying to make sense of what had just happened. He collapsed, shuddered once, and then lay still.

The professor pointed as the puddle of claret formed a corona about Jason's head. 'Is that enough?'

There wasn't any expression on Richard's face. Equally, his mind was blank, having compartmentalised the terrible event he'd just witnessed. This was the nature of the vessel, and the people that were attracted to it. He squatted beside Jason and placed a palm into the warm, bloody pool like a toddler about to produce a handprint for its mother.

He stood and walked forward; his hand held out before him

so as not to soil his own clothing. Without looking back, he crossed the threshold and entered the chamber.

THE VESSEL APPEARED INNOCUOUS, yet Richard knew it to be no such thing. He approached with caution, looking upon the artefact, its blemished surface yielding nothing.

His bloodied hand was a few feet away from the surface, and he looked out at those in the anteroom. Alma had closed her eyes, but he could see her mouth moving soundlessly.

'Are you sure you want to do this, Professor?'

'Just get on with it, White.'

Richard took a breath, held it for three seconds, and then let it go with a drawn-out hiss.

He placed his bloody palm on the vessel. A moment later, the world changed.

COOKE WATCHED as Richard touched the urn. When nothing happened, a sense of frustration began to build in his gut, his anger growing like a canker eating away his innards.

Then he heard the voice; an indecipherable, rhythmic refrain that quelled his frustration and fostered his scientific curiosity. He turned to see the woman still held by Jenkins, her lips were moving, but there was something not quite right with her face.

Because it wasn't Alma's face at all, it had become Howells', and when the professor looked over at the security guard, he saw Howells had no face at all, her head was like an artist's mannequin, featureless and smooth. Aghast, he looked over at the other scientists, their faces were also without features, and in their panic, they each began clawing their featureless heads until the unblemished skin was a mass of tattered flesh, and lumps of bloodied meat splattered onto the floor.

Under the professor's gaze, Jenkins also lost his features, and the hand holding the gun came up to the security operative's head and he blew out his brains, sending them to the ceiling where they stuck like a gory exhibit at a Damien Hirst installation.

No longer supported by Jenkins, Alma fell to her knees, but her chanting continued, a gentle lilt amongst the absurdity and carnage.

The professor felt his own countenance starting to oscillate, and he caught sight of himself in the dead screen of a VDU, the way the bones beneath the skin of his cheeks and eyes juddered as though they were being reworked from the inside by rough, unseen fingers. His nose sank into the writhing mass and his glasses fell to the floor. He screamed, but the sound came from multiple sources - from Howells, from the other scientists, and each of them had Alma's face, and Alma's scream was theirs.

And when Cooke looked upon Alma, she was alternating between every face but her own, swapping them as though trying them for the perfect fit.

Only then did the vessel make itself known.

THE IMAGES in Richard's head were familiar, yet from a place where things such as pasts and futures held no meaning. The vessel was designed to accentuate the present, to keep it stretched out like the smears of comets and dead stars in the infinite cosmos overhead. There was matter, evidenced by the rocks and caves of bloated, battered landscapes that twisted about him, beneath him, and like the dying embers in the grate of a once unfathomable fire, each cave had an ethereal glow, a ghost of something no longer missed by the universe.

Amid all of this, something *probed*, searching for a presence that had been lost, a presence that had evaded its duty, and that duty was penance for crimes that had led to its infinite incarceration, its name removed, its rights annulled forever.

There was no gateway to a new world, there was only imprisonment, and endless pain. So it was that the entity he knew as *Gaoler* searched, and because Richard did not wear Alma's face, he went ignored.

The same could not be said for those now garnering the attention from elsewhere. The Gaoler was so energised by its discovery, it was given form - a great, pulsating mass of yellow and black flesh, quivering with excitement. Tendrils rose from folds of blubber about its belly, and these snaked out towards a fixed point - Richard's innate form now the conduit between freedom and eternal confinement.

The meaty tendrils punched painlessly into his belly and crossed the void between realms. By the time they emerged in the lab, they had morphed into tentacles of brilliant, white light.

And those wearing the faces of the duplicitous escapee were dragged back through the portal, their screams for mercy marking their passage.

ALMA WATCHED the incandescent streaks emerge from Richard and strike those wearing her face. As the brilliant tendrils tore into the bodies, the people rose, dancing on the air until they started to desiccate, substance sucked away to husk, crumbling as they were released and landed on the lab floor.

In mere moments, the deed was over in the world of

humankind. But Alma had known the pain of the vessel, and the fate awaiting those who were now part of it. A small eternity would pass before Gaoler realised the ruse. But in that time, Cooke and his minions would be beyond help, their minds broken. This was their attrition for their crimes.

Alma sighed as the light retreated back into the body of her saviour, and her love for him was renewed. There was no discernment, there was only acceptance.

The lab was unnervingly quiet. Only the bodies of Jason Ritter and Jenkins told a tale outside the realms of normalcy. As Richard emerged from the chamber carrying the vessel in the crook of his right arm, Alma went to him. She was hesitant. The artefact was inert but its implications for her we're profound.

'It has to remain in our keep, Alma. We cannot risk another today.'

She kissed his brow. 'Yes, my love. There is no escape, we are each bound to it.'

Richard sighed. 'You crossed dimensions so that I may rescue you. I fear your power. I fear your past.'

'All of what I am is yours. Overseen by my undying loyalty to you. My gift for my freedom.'

Richard's eyes misted. 'Is this what I am meant to be, your warden for eternity?'

She stood beside him, her arm about his waist, her head on his shoulder. 'If so, then I accept this blissful internment.'

Without another word they left the complex, the vessel in their keep like a child born of their joy and pain and love.

Its parents, forever.

DAVE JEFFERY

Dave Jeffery is the author of 16 novels, two collections, and numerous short stories. His Necropolis Rising series and yeti adventure Frostbite have both featured on the Amazon #1 bestseller list. His YA work features the critically acclaimed Beatrice Beecham supernatural mystery series. Screenwriting credits include award winning short films Ascension and Derelict. Finding Jericho (Demain Publishing) has featured on both the BBC Health and Independent Schools Entrance Examination Board's 'Recommended Reading' lists and is an amalgamation of his 35 years of NHS mental health nursing experience of working with service users who have suffered stigma and social exclusion due to mental illness. Finding Jericho is currently being optioned as a TV miniseries.

Jeffery is a member of the Society of Authors, British Fantasy Society (also as a regular book reviewer), and actively involved in the Horror Writers Association where he is a mentor on the HWA Mentorship Scheme.

THE GULCH

BY ANTHONY SELF

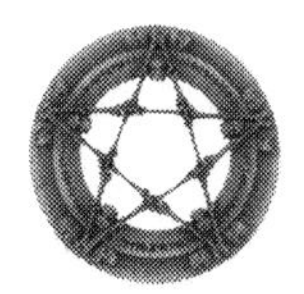

The thuggish looking McAlister pointed the .45 at Control's face.

Harrigan turned, noting the passive stance of the guards in the small armoury. He blinked, wondering why they hadn't descended upon the brute with their electrified stun batons.

'I'll ask ya again missy,' McAlister snarled, 'what's stopping me from blowing your fuckin' skull wide open and just walking out the door, eh?'

Control raised an inquiring eyebrow.

'William,' she said sardonically, 'do you *really* think we would give loaded weapons to convicts down here?'

A transformation spread swiftly across the thug's face, then through his body. Harrigan could barely comprehend the process within McAlister's expression, body language and what it all meant. The muscles in his forearms corded like rope. A tattoo of a spider on his bicep undulated across his arm. His eyes lidded to slits. Harrigan knew that dark look, the countenance of a sloppy drunk that wouldn't be dissuaded from a fight. He had the kind of cadaverous face of a man who had been slighted and would demand retribution one way or another.

'Bullshit.' McAlister's voice was slightly breathless but taut with emotion. The long scar against his cheek flashed white against his blanched skin.

Control tilted her head slightly. It was a small gesture, but Harrigan read it as: *Try me. Try me and see what happens.*

Harrigan thought about all the repellent men Control had met in her time at this grim detention camp. The bullies...the sociopaths...the superficial shows of geniality when they were first introduced, when the hood had been removed from their heads and a warm handshake by an attractive woman showed interest. *First time they'd seen a woman for years, most likely.* But once the tour had been given and the parameters had been set, they would feel cuckolded. They would feel powerless. And men like McAlister hated feeling powerless. Especially when a woman was giving the orders.

Harrigan also liked the way she used the bully's first name. As if she were a teacher chiding a petulant student. *That's why she's called Control,* he thought absently. The truth of the matter was, they were all prisoners. McAlister looked at the pistol in his grip and then back at the woman in the lab coat.

Don't do it, Harrigan implored. *Don't be a fool.*

But McAlister's face held the look of a boy with a secret so monumental that holding it back caused him physical pain. Harrigan knew what McAlister was about to do. The loutish behemoth was that predictable.

McAlister pulled the trigger.

The firing mechanism clicked. McAlister frowned at his weapon. Control deftly moved forward, snatched the gun from his grasp and slapped him across the face so hard Harrigan felt the reverberation in the small room.

The guards reacted. Harrigan observed their precise movements and choreographed routine. *This isn't their first rodeo, Johnny boy. Think about that.* The guards produced their humming batons. Control waved her hand dismissively. They pulled back. With their blackened helmets, Harrigan couldn't see the expressions on their faces. But he sensed they felt cheated.

'The weapons are all designated to your biometrics,' Control said languidly, tossing the gun back at McAlister. He fumbled to catch the weapon and looked at Control with a look of either love or hate...or possibly both. 'They don't get activated until you're in The Gulch.'

Harrigan turned to McAlister.

'McAlister. There are two train tracks. One has five random people tied to it but on the other is a child. You've got to decide which track the train goes on. Which one do you pick?'

He stared at Harrigan coldly and walked away.

'Why am I here?' Harrigan asked.

They were sat in a small amphitheatre. Control stood at the podium, highlighting their insertion point and quickest way through to the lowest levels of the research facility. The soldier, the doctor and the teacher.

'You're the key, John.' Control said.

Harrigan sat silently and stared impassively at her.

Control blinked and adjusted her glasses, and he saw a flicker of something human, something behind her patient, beatific dangerous calm. With his psychology degree, he'd learnt how to read micro-expressions and emotions that jumped to the surface, revealing all in a tremor of a voice, a nonchalant flick of the hair or a nervous laugh. She was sincere.

'Spare us the theatrics,' The doctor said. He didn't sound unfriendly, but his voice resonated with sarcasm and indifference. He sat rigidly in his chair. 'We go down. We analyse. We receive a reduced sentence. Am I missing something?' He sat several feet away from Harrigan and McAlister. 'Oh yes. The part where we all die horribly?'

Harrigan eyed Dr Bannerman. He instinctively disliked the man. The doctor had the kind of body he'd seen on drug addicts and people with eating disorders, supple skin pulled tight on knobbly features and sinewed skin. Hair combed too tightly to the skull. The type that rebuked employees with a pithy remark just because he could. Harrigan had met many men like Dr Bannerman. He disliked them all.

'There are risks,' Control replied, levelling her gaze at the diminutive doctor. 'But you've already read the files. You know what's at stake.'

The doctor looked upward at the ceiling of the amphitheatre. 'Oh my,' he said sycophantically, 'the world crumbling around us. Of course. How could I forget?'

Harrigan had seen the reports on TV. They thought it was a virus. A possible airborne pathogen that caused people to see their wildest nightmares in physical form. They called it '*The Incubo Effect*' and it was spreading. Fast.

Control turned her attention back to Harrigan. 'Every team we've sent down to The Gulch has failed, John. But we've learnt something new from each expedition. It's no coincidence that when communications went down several weeks ago events topside started occurring. Contact has been down too long for the interruption to be perceived as equipment failure. We believe that the head researcher is still alive and may prove pivotal to the answer.'

The Gulch. An underground facility located miles under the surface of the earth – undisclosed experiments. Unsanctioned aberrations. It was the modern era Area 51. Harrigan looked down at his hands. Luke would have loved hearing about it. Luke loved sci-fi shows like *The Twilight Zone*.

Harrigan clamped his hands together to stop them from shaking.

McAlister scoffed. 'Fuckin' nerdy scientists playing God. You guys never watch *Jurassic Park*, eh?'

Control cleared her throat. 'You asked why you were here, John. Let me answer frankly. Yes, we've sent down a myriad of expeditions including scientists, botanists, surveyors...the best kind of person of every conceivable profession. But they always turn on each other down there. Every person that has gone down into The Gulch hasn't made it past the first level. And that's when we realised...we were sending our *best* down there. Good, honest people. You see, gentlemen, whatever is dwelling down there in the depths...lurking in the shadows...feeds on virtuousness and integrity. In the same way a vampire feeds on blood, we think whatever now has control of The Gulch requires the most honourable of us. And its thirst is forever wanting.'

McAlister made a choked, ragged noise that could not quite pass as laughter.

Harrigan's eyes flicked to Dr Bannerman. He was sitting forward.

'We stand a better chance because we're criminals?' The doctor asked.

'It's a theory.'

Harrigan snapped himself out from his own reverie.

'You still didn't answer my question,' he said through dry lips. 'Why am I here?'

Control tilted her head again. The same way when McAlister tested her. 'Although your crimes,' she shot an accusatory glance at McAlister and Dr Bannerman, 'as grievous as they are...may pale in comparison with your other peers, perhaps this could be your shot at redemption. You asked me why you're here? Well, it's simple really. Your ex-wife asked for you.'

Are you a good man, John?

The doctor, the soldier and the teacher stood in a vast chamber. To Harrigan, he sensed being on the edge of a bad smell that wouldn't fully reveal its source. There were floodlights in each corner, permeating a soft, yellow artificial look to proceedings. It felt like he was in an underground parking lot. A large cavity in the middle of the floor dominated the scene, a deep and vast black hole of unquantifiable fathom. Armed guards circled the perimeter, each rifle twitching at any whistling sound that permeated from the depths below.

They had constructed a machine, like a giant three-pronged claw that hung inert above the chasm. Harrigan compared it to the seaside arcade machines that Luke used to play when they went on holiday as a family, the kind that never latched onto a prize because of flimsy pincers.

Each of the fingered 'claws' fashioned a crude seat.

'Express delivery straight to hell,' McAlister mumbled.

Harrigan's mind trailed back to the recording Control had played for them. His ex-wife's flat, monotone cadence rendered tinny by the recording. Rachel had sounded sleepy, her words dripping out like treacle.

I need you down here, John. Luke needs you too...

Rachel never needed him for anything after what happened with Luke. He shuttered the memory away. Better to think about the job at hand.

Control signalled them as they made their way up the mobile air stairs to the platform. Technician staff fastened them to their seats. Harrigan felt like he was about to board an aircraft. Control tapped her ear.

'Testing...testing. One, two. One, two.'

McAlister, Dr Bannerman and Harrigan gave a thumbs up. They were all suited up and could hear Control through their respective helmet earpieces.

'We're not sure of any neurotoxins or contamination at play down in The Gulch. You're wearing state-of-the-art suits like NASA astronauts. Only better. Your helmets display your HUDS to us but with all the layers you're going down, comms may be garbled. I shouldn't have to remind you how important your task is. If there's a threat in The Gulch, neutralise it.'

Harrigan felt Control's eyes on him.

'Good luck, gentlemen.'

Harrigan was buckled tightly into his seat. His rifle secured next to him. His legs dangled over the precipice. Once again, he recalled an image of Luke as they waited for a ride at Alton Towers. The one that slowly *ker-chunked, ker-chunked* as it ambled its way up the railings to its apex on gears and cogs and then dive-bombed into oblivion. Luke loved that ride. Harrigan glanced to his left and wasn't surprised to see Dr Bannerman looking solemn and phlegmatic as he was buckled securely into his seat. McAlister spoke in the same volatile and voluble way as the technicians attempted to seat him.

'This fuckin' thing isn't just going to drop, is it?'

Harrigan couldn't help but look down into the vast darkness. He wondered what awaited them down there. Rachel. She was down there. Head researcher of a top-secret Government facility. She really had gone to work after their divorce. He realised he hadn't spoken to her in over four years. Not since the sentencing.

After the technicians were satisfied that the three men were secured, they disembarked the machine and the ramp stairs slid away. A soothing AI voice started commencing a countdown.

McAlister scrutinised the doctor's storage unit. There was a small leather bag, the kind that splayed out from the middle.

'No weapon, doc?'

Dr Bannerman craned his head round and tapped the side of his helmet. 'My mind is my weapon,' he said curtly, as way of explanation.

Harrigan peered down at the open gorge below. There was something profoundly awful down there. He sensed that McAlister and Dr Bannerman felt the same, even if they didn't voice their feelings. Rational minds objected to unreasoned fear. These weren't rational men. They were all criminals.

The AI voice counted down. He waited for a random gap in his mounting dread, that lull that sometimes occurred in your brain whenever you psyched yourself up for something – like jumping into the swimming pool.

The AI voice counted down.

The claw started its descent into the abyss.

CONTROL TOLD them it had taken decades to construct the facility and to bore down this far under the Earth's surface. Harrigan felt a soft humming resonating through his body with a vibration completely divorced from the rattle of their carriage as they continued deeper.

'Just so you both know, I'm taking point when we touch down,' McAlister said through the comms. 'You listen to my commands and maybe we get out of this alive.'

Control had given Harrigan a crash course in firearms training. An hour shooting at cardboard cut-outs. As far as he was concerned, McAlister may have acted the jacked-up gorilla, but he had experience with this type of thing. Harrigan nodded his consent. He wondered what crime the soldier had committed to have been incarcerated in the first place. His spider tattoo seemed to dance with each contortion of his muscles.

Dr Bannerman's face remained expressionless, with unsmiling blue eyes.

'You...feel...pressure...further down...' Control squawked through their headsets, 'your suits...take care...let...know if you...any dizziness or nausea.'

I need you down here, John. Luke needs you too...

Harrigan knew that Luke wasn't down in The Gulch. He knew because his son had gone missing five years ago. *No,* Harrigan corrected himself. *Not missing. Vanished.*

It had been a cloudy autumn evening. He and Rachel had argued, so to give her space he'd taken Luke to the park. All the other kids had left for the day, but he didn't see any problem with Luke using the monkey bars and slides for half an hour. He would take him to the ice cream shop afterwards. The shadows of the trees were starting to blend into the blackness and their silhouettes would soon be less pronounced. Street-lamps illuminated orange cones of light on the pathways and each break of a simple leaf or twig became magnified in the small playground.

He'd been distracted. Looking on his phone. Scrolling through Instagram accounts of impossibly attractive women.

'C'mon, Luke. Let's get some ice cream bud.'

But there was no answer. Panic filched into Harrigan's chest at the time. He looked up from his phone, over at the swings that eerily creaked in the wind. Those minutes seemed to stretch into an eternity for Harrigan. Kids just didn't vanish into thin air. Luke was playing a game, that was all. Playing hide and seek, ready to jump out from behind a tree and scare him.

'Hey, Luke. Stop messing around.'

A thread of unbridled terror curled itself around his heart when only the wind answered him. He quickly wandered around the small playing area, checking behind rubbish bins and clumps of leaves. Then something insidious crept through his mind. A voice. A dark, malevolent thing that whispered three words.

Luke is gone.

Harrigan had turned into a savage wreck an hour later. He screamed his son's name in the blackened park, tears streaming down his face. He shrieked until his larynx wouldn't physically allow him to. Luke had been taken and the only function left in him was the animal part. The most ancient and bestial part. *This is what being a parent is.* To love a child.

A year later, divorced and jobless, Harrigan relentlessly pursued any lead he could find. He was obsessive. But his obsession led him to a name. A name of a known sex offender in the area at the time.

The claw began to slow. They had reached The Gulch.

THEY DISEMBARKED and made their way across a platform to a metallic door. The air felt fetid here, dense. Their suits would compensate, but Harrigan could already feel himself sweating. Dr Bannerman opened his medical bag and produced a small electronic device to bypass the lock.

'Little bag of tricks, eh?' McAlister noted, his rifle trained at the door.

'You have no idea,' Dr Bannerman said flatly. A few moments later the door hissed open.

McAlister motioned to Harrigan with a swift wave of his hand and he entered the poorly illuminated reception area. He paused briefly to let his eyes adjust in the near darkness. It felt impossibly warm in The Gulch. Too humid for a research laboratory. If the power had gone down here, how could anyone survive?

McAlister quickly followed, swiping his rifle to the corners of the room. Indicating that the way was clear, Dr Bannerman brought up the rear, studying another gadget in his hands. He seemed evidently content physically as well as mentally. Harrigan couldn't understand how the doctor could appear so calm in this place. The thought made him jittery.

'Plenty of inert nitrogen, some oxygen and a low concentration of free carbon dioxide. All looking pretty standard, but I wouldn't advise taking off your helmets.'

McAlister tapped his helmet. 'Control...if you can hear this, we've made it to the insertion point.'

Crackly static confirmed that they were on their own for now.

They surreptitiously made their way down a long corridor. Harrigan was ready to spring backward the instant any fragment of darkness gave hint of movement. Emergency lighting gave the team sufficient sight to show them that nothing hid in the malodourous corridor. Something caught Dr Bannerman's attention. He touched the wall, pulling his hand away in disgust.

'What is it?' Harrigan whispered.

'A thick viscous slime.' The doctor replied.

'Made by what?' McAlister hissed through gritted teeth.

'Your guess is as good as mine,' Dr Bannerman said, before continuing down the corridor. They came to a mess hall. A few tables were upended and dark stains covered the floor in scattered patches. Blood stains. In all the corners of the ceiling a rash of black spores erupted and bloomed out like bacterial varicose veins.

'Looks like there was a standoff,' McAlister said quietly.

Harrigan was seized by an apprehension that hardened under his skin like forged metal. His sense of being watched was acute. He felt a peculiar tension growing inside his ears and eyes, like anticipation. Something was trying to get his attention, not by movement or sound, but through other ethereal means. *I need you down here, John. Luke needs you too...*

He swallowed hard.

The creature unfolded itself from an inky section of the ceiling. Crawling out from its self-contained lair like a spider, it quickly traversed to the wall and unfolded each of its long, dark limbs out, unpacking itself from its hiding spot with the relative ease of a stage show contortionist. It descended in utter silence and conveyed a feeling of tremendous power held in check. It was long in its extremities and bulbous in the middle. Its skin texture was as sheen as a bat's wing; tiny capillaries rippling over its surface. Its arms and legs were nothing but bone wrapped in a thin veneer of skin. Its multiple eyes all seemed focused on the trio, saliva dripping from its gaping maw that exposed sharp, jagged teeth.

Harrigan's larynx was snatched by a pervasive terror. There wasn't any time to warn the others, he simply raised his rifle and fired.

His aim was off. A chunk of wall exploded behind the creature, and now its presence had been revealed, it bellowed a deep and guttural cry, something inhuman and primeval. Harrigan heard other rustling noises coming from the ceiling and in his peripheral vision counted at least three more shapes descending from on high.

Dr Bannerman ran for the far door. McAlister volleyed off a few shots as he barked commands at Harrigan. The rapport of gunfire and muzzle flashes created a strange, strobe-like effect in the mess hall. Harrigan fired again as they withdrew to their only exit. One of the creatures slumped to the floor as a bullet pierced its skull. They were fast, crab-like in their movements.

More creatures poured into the mess hall from the door they had just entered. *They had been hiding in the shadows,* Harrigan thought grimly. *Waiting.*

'Go! Go!' McAlister shouted through his comms, and they raced through the doors and down another dimly lit corridor. Harrigan felt his heart pumping like a drum in his chest, running blindly, madly, neither thinking nor caring. At the end of the junction, Dr Bannerman was crouched, working his electronic device on the lift that would take them down to the second level. Behind, Harrigan could hear the shrieks and wails of the creatures as they gave chase.

McAlister turned, firing at the mottled shadows as they spread closer towards them.

'How long, doc?' he said over the cacophony of insectoid screams.

'A few minutes,' Dr Bannerman said calmly.

'We don't have a few minutes.'

The doctor didn't answer.

Harrigan licked his lips as he stared down the iron sights and began shooting. The creatures were vast in number, grappling over their dead and stumbling into one another with talons and claws swiping in a frenzied manner. Panels on the walls were ripped apart as the monsters flailed wildly at the air in front of them. They were getting closer, so close that Harrigan could hear hissing from the advancing abominations. His ears rang with gunfire tinnitus until he squeezed the trigger and nothing happened. He was out of ammo.

He had another magazine in his utility belt but it would cost precious seconds to reload.

'Get to the doctor,' McAlister ordered, firing into the shadows. 'I'll provide supressing fire.'

Harrigan nodded and ran back to where the doctor was busily concentrating on his task at hand.

Harrigan fumbled for the magazine and quickly ejected the empty one. When he glanced up, he saw the floor panels erupting around McAlister's feet. Clawed arms seized him, powerful limbs and insectoid fingers locking around his ankles and dragging him down. The wave of dark creatures engulfed him and he was gone in seconds, swallowed by the subfloor space.

The lift doors opened. They bundled in.

Harrigan was able to slap in the new magazine and fired again before the wave of darkness descended upon them. The lift doors slid shut just as a talon swiped at his face and Harrigan jolted back, hearing dull thunks against the steel alloy.

'What were those things?' Harrigan asked.

'I don't understand why they named this place The Gulch,' Dr Bannerman said impassively. 'A gulch is a deep V-shaped valley formed by erosion. Usually contains a small stream or dry creek bed and is usually larger in size than a gully. Doesn't really make sense to me.' He shook his head, as if the joke was lost on him.

Harrigan stared at the doctor behind his visored helmet. Up close, Dr Bannerman looked unwashed, oily, sebaceous.

'We just lost McAlister,' Harrigan said slowly.

The lift sank deeper into the bowels of the facility. Dr Bannerman turned his head in an exaggerated and slow fashion, as if he were a ventriloquist's dummy. He glared at Harrigan, his blue eyes shimmering like someone inspired.

'My initial conjecture is that this facility manifests our deepest, darkest nightmares into reality,' he said. 'McAlister was averse to bugs. Spiders, most likely. The tattoo on his bicep was likely some crude response to try and overcome his phobia...much in the same way superstitious sailors would ink their bodies with sea creatures. This place is alive...have you not heard it talk?'

Harrigan remained silent. *I need you down here, John. Luke needs you too...*

'Tell me, Harrigan...what do you think we'll find on the next level?'

Their comms crackled to life. It was Control.

'Things...topside...escalating...compromised...Incubo...out of...control...'

The lift pinged, announcing they had reached the second level.

INSTEAD OF AN ATRIUM befitting a research facility, Harrigan was surprised to find himself in a surgery room. Sleek floors and beige tiles seemed uncharacteristically out of sync from the upper level they had just escaped from. Art on the walls depicted graphic surgical procedures and organs of the human body. One picture had a surgeon smiling towards the camera, a cadaver on the table in front of him with an exposed ribcage. The air had a pure fragrance, not sterile, just clean. But there was something else, too. The room was alive, vibrating with a black energy that pressed solidly in Harrigan's mind.

In the background, strange music played at just the right level to give patients and staff an emotional lift. In the middle of the room a green dentist chair took precedence, and a young girl sat with her arms crossed over her chest. She was dressed in a cheerleader's uniform.

Dr Bannerman let out a derisive snort.

'Harrigan, I would suggest you leave this room and find the

source,' he said dryly. 'It appears we have entered *my* nightmare.'

The young girl sat up from the chair and smiled at Dr Bannerman.

'What's up, doc?' She giggled.

'Look,' Dr Bannerman began, in what he hoped for was his best conciliatory manner, 'whatever you are, we don't have time for this. We –'

The girl's smile morphed imperceptibly into a frown.

'You don't remember me?' she murmured. She buried her head in her hands and rubbed her eyes hard, as if she had shards of glass stuck in her irises. She began to sob, her shoulders shuddering with each exhalation. It seemed a little theatrical to Harrigan. But that wasn't the worst part. As he surveyed the room other little things began to gnaw at him. The door on the opposite side of the room was crooked. Not by a lot but canted just the tiniest bit to the right. The picture frames also appeared to be slanted, not completely but enough to give Harrigan a feeling of seasickness. The picture of the smiling surgeon had now changed. The corpse with the exposed ribcage was standing and it held the severed head of the surgeon like a lantern.

The girl looked up at the doctor. She lifted her top, baring her breasts. She held one in each hand. A drop of blood trickled from each nipple.

'How about now, doc? Remember me now?'

Dr Bannerman moved forward, his hands up in a placating manner.

The ground beneath Harrigan seemed to shift lightly. This room was wrong. Everything about this place was wrong. He felt light-headed and he dropped the rifle to the floor. He felt heavy.

'You liked the control, didn't you? Liked it when we were under anaesthetic.'

Harrigan moved towards the door, but his body seemed slow, almost like he was treading through syrup. Dr Bannerman also seemed to be suffering from the same fatigue, his eyes lidded and straining to remain open.

'We all remember you, doc.'

The girl leapt at Dr Bannerman. He was sluggish to react, slowly putting his hands up to defend himself. But it was to no avail. The girl laughed manically as her hand arced through the air - in her curled fist a scalpel smashed through the visor of his helmet. He let out a guttural moan as the blade sunk into his left eye socket.

Harrigan languidly trudged to the door. He heard other voices in the room now, other girls giggling and crowding round the lifeless doctor's body. Harrigan was panting, like he'd just broken across the finish line of a marathon. He felt so tired. So. Very. Tired.

He didn't look behind him. His sole focus was the door. The crooked door that now seemed lopsided. He wouldn't fall.

The world spun in a kaleidoscope of dark images. A vignette of darkness crawled and clawed from the corners of his eyes. He was about to collapse.

I need you down here, John. Luke needs you too...

With the last vestige of strength remaining, he staggered towards the door.

He fell through. And then the world went dark.

'You're looking good, John.'

Harrigan opened his eyes. Slowly, he propped himself up on his elbows and lifted his head. He was in an office. His helmet had been taken off. A moment of panic shuddered through him but then he realised this room had air. For the first time since he'd been in The Gulch, he didn't feel the oppressive heat. Rachel looked down at him with a half-smile.

'You shouldn't have come here,' she said slowly. Harrigan picked himself up. The exhaustion he felt in the surgery room had dissipated.

'You sent a message,' he said, 'you asked for me. What happened down here?'

Rachel nodded beatifically, as if she was half-listening to what he had to say. 'Time moves...differently down here. Since we woke it up. We never should have awakened it.'

She sat back in her chair, radiating her arms out and mimicking an explosion. 'Just like Oppenheimer. Now I am literally the destroyer of worlds.' Rachel smiled again, but Harrigan noted a harried pinch beneath it. He scanned Rachel's table, opened pill bottles and syringes.

She followed his gaze and winked at him. 'Ah. Yes. It's the only way to survive down here. Sedation. It can't control me if I'm not in my right mind...so to speak. But sometimes they get through.'

Harrigan remembered the recorded message. The way Rachel sounded half-asleep. Mentally, a puzzle piece slotted into place.

'*You* didn't send the message.'

Rachel shook her head. Her eyes started brimming with tears.

'We found something down here, John. Something that had been buried for a long, long time...Fossils of an ancient, celestial being. Maybe.' She craned her head, as if the sheer notion of talking pained her. 'We don't really know...all the best minds in the world...and we don't really know. It's funny,' she closed her eyes and a single tear ran down her cheek. 'Perhaps it was something that came to Earth hundreds of years ago...or maybe it's always been here. Fact is, we dug it up. Then it started to happen. Small things, at first. Scientists locked themselves away in labs...talking to themselves. But we started coming up with formulas that would change the world. It showed us things, John. Marvellous things. The cure for cancer. Alzheimer's. Everything.'

Harrigan stared at Rachel.

She slid off her chair and stumbled to another door. Harrigan followed.

In the middle of the room a large circular tube filled with bubbling liquid monopolised the workspace. Inside it, brown leathery flesh of elongated arms ended in hands too finely detailed with multiple digits and fingernails. The small, withered head was entirely obsidian, almost black enough to obscure its features. The mouth was hung open, or what remained of the lips were parted, and a small row of yellow teeth were revealed in a grin. The eyes were closed, something for which Harrigan was deeply grateful.

Several transparent hoses ran from the sides of the main cylinder, each trailing off like tendrils to tables, and it appeared that liquid was being pumped into the central container from them. Harrigan stood immobile. Sheets had been placed deferentially over the tables. Small protrusions suggested bodies underneath.

'I...I don't understand.'

Rachel fell to the floor. She sobbed, great wet gurgles. 'There's a price, John...always a price.'

Almost hypnotically, Harrigan slowly uncovered one of the sheets on the table. The expression of revulsion and fear must have registered to Rachel because she turned her head so quickly as not to meet his eyes.

'These...these are children.'

With a tremulous arm she pointed at the corner of the room.

'Look in the mirror.' She said dully.

Harrigan turned and looked at the half-length mirror situated in the corner. He walked over and peered at his reflection. But there was none. Something else shimmered in the glass.

A cloudy autumn evening. Monkey bars and slides. Streetlamps illuminating orange cones of light on pathways and each break of a simple leaf or twig became magnified in the small playground. Harrigan could see his son on a swing. When he leaned towards the glass, he could see himself standing in the distance, concentrating on his phone. Harrigan knew that if he reached out and put his hand through, he would be able touch the coat of his son through the portal.

Inside the main tube, and within the small black head, a pair of marble-white eyes opened.

'It feeds on the innocent, John. That's what it does.' Rachel said with a flat, emotionless inflection. 'That's the price we have to pay.'

He turned to her.

'No...' he stammered. 'I found the guy, Rachel. I found who took our son. And I...I dealt with him.'

Don't you want to see your son? A voice inside his head whispered. *Don't you want to see him again?*

Rachel's face crumpled and her lips trembled. 'No...John. Everything going on in the world...it demands the most innocent. The purest. Everyone started going crazy down here...one scientist...he...he pulled a child out. His own child. That's the sacrifice we must make. It told me...in my head. It just needs one more. One more and then it'll stop everything that's going on...don't you see? We tried everything. To seal it from the inside. But it was already out. There's only one left. But I can't. I just...can't.'

There are two train tracks. One has five random people tied to it but on the other is a child. You've got to decide which track the train goes on. Which one do you pick?

The very idea of what he was about to do made his feelings crawl on all fours in the form of guilt and grief. His vision shook.

'I can't do it. No. This is madness.'

Rachel looked at him with a resigned look that decimated every atom in his body. She wiped fresh tears from her eyes. 'It's the only way. That's why it wanted you down here. Because I...I can't...even though I've been on the verge. So many times.'

Harrigan looked back at the mirror. Heard his son's voice squeal with delight as he swung in the park. Oh God, how he missed that sound.

'Is this my nightmare?' he asked, before he sauntered towards the mirror, putting his arms into and through the glass, touching the back of his son...pulling him back into the abyss.

Is this my nightmare?

ANTHONY SELF

Anthony Self is a writer based in West London. He is the co-director and manager for STORGY.com, an independent online magazine and book publisher, as well as Inside Your Screen, a YouTube channel specialising in horror gaming playthroughs.

In 2021, he released his debut novel, 'Birthday Treat,' a dystopian look at a post Brexit London. It's an unflinching account of oppression and resistance.

He is currently writing his second book, an anthology of short stories called Cat Box. You can find him on twitter @Mr_Selfy

PANDORA'S NEW BOX

BY SARAH J HUNTINGTON

By the year 2021, the Earth was dying a slow, brutal death. Ravaged by humankind, flesh hurt from the testing and dropping of nuclear bombs. The destruction of the oceans and forests.

The poison, the chemicals, the pollution, the barbaric treatment.

A perfect ecosystem fell out of balance. Harmony shifted.

Humanity swarmed like a plague, all take.

The heartbeat of the planet began to fail. Fearing it was too late to act, select groups took many paths to seek salvation and repair. New ways, old ways, ancient ways.

Deep in the dark British countryside, beside Serene Lake, forbidden rituals flourished.

Dark vile magic, the blackest of all.

Freemasons, Occultists, those in positions of political power, gathered in a secret cluster.

Not satisfied by the split of an atom, they sought to part the veil between worlds, penetrate the membrane between dimensions. Sought contact with life existing in a higher realm.

A circle of focused power, selfish, arrogant intent.

Collective mind power. A sacrifice of innocent life, a bloody gift to ancient gods, an offering. Forgotten guttural language spoken aloud with force. Unknown forces conjured, called, summoned, invited.

A tear in reality, a hole in the fabric of the universe ripped open.

The powerful cult was seen, observed, and found lacking, savage, and inferior.

A knock on the wrong door, a key in the wrong lock, cursed humanity.

A reply was sent, a tiny spark, origin elsewhere. Carried by interdimensional winds, blown by a mouth of incomprehension. A weapon like no other.

The Earth in turmoil absorbed the damned gift and fashioned anew. Changes occurred deep underground. Created chaos, bound and spliced.

A chamber opened. A seed from Hell itself unleashed.

Great Britain

Red sky at night, shepherds delight. Red sky in the morning, shepherds warning.

Those are the first words that come to her. She can see red, the vibrant colour of blood somewhere above her.

I'm Lisa and I'm...

She struggles to make sense of where she is, until her mind sparks, catches and lights. Knowledge floods and none of it is pleasant. She knows. She understands.

She has fallen. Straight into the hole and all the way down.

That's why the ground feels rocky underneath her. She realises she must have banged her head too, it hurts, stings.

Her thoughts are confused, jumbled. As if her brain is underwater.

'Adam?' She croaks. Did he fall too?

She tries to test her legs, tries to focus on moving. She can't. Surely something essential must be broken? She wonders if she has a jagged bone sticking up out of her flesh and the shock of her plummet down is preventing her from feeling it.

In truth, her lower spine is shattered. Internal bleeding is rife. Time is short, almost an empty sandglass.

'Adam?' She cries. Where is he?

She can feel the tight safety rope digging in below her chest. What use was it if it couldn't save her?

She only wanted to peer in, just a little, just a peek into the never-ending blackness inside the unknown depths. But now it surrounds her. All bleakness and pressure.

She blinks rapidly, the red sky she thought she saw shifts. Not sky at all but blood cascading from a wound.

I'm hurt. I can't feel my legs.

Still, she feels numb and cold. She wishes she had a blanket and almost laughs. Just how deep has she fallen? How long will it take them to get her out?

They were making a film, a documentary for class at school. About the curious new sinkhole in the woods near Serene Lake. It was supposed to be an adventure, something fun.

Her boyfriend Adam was behind the camera, her brother, Luke, in charge of sound, and her in front of the camera, the place Adam says she belongs.

Have they gone for help? The fire service?

Lisa wonders if they might have to send down a cage for her, she will have to climb inside and make a dramatic entrance on the surface.

She closes her eyes briefly and wonders if their film will win a prize now.

Her lungs begin to hurt. As if she is breathing glass shards.

Wait, she hears a sound.

A slight scuffling. It is so black that she cannot see a thing, only blood reflecting off her head torch. So dark it might be the edge of the world.

It's Adam. He's come for me.

Alone, in the black, shaking and without her knowledge, bleeding to death, Lisa waits. Waits to hear the echoing sound of her boyfriend's soothing voice.

When she is safe, back on the surface, all that way above her, they will laugh about her fall. She feels sure. Adam will take care of her, in the way he always does.

"It's slippery. Don't get too close to the edge," he'd warned her.

But she had, hadn't she, and then down she went.

'Adam?' This time her voice is a fading whisper, the pain in her lungs increases. Something is with her. She hears it writhing in the blackness, feels its presence. Something awakening, approaching.

Her mind plays out horror movie scenes, the one about the fearless women scuttling around in caves with greedy monsters.

Lisa wishes she hadn't seen it now. She thinks of old stories of demons hiding underground, monsters rising from unknown depths.

I'm okay, I'm okay. She chants. *They'll get me out.*

In reality, she is not okay and they cannot get her out. Up on the surface, Adam has raced away, searching for help while Luke sits crying, wondering what he will tell their parents.

She hears the slithering again. Closer, closer, snake-like swishes. Flesh crawling on rock.

She moans loudly, hoping to scare away whatever creature it is.

Something vicious, savage, wraps around her foot. Lisa cannot feel it, cannot see it.

It slithers up her jeans leg, finds the nearest entrance, seeking the nourishment that is inside her body.

Inside it crawls, leaving ripped flesh and blood in its struggle.

All she feels of the invasion, all she knows is that her heart turns cold. Her body begins to jerk in wild spasms. Sudden panic fills her, her eyelids close without her agreement. No, not closed, they seal.

Flesh, or a perversion of, grows rapidly, within brutal short seconds the matter covers her mouth and nose, every orifice of her body.

She cannot breathe, has no way to get air. Deep down in the sinkhole, in the Pandora's box of Earth, she becomes the same. She knows she is dying, trapped inside herself. Panic takes hold. Her lungs burn like fire, impossible white-hot agony tears through her. Her mind explodes in fear and shatters. A thousand thoughts race across her mind and then none at all. Her heart stops, gives up the fight.

Dead.

Dead and lying surrounded by a type of life humans have never before seen or even imagined. Parasites seeking warm hosts, seeking food, and annihilation.

26 hours later

Grace Mack opens the body bag and flinches. For a moment, all of her confidence flees to a dark corner and hides. She sees the young girl's face and cannot imagine what might have happened to her.

Glue is her first thought. Some kind of industrial adhesive?

She sees that her eyes, ears, nose, and mouth are sealed shut. It looks as if skin has grown and formed a layer, a barrier, but that she knows, is impossible.

With a gloved finger, she pokes at the strange substance. It feels firm, almost like elastic.

What the hell is this?

She sees the girl's neck and shoulders.

Tiny stem-like buds grow from the tissue of her body, bursting out and seemingly thriving.

This looks like fungus, she realises. *Something rare or unheard of.*

She will have to be extra cautious when slicing away at the growths for samples.

Fungus has spores?

She steps back, suddenly unsure and afraid. She feels as if she has been dipped into a freezer.

The dead body is wrong on a level she can't explain.

A sense inside her, primal instinct, or maybe ancestor memory screams at her to leave. Corruption and evil lie on her table.

Under the bright lights of the autopsy room, she makes sure her mask is secure and takes a deep breath. The world for her, feels upside down and back to front.

Be rational. Be calm.

She grabs the file and reads again. According to the notes, the girl fell down a new sinkhole.

After a twenty-hour rescue attempt, her lifeless body had been winched to the surface and shuttled to her, in the morgue, underground at the nearest main hospital for answers.

Grace closes her eyes and takes a moment for herself, just a few seconds for composure before she begins. She reminds herself that yes, the girl is an unusual puzzle to be solved, but she is also someone's daughter, sister, and friend. Was.

It is important they understand what killed her, the fall, or the environment she landed in.

What kind of toxin or pathogen would seal a body up tight and why? It's unheard of, an alien concept.

A knock at her door makes her jolt.

'Come in,' she calls and moves to shield the body with her own.

The senior pathologist and her boss, Frank, pops his head around the door. He looks gravely unwell, pale and sweaty.

'Frank?' Grace says, worry in her tone. 'What's...'

'Four more came in,' he interrupts. 'Every orifice sealed up tight. We're on lockdown, possible biohazard. I made the call.'

'What?'

'Four more, the men that got this one out of that sinkhole,' he says and points to the body as if the surreal situation is all her fault. 'The hospital is on full alert.'

Grace feels her own stomach fall to her feet. Her body hisses with fright.

Something down that hole killed them. A contagion?

She is known as being talkative, non-stop in fact. Yet for once in her life, she has no idea of what to say. Curiosity and determination flee. Fear is her only companion in the sterile room.

For her, scenes flicker as Frank leaves. Autopilot. Until she zips up the body bag and freezes.

The corpse moves, she feels sure. Her heart thuds loudly, white static fills her mind.

It's my imagination, I'm spooked that's all.

She pushes the trolley back to cold storage, almost laughing at herself.

She *is* spooked, she knows it. A strange event, a possible new pathogen, and a lockdown. It would be enough to scare anyone.

Still, she is almost sure the substance covering the girl's eyes, nose, and mouth is an organic material, and that troubles her a great deal.

Fear crawls up her spine as she cleans, her mind struggles to think clearly.

Fungus, mould, spores, or something new? She creates a checklist in her head.

Grace is no expert or epidemiologist, but she feels fairly certain that nothing she has ever heard of can cause what looks like flesh to grow at such a massively accelerated rate.

How does it spread? Do I have it?

She fights a growing tide of nausea and retches. She has to get a handle on herself.

It won't do to be seen as weak in front of her superiors. She mustn't panic.

By the time she makes it to the room they keep aside for breaks, a cluster of people has gathered. Grace knows them all, from the head pathologist to the cleaner. Each person has the same frightened expression.

No one speaks. All work has ceased.

'Does anyone have any ideas?' Grace says. 'Or ever heard of this before?'

She tries to sound bright, hopeful and fails.

Several heads shake in reply and now she feels more troubled than ever. She heads to her locker and fiddles with the code, she can never remember the correct sequence, and her hands are shaking. She wants her phone, she needs to be able to speak to Karl, and tell him she likely won't be home for the night.

'No contact with the outside,' Frank appears and reminds her. 'You know the rules.'

'Please, he's my son,' she says.

Frank, kind, gentle Frank, points her to his office. She slips inside and closes the door quietly. Dials.

'Hey, Mum.'

'Baby listen,' she says. Karl is not a baby, he is seventeen but still, her baby. 'Something happened at work, we're locked down as a precaution. There's money for a pizza in the top drawer. Okay?'

'What's happening? Not Covid again?'

'No, don't worry. Listen, keep an eye on the news for me? Text me anything important.'

'Like what?'

'Anything...erm...weird yeah?'

'K.'

'Love you, bye.'

She ends the call just as a fire alarm begins to sound.

Shit, now what?

'What does protocol say?' Someone yells over the noise. 'Do we stay or leave?'

Grace presses her fingers to her temples. Today was supposed to be a quiet shift and now she can't think clearly, her head is thudding hard.

She knows it's likely a false alarm or a small fire upstairs. They are quarantined, they cannot leave unless their lives are under immediate threat. They can only sit and wait for public health officials to arrive and take charge.

'The main doors are locked, we're locked in!' The cleaner wails.

Frank takes charge and calls upstairs. The hospital is old but large, the main one in the county, an evacuation would be all but impossible. The alarm stops and that's when she hears the sound.

Thud, thud, thud.

The noise is coming from the room she works in.

Is someone in there?

Her hand reaches for the door but she stops, she cannot find the bravery inside herself to peer in. All she can hear now is her own heartbeat, the rush of blood around her body. The sense that she has stepped into a dream fills her, a nightmare of epic proportions.

Thud, thud, thud.

'False alarm,' Franks says from behind her. 'Something set off our smoke detectors.'

'Ours, down here?'

'Yes.'

She pushes that thought to the back of her mind, she will think about that later, not now.

Thus, thud, thud.

'Shhh,' Grace whispers. 'Listen.'

Three thuds again.

Frank narrows his eyes but does not hesitate. As the boss, the entire morgue is his kingdom of death. He pushes open the door and stares around the small sterile room. The sound is coming from the wall of body storage units.

'What is that?' He gasps.

Grace has no answer, she wants to tell him to stop walking, wants to tell him not to open the door.

Something is very wrong, she can feel undiluted evil. The hair on her neck rises.

'Which body is in here?' Frank says. As if he needs to ask.

She opens her mouth and closes it again, her words and warnings fail to strike and die like a damp match that won't light. She cannot answer, her mind has flatlined.

Frank takes hold of the handle and opens the storage door.

Grace fails to understand what it is she is actually seeing. She only knows something white erupts from the girl's torn-open body bag. It hits Frank and bounces away as if it is nothing more than a harmless ball.

She hears frantic screaming and realises the sound is her. Others pile in, they shove her aside and act fast. She hears shouts and orders but all she knows is relentless hissing in her head.

Danger. The word comes to her. Instinct acts and propels her backward.

She cannot be here. Franks falls to his knees as she watches, he claws at his face with both hands. He is wild, frantic. He jerks back and forth in desperation. The unknown is sealing him inside himself.

He's suffocating. Grace knows this, still, she cannot move.

She sees a flash of white darting and moving among clustered bodies trying to help Frank. It is snake-like and fat, slimy and greasy. A giant worm or a huge slug. A thing that doesn't belong in her world.

It stops and shudders, a cloud of white bursts out from it.

The fire alarm begins to sound once more. To Grace, the noise is a war cry, a call to arms.

Frank is jerking, frenzied, a puppet with its strings cut.

He pounds his head against the freezer doors until blood sprays. She hears the crack of his skull over the noise of the alarm and her own screams.

The thing that burst from inside the girl slithers wildly across the floor.

Grace turns and runs.

Down the long, twisted corridors.

Out through the emergency fire exit and up a set of darkened stairs. Her breath wheezes, ragged and frantic. She has to get out, out into clean air and safety.

She has seen the impossible and she is terrified. She bursts out of a main door, into the big foyer, and falls. People stop and stare at her. Visitors and patients only gaze, startled.

'Run,' she shouts. 'Run, please!'

No one runs. They only look at each other, waiting to see who might take charge.

She feels a burst of pain in her lungs, a quick sharp dagger striking.

No, no.

She hauls herself up and reaches out. She needs help, she can feel it, an invasion in her body, a presence taking over. One eye begins to close and she screams. Her vision is replaced by a layer of skin. Pain rips through her.

She tries to say *spores,* her tongue won't work.

She thinks of the ancient air vent system in the hospital, a perfect delivery system. The body in the morgue, a human bomb.

She scratches at her mouth, too late. Her lips are sealing, closing. In her ears is a high-pitched ringing, a warning bell. Her mind is on fire.

She thinks of her son, her beautiful son, at home alone, thinks of all the people in the hospital. There must be thousands. Disbelief and terror grip her tightly. No air. There is no air, only blackness welcomes her.

Down she falls, dead.

Six hours later

'Christ,' Tom Harrison utters. He has no other words.

He has never seen such a massacre before. Not even in Africa during the last Ebola outbreak.

Inside his biohazard suit, he does not feel safe. His skin feels itchy as if electricity is crawling all over him.

People, fallen human beings, scattered like toy soldiers spilled from a tin lie still. There are hundreds of bodies, each with faces that look as if they have been dipped into wax. The team around him kneels carefully to take samples.

He wonders if he has stumbled into Hell somehow. A war has taken place and humans have lost.

Biological warfare? Terrorism? He can't imagine the cause but he needs to find one quickly. He needs theories, ideas and he needs them fast. His superiors shout orders for him down his internal headset. They want a closer look via his attached camera.

Tom breathes his own air supply and focuses on the woman lying near the main door.

A badge pinned to her white coat tells him her name was Grace, autopsy technician.

He guesses enough pieces of the puzzle to understand she carried a plague up to the main floors, or maybe the air vent system did a better job. He has not been downstairs yet but assumes patient zero awaits him in the morgue.

What a fucking mess. What now?

The Public Health Authority had arrived too late. Delayed by red tape and bureaucracy. Police and the fire service had already cordoned off the area, but too slowly and doing so killed them all.

Tom has no idea how many people fled the barriers, or how such a contagion might be able to spread so fast.

The hospital ground is also covered in bodies, a mass exodus of escape failed for the majority.

There are too many bodies for anything less than airborne.

The knowledge stuns him, terrifies him. In all his years, he has never seen anything like this. An instinct inside him longs to call his wife and grown-up children and tell them all to get very far away, as fast as they can.

'Sir,' his assistant says. 'Look at this.'

He hears her voice through his headset. Her worried tone echoes and bounces around his skull like gunfire.

She is taking a sample of the exposed abdomen of a corpse. Tom squints and sees that a clear greasy substance has covered the body partially. It looks to him like the secretions of a slug's trail.

What the hell is that?

He peers closer and sees the skin of the corpse undulate. Something is moving and writhing inside the dead body, under the flesh. Vomit rises in his throat and burns.

Parasite?

He gags and steps back. This is unknown. Utterly unknown.

Tom likes data and genetic breakdowns of viruses. He does not like something so...alien in nature, so violent.

A sense inside him forces him to move back further.

'What is it?' His assistant asks. 'A tapeworm?'

He has no idea. It's all happening too fast. People dying where they stand. It makes no sense. Bacteria, pathogens, all need time to infect a host, parasites too.

'Get back,' he manages to say.

They can't investigate, it's too dangerous. Some kind of toxin he has no word for, some kind of brutal, fast contagion. The perfect killing machine is loose.

Voices shout orders down his headset. He cannot understand a word. It all sounds like incoherent sentences.

The body they are both staring at spasms. The lifeless corpse is not so lifeless after all. Its throat begins to bulge and ripple as if something is pushing its way up and out.

Whatever it is, it can't escape, every orifice is sealed.

Tom is wrong.

The incubation period is over. The nice dark and confined space the lifeform needed is no longer required.

It has fed on still, bloodless organs and ate its fill.

It wants to be born. It wants to ruin and destroy. The only nature it knows.

The seal on the corpse's mouth begins to split, starts to rupture until a gap forms. Tom watches in horror and hears the shouts to evacuate from the control room.

He wants to run but he needs to see, has to.

He is mesmerised by the horror.

A sightless white, fat worm emerges. Long in shape and thick, it forces its way out of the stretched wide open mouth. Sharp barbed fins line its spine, inside it is almost clear. It looks as if it belongs in the depths of the oceans, not on the surface, never on the land.

Tom can see organs, blobs of darker colour, and pulsing veins through its translucent flesh. Obscene growths cover its sides. A painfully high-pitched sound he can barely hear bursts out from it. Immediately, Tom feels confused and agitated. It shudders and sends a white cloud into the air.

Someone pulls him back. Other bodies begin to quake.

They're inside people.

The knowledge he wishes he didn't know hits him.

'Evacuate!' A voice in his headset repeats. Tom throws up in his suit but runs, gripped by the need to survive, stepping over bodies as he flees. Out through a useless rigged-up plastic tunnel and through showers of chemical sprays.

He can't understand. The things he witnessed can't be real.

He is cold all over, yet sweating, shaking, crying.

Tom is shuttled into a room with the others and needs to be told what to do. A vague part of his mind understands he is in shock.

Suit off, another chemical shower. He knows one cold truth.

He needs to tell someone it's all pointless. The growths. The burst of barely-there cloud. He knows what it is, what it means. Spores.

It's in the air. It's too late.

It's not a new pathogen or a virus. It's an invasion. It's an attack and humanity has already lost.

52 HOURS later

Grace's son Karl paces the living room. It's been days since his mum called. Two days, almost three.

He wonders if she is still alive. Deep down in the layers of truth inside him, he knows she is gone.

He has no idea of what to do or where to go. The windows and doors are sealed tight. Duct tape, just like the news said everyone should do.

There is no food left in the small house, only a few tins of soup. He cannot go outside. To do so means certain death. The air is poisoned, to breathe is to die.

For two days he watched the news with wide eyes and texted his mum and his friends. Neighbours were leaving, escaping. Karl doesn't know if they made it, he doubts anyone has survived.

The news stopped four hours ago. The only thing being broadcast is an emergency message playing on loop. Endless repeats to shelter in place.

Karl sits on the couch and bites his nails.

He has never been so scared in his entire life. He cannot sit still, his body pulses with nervous energy. He stands and tries the radio once more. Only static for company, no voices or sounds of life. As he turns the dial, searching, the power shuts off. He is not surprised. No one can run the power grid when everyone is dead.

He returns to the couch and curls himself into a ball.

Once again, he thinks over what he knows. The news said it started at his mother's hospital. A fast-acting fatal contagion, nicknamed 'Sealed,' that only infects human beings.

A quarantine failed. There was no time, it happened too quickly. A shock and awe attack. Cases began to be reported as far away as ten miles, then twenty, and so on. A radius spread like ripples in a pond.

People fell like dominoes, one after another, cascading down. A news helicopter filmed the carnage live and then crashed into a fireball.

It looked like a disaster movie made real and come to life.

Quickly, news presenters lost their excitement, and they too were powered by fear.

An expert via video link talked about the efficiency and resilience of Ophiocordyceps, a fungus. She claimed the fungus spores were carried by the wind and migrating birds. An unknown version, ancient or new, was decimating the world. Perhaps it had arrived on a meteorite, or come from elsewhere, somehow.

Another talked about parasites and hosts, sinkholes, dormant contagions emerging from under the ground.

Biological horrors said someone, lab-made terrors.

The fungus causes a rapid takeover and makes a complex cellular network inside the body. Chemical control, a hijack.

All of the experts agree on two things.

An organic material mimicking skin covers the victim's orifices until fast suffocation occurs. The parasite, traveling on a tiny spore, invades the body. It kills, cocooned inside, grows rapidly, and makes an exit.

Others said such a thing is impossible and yet, it happened at speed. Hundreds of victims became thousands, thousands became millions. City after city fell within hours.

Great Britain, an ancient nation, was not great anymore. Europe came next. France began to fall.

Any survivors sealed themselves inside their homes, a tomb in which there is no escape. A method to prolong suffering.

Religious people claim the new epidemic is wormwood, an old prophecy made real. They claimed God had declared war, a second flood, not of water, but of horror. Others said the environment was fighting back. They blamed fracking, pollution, and melting polar ice caps. They said Earth unleashed the end and was busy culling the population.

No one agrees, no one knows the truth and now everyone is silent. No one can tell Karl what to do.

The internet is down, there are no phone signals. He wishes his mother would walk through the door and tell him everything is fine.

What will he do without power? He has never known a life without electricity and mobile phones, never known a life without convenience.

He picks up his mother's favourite sweater and brings it to his face. The smell of her is comforting.

He wonders what the point is in living any longer. He is only waiting for death. He will either starve or run out of air, sealed inside his house instead of himself.

Would it not be better to face extinction on his own terms? Would it not be better to throw open the door and breathe fresh air one last time before he joins his mother?

Karl stands, full of determination. Yes, he will die on his own terms. He can't live waiting for the inevitable.

He scrambles to the main door and rips off thick tape seals. He wonders if his death will hurt.

A small part of him, hope, thinks that maybe the air will be clean, maybe winds have carried the plague overseas and away.

One, two, three, four, five. He opens the door.

Sunshine greets him, the sounds of birdsong and vibrancy. It is a beautiful day. He squints and uses his arm as a shield against the brightness. He smiles. He can breathe.

Karl begins to laugh and races down his path.

It's over. The danger has passed. Or so he thinks.

Sharp pains in his lungs take him by surprise. It is agony, unbearable burning. Panic quickly takes hold.

'Mum,' he manages to cry. He falls to his knees as the spores take hold of his body. His eyes seal and he can no longer see the beautiful day. His ears close, he can no longer hear the singing birds. His mouth is next. No poisoned air to breathe.

Down, down, impossible blackness. Consciousness lost. Dead.

His body joins thousands lying in the streets alone.

Overhead, great flying beasts swarm the skies. A takeover. The ground vibrates with new life on its surface. Nightmares, slithering, nasty things.

A doorway was opened, yes, a door no one closed. Obliteration followed.

The world does not belong to humans any longer.

SARAH J HUNTINGTON

Sarah J Huntington is the author of three short story collections and one recently released horror novel. She has been lucky enough to have stories in several anthologies so far.

Sarah is a nurse in a secure unit, she lives with her dog and cats. She also enjoys walking, martial arts, reading, writing, horror, and science fiction movies.

THE DISINTEGRATOR

BY DENIS BUSHLATOV

On Friday, at 7pm on the dot, Startsev opened the door of The Disintegrator.

'Why would you do that?' Kudrya was trying to stop him. He was untidy and drunk, and his words were slurring, 'How much time do you have left? Ten years? Twelve? Everyone will have the same ending. Look around!' He pointed in a vague direction, 'Look at all this beauty!'

Startsev obediently glanced over his shoulder. In the putrid semi-darkness of the pub, the faces of other guests looked like death masks that were put on the half-rotten heads for the sake of the joke. They sat bent at the spotted tables, gulping a disgusting foaming swill from dirty mugs covered in fingerprints. Now and then, squealing pointless phrases were breaking forth from the monotonous, animal-like sound of their voices. A long-nosed wrinkled dwarf sat on a children's chair in the corner, passionately playing an absolutely wild melody on the out-of-tune piano. His dark, bumpy face was full of festering pimples.

'Besides!' Kudrya continued, howling hysterically, 'There's a chance that scientists may fix that thing with the gen... the gen of', he stumbled and look at his big swollen hands with hatred - they were almost black because of the flesh-eating disease, 'The gen of death! And then we will live... believe me. Not just for hundreds of years! Way longer, brother, way longer!'

'And what about the politics?' Startsev asked wearily. He had to raise his voice to drown the piano, and immediately hated himself for how pitiful and unconvincing it sounded.

'What about it? We defeat that plague from the East!' Kudrya shook the swollen fists in the air, but instantly dropped them down on the table, sticky of the spilled stinky booze, and quickly looked around with fear, 'And then we will live! Like kings! With our potential! Think for yourself!' he loudly sipped from his mug. With a fainting curiosity, Startsev noticed how two fat maggots, that actually looked more like silkworms, insidiously sneaked into his mouth with the thick foaming liquid, 'We've got the brains! And the gas! And the chernozem soil! And what do they have? What do they have?!'

'We're fucked,' Startsev's whispering was barely audible.

But Kudrya heard him anyway, and looked around one more time. Two men were sitting at the table next to theirs - fat, unshaven, dressed in Camo clothing. The one, who sat closer, had a poorly tattooed swastika on his shaved occiput.

'We got such a big potential here!' Kudrya repeated, but somehow with less confidence, choking. Perhaps, the worms in the gullet caused him a great deal of discomfort.

'But what's the bloody difference?!' he suddenly exploded, 'You think you're better than others, don't you? Like smarter or something? Everyone dies!'

'And then what?' Startsev wheezed out another question.

He wanted to go to the piano and spew onto the head of the hardworking dwarf, but he was afraid he might get judged.

Kudrya oinked.

'What then? Well, opinions vary about that,' notes of mentorship appeared in his voice, 'Some believe that Heaven and Hell are only projections,' he hiccupped and got silent - he obviously lost his thought.

'And what if there is nothing?' Startsev asked listlessly.

'Then so be it! If there's nothing, you won't feel jack! You die and that's it! Puff, gone!'

Startsev wiped his face, feeling how tiny drops of Kudrya's saliva were burning his skin like acid.

'How could it be nothing? I can't imagine that! Nothing!'

'But there was nothing before you were born, was there?' Kudrya hideously burped. Something was constantly moving between his lips, Startsev only hoped that those previously seen maggots weren't summoned back by the perky piano music.

'It was... something different.' He shrugged his shoulders.

'And I think that was exactly it!' Kudrya smiled widely. He indeed had worms in his mouth. And not just a couple... but a lot of them.

'Isn't it odd that they don't stifle his speech?' Startsev thought, without any real interest.

'Before I was born... there was no me, I suppose.'

'And there will be no you after the death' Kudrya summed up triumphantly, 'Puff, gone!' he spat, 'And that's it!'

Startsev sat quietly for a moment, choosing the right words.

'It doesn't scare me,' he finally said, 'But the knowledge of what will become of my body disgusts me. All those...' he helplessly looked around, realising how pointless it was - trying to explain something to Kudrya, '...gases, body liquids. Also! Also! I don't want them to dig in me, to stitch me, to put inside me all those... I don't know...' he was almost screaming, and to his own satisfaction, could hear that his voice was hard as steel, 'Probes and all that! Have you seen a morgue? Have you? Dirt and rust... and granite tables, I think. I can't do that! It's such a shame, such an impotence!'

Kudrya finally won the battle against the annoying worms. Now he focused on chewing and making small and frequent swallows.

'Of course you can!' What came out of his mouth sounded more like 'of couth youth can', 'As I said, you won't be bothered by it.'

'But they will!' Startsev thought about his wife, about his daughter who couldn't walk for almost four years - they had been no more able to buy her vitamin supplements, and so rickets turned her legs to tuberous roots. He thought about his grandfather, who was crawling around the house like a snake. The old man made a bleating noise every time he dove his hairy face into a bucket of bran.

'They will!' he stubbornly said one more time.

'But what about... God?' Now it was Kudrya's turn to whisper. It was dangerous to talk about God in such a decent place. More dangerous was only to say out loud that the politics of the Party wasn't exactly right or that it was totally wrong, or to mindlessly state that the hunger, deaths, rampant inflation and the 98% child mortality rate wasn't the result of the targeted foreign aggression, but, in fact, was the government's fault and the fault of those who actively supported... Kudrya squeezed his eyes shut. How could such... ill-thoughts come to his mind? What if he was talking in his sleep? The noseless incorruptible face of his son Pavlik flashed before his eyes. No, it was absolutely, absolutely unacceptable... Deadly dangerous!

'And where is that God?' Startsev asked without even trying to be secretive.

'Think about the kids,' said Kudrya. He no more liked their conversation.

'That's what I did.'

Statsev got up, straightened his worn-out, patched here and there frock-coat, and woodenly walked towards The Disintegrator.

Kudrya followed him with his eyes.

When the door closed behind Startsev's back, Kudrya suddenly thought that he had never been inside The Disintegrator's cabin. How strange! The machine had been installed in the pub... since forever, and anyone could walk in.

He sipped the greasy brew once again and let himself think a bit further. *I wonder... what will Startsev feel when his body gets... disintegrated? Will it be like a bright flash? Maybe a flash of pain, that tears your entire being into atoms, giving back to the universe all the shards of stars that once were borrowed? Or will it be... nothing? A curtain of black dust...*

No suffering.

No sorrow.

No thoughts.

He will just see a dream within a dream. And in that dream, he will be sleeping and seeing another dream...

For a brief moment, the pub went dark. And yet people carried on their loud chatter – lately, The Disintegrator got used more and more often. The dwarf kept playing the piano, screeching in unison with the most successful accords now-and-again. His voice, alloyed with the music into a rusty knife, was cutting the dense smoke that hung over the tables.

Kudrya flinched. First, he glanced at his watch that had stopped at 7pm on the dot several years ago, then he looked at The Disintegrator. The simple iron door was open a crack. The light bulb inside it was shining with the inviting warm green light.

'I should try it sometime' he decided, talking either to his mug or to his ashtray filled with a viscid black goo.

He was thinking about the granite tables.

About the probes.

DENIS BUSHLATOV

Denis Bushlatov is a Ukrainian horror writer. At present, he has published two short story collections: Devolution and The Gift, which are sold worldwide in more or less every bookstore featuring Russian literature.

Unfortunately, up till now, few of his works have been translated into English. Nevertheless some of them (e.g., Safe Heaven novella) were published in such magazines as Bewildering Stories, Black Petals and Dissection.

He currently lives in Odessa, Ukraine, with his wife, his 11-year-old son and full-of-nuisance cat, Richard.

THE KELP

BY WILLIAM MEIKLE

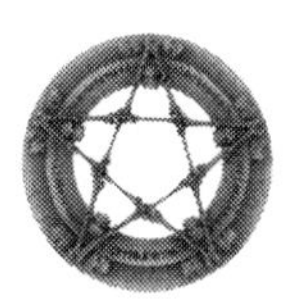

I didn't know what to expect. All they'd said was that it was a *matter of national security*. Just what the RNAD wanted with a fifty-year-old doctor of Botany with a gammy leg and a drink problem I wasn't told. I was given a train ticket and a contact name and sent off to Helensburgh.

Once there I was met by a sergeant and a truck – both of them well past their best. We rattled along an unlit road for what seemed like hours, coming to a sudden halt at a manned checkpoint alongside a long, moonlit loch. An attendant waved a torch and a gun in my face, I showed him my paperwork and we were allowed through. I was driven to a Nissen Hut, shown inside to a bed, and given an order to see the Colonel in the morning.

I sat on the edge of the bed for several minutes, unsure of my next move. It felt cold and quiet, and I was already missing the comfortable clutter and noise of my university apartments back in Glasgow. I went outside and studied the lie of the land. There was a loch, and a lot of huts. Beyond that there was little to see but the moon on the water. It was very pretty, if a bit chilly. I watched it for a while as I tried to get used to my new situation. It took three slow cigarettes before I even felt like settling. When I finally lay down I soon found that my allocated bed was little more than a few sheets thrown over a stiff board.

I slept badly. Things didn't get much better when the morning started on a wrong note.

I'm afraid the Colonel, a stiff little man with a stiffer little moustache, didn't take to me. From what I understood of my short briefing, I was to be seconded to this unit for the duration, to '*do my bit against the Jerries*'. But by the time he led me via a warren of corridors through and between a maze of Nissen Huts and showed me into the lab I was still none the wiser.

It was only when I was introduced to the head of the team that I began to have some inkling as to why I had been summonsed.

I knew Professor Rankin by his reputation of being an iconoclast, a visionary and as mad as a bag of badgers. Last I'd heard he had gone over to the Yanks for a huge stipend at one of the West Coast think tanks. I never expected to meet him in a Nissen Hut on a Scottish loch-side.

His unruly mop of white hair shook as he grasped my hand. He was as thin as a rake, but his grip was as hard as cold steel.

'Ballantine. And not a minute too soon. Come over here man. You need to see this.'

It all came out of him in a rush, as if it had been bottled, shaken and released. 'It's a complex hydrocarbon all right. But it's much more than that. It's alive... or at least it was before it was frozen. There's Golgi apparatus, and mitochondrial DNA, but no real cell wall structure to speak of. It's like nothing I've ever seen before... like nothing *anyone's* ever seen before.'

I wasn't given any chance to answer. He dragged me over to a microscope.

'Look at it,' he said. 'Just look.'

I looked. I had no idea what it was. It looked almost like the internal structure of an amoeba.

'It's going to change *everything*,' Rankin said. 'Do you remember the Pabodie Expedition in the early thirties?'

'The great Antarctic failure? Wasn't there some kind of mass delusion on that one?'

'So everyone thought at the time. But the story goes that they discovered an ancient city under the ice. A city built by beings genetically engineered for the purpose. Beings that could take any shape required to get the job done... and at least one of the beings was still alive. They called it a *Shoggoth*.'

I barked out a laugh.

'Cabin fever and too much booze more like.'

Rankin looked down at the desk. He'd obviously prepared the microscope slide from something in a petri-dish at the side. It looked like nothing more than a pool of thick oil.

'They were asked for proof, but could provide none. Save this. They brought back a sample,' he said. 'It cost an arm and a leg to get it, but we finally managed to persuade the Yanks to give us some of the material for experimentation.'

He lifted the petri-dish, studying the contents.

'OK,' I said softly. 'You've got *something*. But what has it to do with me?'

He smiled.

'This material was *manufactured*. It bonds with other living tissue, and builds.'

'Builds what?'

He laughed loudly.

'Anything we want it to. Don't you see Ballantine? You and I are going to change war forever. We're going to make the ultimate defensive weapon.'

The protoplasm in the petri-dish suddenly *surged* against

the glass, with such force that the dish jumped out of Rankin's hand and shattered as it hit the ground. The tarry substance started to make its way across the floor, scuttling like a manic spider.

Rankin nonchalantly stepped forward and poured some of the contents of a glass jar on it. Steam rose. A vinegar-like tang caught at the back of my throat and forced me to close my eyes. When I looked again there was nothing left but a smoking pool of oily goop on the floor.

'Molar Hydrochloric acid,' Rankin said, holding up a half-empty jar and almost smiling. 'It seems to do the trick.'

OVER THE NEXT few weeks I began to understand the detail and scope of what Rankin hoped to achieve... and my part in it. The tarry material did indeed prove adept at recombining existing biological materials into things rich and strange. And it did it at a prodigious rate. He had me trying combinations of various plant-life. We had a spectacular disaster when we introduced the tarry material to pond algae, which left a green scum covering the whole interior of the lab that had to be removed with bleach and blowtorches. Still Rankin refused to be depressed.

'We're getting there,' he said, even though I had no real idea of the required destination.

Not yet.

I began to get an idea what he was looking for when we set the substance to work on some seaweed. It took a particular liking to *Ascophylum Nodosum*, one of the bladder-worts common along this coastline. It seemed like a marriage made in Heaven. Although contained in a tall sealed jar, the weed-tar combination filled all the available space within minutes and was soon a seething mass of crawling vegetation frantically trying to escape.

Rankin clapped me heartily on the back, phoned the MOD and returned to break open the whisky. We sat on the harbour wall smoking and drinking, and after a few drams his tongue finally loosened.

'They approached me last year,' he said. 'They're frightened of the power of the German fleet, and wanted some way of locking them in port and making them vulnerable to attack.'

He took a long drag of smoke before continuing.

'By coincidence I had been talking that very day about the *Shoggoth* material. I put two and two together, the brass came up with the cash, and here we are. We've done it Ballantine. All we have to do is introduce a scrap of the new stuff to the waters around the Hun's anchorages and they'll be clogged up in no time. The perfect defensive weapon.'

I could see several flaws in this plan but kept my mouth shut... I didn't want to cut off the only supply of whisky I'd had in weeks. So far he hadn't noticed that I was managing to get twice as much of it inside me as he was... I wanted to keep it that way.

I regretted it the next morning of course... I always do. And I regretted it twice as much when I walked into the lab to be confronted by two admirals of the fleet and a Secretary of State. Luckily Rankin wanted to showboat so I hung at the back and let him get on with it.

He gave them the spiel about the Antarctic expedition and the *Shoggoth* material but even in my hung-over state I could see that they were seriously under-whelmed. They perked up slightly when he started the experiment proper. He used an even larger jar this time, one near six feet tall. The tar combined with the weed and *surged,* filling the space in seconds, fronds flapping and slapping against the glass in frenzy.

The brass sat in stony silence.

'That's it?' the Secretary finally said. 'All this time and effort and you give us some bloody energetic seaweed?'

Rankin gave them the same line he'd given me the night before, about clogging up harbours and stifling the Jerry fleet.

The Secretary sighed theatrically.

'Look Rankin, the reason we got you for this job was because we *expected* something flamboyant, something that would show our people that we are ahead of the game compared to Hitler's scientists. But this just won't do. They throw the Doodlebug at us and what do we do in reply? Send them some fucking lively seaweed? No. This just won't do at all.'

RANKIN WAS A DRIVEN man after that. He would be found in the lab, alternatively shouting at the *Shoggoth* material, and muttering under his breath.

'Flamboyant? I'll show them flamboyant.'

I first guessed his intent when he had me procure some material from the Botanic Gardens in Glasgow. Venus fly trap mostly, but also three different types of pitcher plant and a particularly sticky sundew that was both rare and expensive. I also heard from a colleague that he had requested several jellyfish be tracked down... the more poisonous the better. I tried to get a look at what he was working on, but by that time he had locked the lab down to all but himself. The rest of us were reduced to bit-players, and spent most of our time in the mess hall drinking beer and playing cribbage... although in my case I didn't join in the card games.

It was nearly two weeks before we were summonsed for a demonstration. There were no brass present this time... Rankin wanted to be sure of his *flamboyance* first.

He had made some drastic changes in the lab. A full fifty per cent of the area was taken up by a large glass tank. In the centre of the tank sat a metal box. A chain was attached to its lid and led, via a winch, to a pulley next to Rankin. On the far side of the glass tank a small pony munched contentedly on a pile of hay. Suddenly I wanted to be back in the mess cradling a pint of lukewarm beer, or back in the postgraduate club at the university getting beat at chess.

Anywhere but here.

Several others shuffled nervously. Indeed, there might even have been a revolt... if Rankin had given us time to think about it. But before we could stop him, he yanked on his end of the chain.

The metal box opened.

The pony pricked its ears. That was all it had time for. Thrashing tentacles came out of the box. They waved in the air as if tasting it and sought out the pony like snakes zeroing in on prey. They struck as one, wrapping themselves in long strands around the pony's flanks. The beast started to whinny, and tried to pull away. One of the tentacles tore off from the animal, taking a long strip of flesh with it. The other tentacles merely tightened and pulled harder.

Something climbed out of the metal box; an amorphous mass of thrashing fronds that might once have been seaweed. It opened in two halves, spreading itself wide like bat-wings. The tentacles pulled the pony across the tank. Foam bubbled at the pony's mouth, its tongue lolling, red and steaming. But it was still alive as the *thing* took it into its folds, still alive as the carpet of vegetation wrapped itself around the body and *squeezed.* We all heard the bones crack. As if from a far distance there was a piteous whinny.

Someone behind me threw up and I smelled beer and cigarettes.

'For pity's sake Rankin. Do something,' I shouted.

He turned and smiled.

He yanked on another chain and a rain of what looked like water came from a series of pipes above the tank. The vegetation started to smoke and curl and once more I smelled the tang of vinegar as the hydrochloric acid turned everything to oily sludge.

'How was that?' Rankin asked. 'Flamboyant enough do you think?'

I spent that night getting roaring drunk in the mess. I wasn't the only one.

In the morning we started preparing for the field test.

On the night before the big demonstration Rankin sought me out in the mess.

'Come with me Ballantine,' he said. 'You're the only one who will understand the import.'

I put my beer down reluctantly. I was on my fifth, and already looking forward to the sixth. But I couldn't refuse him. Technically he was my commanding officer, and I wasn't exempt from military justice. With a heavy heart I followed him down to the lab.

The place had changed. The heavy glass tank had been removed. But the network of piping was still in place overhead, and the metal box still sat in the middle of the floor, its walls etched and pitted by the acid.

'If you're going to be slaughtering some poor animal, I want nothing to do with it,' I said.

He smiled grimly.

'Not this time. Come. You need to see this.'

He led me to the long trestle. A thick forest of thrashing kelp and tentacles completely filled a tall glass jar.

'For pity's sake Rankin... how much of this thing did you make?'

'Enough,' he whispered. 'But that's not why I brought you here. Watch.'

He walked away to our left. The kelp followed him, the thrashing fronds and tentacles now concentrated on that side of the glass. Rankin turned and came back towards me. The kelp tracked his movement, the thrashing becoming ever more insistent.

'It knows me,' Rankin whispered. 'I think I've made it angry.'

'That's not possible,' I started.

'Neither is this,' he said, and walked forward. He stared at the kelp and spoke in a loud voice, as if ordering a disobedient dog.

'Quiet!'

The kelp stilled.

Rankin motioned me forward.

'Look,' he said. There was wonder and awe in his voice. I saw why seconds later.

I looked at the kelp.

And the kelp looked back.

A single, lidless eye, pale green and milky, stared out from the fronds. Even as I watched it changed, being sucked back into a new fold. A wet gash opened, like a thin-lipped mouth. It stretched wide and a high ululation filled the Nissen Hut, like a seagull on a storm wind.

Tekeli-Li! Tekeli-Li!

'What the hell is this shite?' I said softly.

Rankin dragged me away. Three new-formed eyes watched us intently.

'I've been reading the journals from the Antarctic expedition,' he said. He led me to the far end of the trestle and picked up a leather-bound book. He opened it and started to read.

It was a terrible, indescribable thing vaster than any subway train – a shapeless congeries of protoplasmic bubbles, faintly self-luminous, and with myriads of temporary eyes forming and un-forming as pustules of greenish light all over the tunnel-filling front that bore down upon us... slithering over the glistening floor that it and its kind had swept so evilly free of all litter. Still came that eldritch, mocking cry...

Tekeli-li! Tekeli-li!"

I leaned over and read the words for myself.

'That's just a story to frighten the gullible,' I said.

'Maybe,' he said. 'But I've sent a sample back to the Yanks. They've got more sophisticated equipment than we have. Maybe they can make something of it.'

From inside the glass the noise grew louder.

'Tekeli-Li. Tekeli-Li.'

THE FIELD TEST was scheduled for noon the next day. I spent most of the morning trying to convince the Colonel to postpone it, but a combination of the smell of beer on my breath, and a fear of disappointing the top brass, led him to dismiss me out of hand. I watched the preparations in the harbour with a terrible sinking feeling in my gut that had nothing to do with the booze from the night before.

Rankin was back into his full-blown show-off strut. He

marched around the harbour barking orders, a conductor marshalling his orchestra. By the time the brass arrived at quarter to the hour everything was in place.

We stood in a rough semi-circle just above the shoreline. Several yards beneath us sat the now familiar metal tank. From where I stood I could hear the thing thrash against the inside walls. A chain led from the top of the cage along the shingle to lie at Rankin's feet.

The harbour wall stretched away to our left and ahead of us in the water a small flotilla of boats made a rough semi-circle encasing a drift-net full of locally caught mackerel. Rankin had wanted to use a couple of convicted murderers from Barlinnie, but even the Colonel had drawn the line at that. The men on the boats were equipped with flame units and each boat contained several bottles filled with acid.

I hoped it would be enough.

Rankin stood, centre-stage, and waited for the brass to move into their place along the harbour wall. When he spoke, it was in a voice honed by many years of addressing large lecture theatres. His voice carried, loud and strong in the still air.

'You wanted *flamboyance*? Here it is.'

He dragged on the chain. The lid started to open, slowly at first. Tentacles found the edges and *tore*. A chunk of metal flew like a discus, passing less than three feet over the head of the Secretary of State. The kelp came out of the box like a greyhound from a trap, expanding as it came into a roiling mass eight feet wide and near again as thick.

It completely ignored the net full of fish. Instead it threw out a writhing forest of tentacles... straight towards Rankin.

He had to step back sharply, and even then the leading tentacle caught him around the left foot and tugged, hard. He fell, slightly off balance and a second tendril reached for him. He just had time to kick off his shoe and scuttle, crab-like back up the shingle beach. The tentacle dragged the shoe back to a maw in the kelp. The moving carpet of fronds came up out of the water, still focussed on Rankin.

The air was full of the high ululation.

Tekeli-Li!

A gull flew down, attracted by the noise. Two tentacles plucked it out of the air. A new maw opened and took it as fast as a blink. The body of kelp did not slow. It came up the beach, shingle rattling like gunfire beneath it.

It was then that I saw the fatal flaw in the planning. All of the men with the flame units and acid had been placed out on the boats in expectation that the fish would be the target. They were now frantically trying to reach shore, to get at the creeping creature, but they were still too far out to be of any help.

Up on the harbour wall security guards ushered the brass to safety, but down on the shore we were in disarray. A fresh-faced young squaddie stepped between Rankin and the creature. He raised a rifle and took aim, pumping three quick shots into the main body. The bullets had no effect. The tendrils wrapped themselves around the lad and dragged him off his feet. He scrambled amid the shingle as he was dragged backwards. At the same time the carpet of kelp *surged* and fell on him like a wet blanket. His screams cut off mercifully quickly.

All along the back of the kelp more moist mouths opened and squealed.

Tekeli-Li! Tekeli-Li!

The rest of us turned and ran.

The kelp followed us up into the warren of huts. A group of men tried to set up a rear-guard action, blocking one of the alleys with volleys of gunfire. The kelp swarmed over them without a pause. Man-shaped forms squirmed and writhed within the kelp then went still.

I ran faster.

When I turned to look again the kelp had more than doubled in size.

I saw Rankin's white mop of hair among the people just ahead of me.

The kelp saw him too. Tentacles raised in the air, thrashing wildly.

'Rankin,' I called. 'It's only angry at *you*. Nobody else has to get hurt here.

I wasn't sure that he'd heard me until I saw him duck inside the lab. Soldiers ran past the open door, heading for the road out of the base and I was sorely tempted to go with them. But despite his faults Rankin had believed in me, and I owed him for that. I threw myself into the lab, just ahead of a nest of tentacles.

'Get into the corner,' Rankin shouted at me. 'Pull the left hand chain.'

That was all he had time for. The kelp flowed through the door, blocking all escape. I pushed myself as far into the corner as I could and grabbed at the chain.

'Not yet!' Rankin shouted. He danced aside, avoiding thrashing tentacles, until he stood on the spot where the metal cage had sat. 'Wait until it's all inside.'

The first tentacle took him around the waist. He screamed as it started to tug at him, but he held his ground, forcing the main body of the kelp to come to him. More tentacles struck, at his chest and his ankles. He struggled to stay upright. By now most of the kelp was inside the room.

Once more I reached for the chain.

'Not yet!' Rankin screamed. 'None of it can escape.'

The kelp rolled over the lab floor. It opened out like a huge umbrella towering over Rankin, then fell on him, his white hair the last thing to disappear from view.

'None of it can escape,' he called at the end.

I agreed.

I pulled the chain.

The acid rain did its job. In five minutes all that was left of Rankin and his creation was a pool of oily goop on the lab floor.

It was only later, as I downed the first of many drinks, that I remembered his words.

I've sent a sample back to the Yanks.

I spent weeks after that checking. I found the shipping order, and the name of the boat, the Haven Home. Records show it was sunk by a U-Boat, somewhere off Rockall. In my dreams I see a glass container, lying in a flooded cargo hold. Inside the kelp sits, dormant, waiting.

And I worry.

I worry about breakages.

WILLIAM MEIKLE

William Meikle is a Scottish writer, now living in Canada, with over thirty novels published in the genre press and more than 300 short story credits in thirteen countries. He has books available from a variety of publishers including Dark Regions Press and Severed Press and his work has appeared in a large number of professional anthologies and magazines. He lives in Newfoundland with whales, bald eagles and icebergs for company. When he's not writing he drinks beer, plays guitar, and dreams of fortune and glory.

OTHER ANTHOLOGIES BY KEITH ANTHONY BAIRD

Horror anthology with proceeds going to the UK's National Health Service.

Available from Amazon.

CONTENT WARNING CONTINUED

Holocaust Reference
(Born Of A Barbed Wire Womb)

Physical Abuse Of Children
(The Great Withering)

Surgical Detail
(Born Of A Barbed Wire Womb / Cerebral Salvage)

Experimentation
(The Great Withering / Born Of A Barbed Wire Womb /
Cerebral Salvage)

Child Abduction
(The Gulch / Cerebral Salvage)

Child Death
(Those Damn Trees)

Pandemic References
(The Dumb Supper)

Printed in Great Britain
by Amazon